PENGUIN BOOKS

Picnic at Hanging Rock

Joan Lindsay was born in Melbourne, where she went to school as a day-girl for a few years at Clyde Girls' Grammar, then situated in East St Kilda. She knew and loved the Macedon district from early childhood.

In 1922 she married Sir Daryl Lindsay in London. The Lindsays travelled together in Europe and the USA, Daryl with his paints and Joan with her typewriter. Sir Daryl died in 1976. Joan lived at their country home on the Mornington Peninsula, Mullberry Hill, Victoria, Australia until her death in December 1984.

W9-ARK-201

PICNIC AT
HANGING ROCK

—————

JOAN LINDSAY

PENGUIN BOOKS

PENGUIN BOOKS

Published by the Penguin Group
Penguin Group (Australia)
707 Collins Street, Melbourne, Victoria 3008, Australia
(a division of Penguin Australia Pty Ltd)
Penguin Group (USA) Inc.
375 Hudson Street, New York, New York 10014, USA
Penguin Group (Canada)
90 Eglinton Avenue East, Suite 700, Toronto, Canada ON M4P 2Y3
(a division of Penguin Canada Books Inc.)
Penguin Books Ltd
80 Strand, London WC2R 0RL England
Penguin Ireland
25 St Stephen's Green, Dublin 2, Ireland
(a division of Penguin Books Ltd)
Penguin Books India Pvt Ltd
11 Community Centre, Panchsheel Park, New Delhi – 110 017, India
Penguin Group (NZ)
67 Apollo Drive, Rosedale, Auckland 0632, New Zealand
(a division of Penguin New Zealand Pty Ltd)
Penguin Books (South Africa) (Pty) Ltd
Rosebank Office Park, Block D, 181 Jan Smuts Avenue,
Parktown North, Johannesburg 2196, South Africa
Penguin (Beijing) Ltd
7F, tower B, Jiaming Center, 27 East Third Ring Road North,
Chaoyang District, Beijing 100020, China

Penguin Books Ltd, Registered Offices: 80 Strand, London, WC2R 0RL, England

First published in Australia by Cheshire Publishing Pty Ltd 1967
First published in Great Britain by Chatto and Windus Ltd 1968
First published in the United States of America by Penguin Books 1977
Published in Great Britain by Penguin Books 1970
First published by Penguin Books Australia Ltd 1997
This edition published by Penguin Group (Australia), 2009

Copyright © Joan Lindsay 1967

Printed and bound in Australia by Griffin Press

National Library of Australia
Cataloguing-in-Publication data:

Lindsay, Joan.
Picnic at hanging rock.
ISBN: 978-0-143-20272-1
A823.3

penguin.com.au

MRS APPLEYARD, *Headmistress of Appleyard College*
MISS GRETA MCCRAW, *Mathematics mistress*
MLLE DIANNE DE POITIERS, *French and Dancing
  mistress*
MISS DORA LUMLEY, MISS BUCK, *junior mistresses*
MIRANDA, IRMA LEOPOLD, MARION QUADE, *senior
  boarders*
EDITH HORTON, *the College dunce*
SARA WAYBOURNE, *the youngest boarder*
ROSAMUND, BLANCHE, *and other boarders*
COOK, MINNIE AND ALICE, *domestic staff at the
  College*
EDWARD WHITEHEAD, *the College gardener*
IRISH TOM, *handyman at the College*
MR BEN HUSSEY, *of Hussey's Livery Stables, Woodend*
DOCTOR MCKENZIE, *a family doctor from Woodend*
CONSTABLE BUMPHER, *of the Woodend Police Station*
MRS BUMPHER
JIM, *a young policeman*
M. LOUIS MONTPELIER, *a Bendigo watchmaker*
REG LUMLEY, *brother of* DORA LUMLEY
JASPER COSGROVE, *guardian of* SARA WAYBOURNE
COLONEL AND MRS FITZHUBERT, *summer residents
  at Lake View, Upper Macedon*
THE HON. MICHAEL FITZHUBERT, *their nephew
  from England*
ALBERT CRUNDALL, *coachman at Lake View*
MR CUTLER, *gardener at Lake View*
MRS CUTLER

Major Sprack and his daughter, Angela,
English visitors at Government Cottage, Macedon
Doctor Cooling, *from Lower Macedon*

And many others who do not appear in this book.

Whether *Picnic at Hanging Rock* is fact or fiction,
my readers must decide for themselves. As the fateful
picnic took place in the year nineteen hundred, and
all the characters who appear in this book are long
since dead, it hardly seems important.

I

Everyone agreed that the day was just right for the picnic to Hanging Rock – a shimmering summer morning warm and still, with cicadas shrilling all through breakfast from the loquat trees outside the dining-room windows and bees murmuring above the pansies bordering the drive. Heavy-headed dahlias flamed and drooped in the immaculate flowerbeds, the well-trimmed lawns steamed under the mounting sun. Already the gardener was watering the hydrangeas still shaded by the kitchen wing at the rear of the College. The boarders at Mrs Appleyard's College for Young Ladies had been up and scanning the bright unclouded sky since six o'clock and were now fluttering about in their holiday muslins like a flock of excited butterflies. Not only was it a Saturday and the long awaited occasion of the annual picnic, but Saint Valentine's Day, traditionally celebrated on the fourteenth of February by the interchange of elaborate cards and favours. All were madly romantic and strictly anonymous – supposedly the silent tributes of lovesick admirers; although Mr Whitehead the elderly English gardener and Tom the Irish groom were almost the only two males to be so much as smiled at during the term.

The Headmistress was probably the only person at the College who received no cards. It was well known that Mrs Appleyard disapproved of Saint Valentine and his ridiculous greetings that cluttered up the College mantelpieces right up to Easter and gave as much extra dusting to the maids as the annual prize-giving. And such mantelpieces! Two in the long drawing-room of white marble, supported by pairs of caryatids as firm of bust as Madam herself; others of carved and tortured wood embellished with a thousand winking tiddling mirrors. Appleyard College was already, in the year nineteen hundred, an architectural anachronism in the Australian bush – a hopeless misfit in time and place. The clumsy two storey mansion was one of those elaborate houses that sprang up all over Australia like exotic fungi following the finding of gold. Why this particular stretch of flat sparsely wooded country, a few miles out of the village of Macedon crouching at the foot of the mount, had been selected as a suitable building site, nobody will ever know. The insignificant creek that meandered in a series of shallow pools down the slope at the rear of the ten acre property offered little inducement as a setting for an Italianate mansion; nor the occasional glimpses, through a screen of stringy-barked eucalyptus, of the misty summit of Mount Macedon rising up to the east on the opposite side of the road. However, built it was, and of solid Castlemaine stone, to withstand the ravages of time. The original owner, whose name is long ago forgotten, had only lived in it for a year or two before the huge ugly house was standing empty and up for sale.

The spacious grounds, comprising vegetable and flower gardens, pig and poultry pens, orchard and tennis lawns, were in wonderful order, thanks to Mr Whitehead the English gardener, still in charge. There were several vehicles in the handsome stone stables, all in excellent repair. The hideous Victorian furnishings were as good as new, with marble mantelpieces direct from Italy and thick piled carpets from Axminster. The oil lamps on the cedar staircase were held aloft by classical statues, there was a grand piano in the long drawing-room and even a square tower, reached by a narrow circular staircase, from which the Union Jack could be hoisted on Queen Victoria's birthday. To Mrs Appleyard, newly arrived from England with a considerable nest-egg and letters of introduction to some of the leading Australian families, the mansion, standing well back from the Bendigo Road behind a low stone wall, was immediately impressive. The brown pebble eyes ever on the alert for a bargain summed up the amazing place as ideal for a select and suitably expensive boarding school – better still a College – for Young Ladies. To the delight of the Bendigo house agent who was showing her over the property she had bought it then and there, lock, stock and barrel, including the gardener, with a reduction for cash down, and moved in.

Whether the Headmistress of Appleyard College (as the local white elephant was at once re-christened in gold lettering on a handsome board at the big iron gates) had any previous experience in the educational field, was never divulged. It was unnecessary. With her high-piled greying pompadour and ample bosom, as rigidly controlled and disciplined as her private ambitions, the cameo portrait of her late husband flat on her respectable chest, the stately stranger looked precisely what the parents expected of an English Headmistress. And as looking the part is well known to be more than half the battle in any form of business enterprise from Punch and Judy to floating a loan on the Stock Exchange, the College, from the very first day, was a success; and by the end of the first year, showing a gratifying profit. All this was nearly six years before this chronicle begins.

Saint Valentine is impartial in his favours, and not only the young and beautiful were kept busy opening their cards this morning. Miranda as usual had a drawer of her wardrobe filled with lace-trimmed pledges of affection, although Baby Jonnie's home-grown cupid and row of pencilled kisses, addressed from Queensland in her father's large loving hand, held pride of place on the marble mantelpiece. Edith Horton, plain as a frog, had smugly accounted for at least eleven, and even little Miss Lumley had produced at the breakfast table a card with a bilious looking dove bearing the inscription I ADORE THEE EVER. A statement presumably coming from the drab unspeakable brother who had called on his sister last term. Who else, reasoned the budding girls, would adore the myopic junior governess, eternally garbed in brown serge and flat-heeled shoes?

'He is fond of her,' said Miranda, ever charitable. 'I saw them kissing goodbye at the hall door.'

'But darling Miranda – Reg Lumley is such a *dreary* creature !' laughed Irma, characteristically shaking out blue-black curls and idly wondering why the school straw hat was so unbecoming. Radiantly lovely at seventeen, the little heiress was without personal vanity or pride of possession. She loved people and things to be beautiful, and pinned a bunch of wildflowers into her coat with as much pleasure as a breathtaking diamond brooch. Sometimes just to look at Miranda's calm oval face and straight corn-yellow hair gave her a sharp little stab of pleasure. Darling Miranda now gazing dreamily out at the sunlit garden. 'What a wonderful day ! I can hardly wait to get out into the country !'

'Listen to her, girls ! Anyone would think that Appleyard College was in the Melbourne slums !'

'Forests,' said Miranda, 'with ferns and birds ... like we have at home.' 'And spiders,' Marion said. 'I only wish someone had sent me a map of the Hanging Rock for a Valentine, I could have taken it to the picnic.' Irma was forever being struck by the extraordinary notions of Marion Quade and now wanted to know whoever wanted to look at maps at a picnic?

'I do,' Marion truthfully said. 'I always like to know exactly where I am.' Reputed to have mastered Long Division in the cradle, Marion Quade had spent the greater part of her seventeen years in the relentless pursuit of knowledge. Small wonder that with her thin intelligent features, sensitive nose that appeared to be always on the scent of something long awaited and sought, and thin swift legs, she had come to resemble a greyhound.

The girls began discussing their Valentines. 'Somebody had the nerve to send Miss McCraw a card on squared paper, covered with little sums,' said Rosamund. Actually this card had been the inspired gesture of Irish Tom, egged on by Minnie the housemaid, for a lark. The forty-five-year-old purveyor of higher mathematics to the senior girls had received it with dry approval, figures in the eyes of Greta McCraw being a good deal more acceptable than roses and forget-me-nots. The very sight of a sheet of paper dotted over with numerals gave her a secret joy; a sense of power, knowing how with a stroke or two of a pencil they could be sorted out, divided, multiplied, re-arranged to miraculous new conclusions. Tom's Valentine, though he never knew it, was a success. His choice for Minnie was a bleeding heart embedded in roses and obviously in the last stages of a fatal disease. Minnie was enchanted, as was Mademoiselle with an old French print of a solitary rose. Thus Saint Valentine reminded the inmates of Appleyard College of the colour and variety of love.

Mademoiselle de Poitiers, who taught dancing and French conversation and attended to the boarders' wardrobes, was bustling about in a fever of delighted anticipation. Like her charges she wore a simple muslin dress in which she contrived to look elegant by the addition of a wide ribbon belt and shady straw hat. Only a few years older than some of the senior boarders, she was equally enchanted at the prospect of escaping from the suffocating routine of the College for a whole long summer day, and ran here and there amongst the girls assembling for a final roll call on the front verandah.

'Depêchez-vous, mes enfants, depêchez-vous. Tais-toi, Irma,' chirped the light canary voice of Mademoiselle, for whom la petite Irma could do no wrong. The girl's voluptuous little breasts, her dimples, full red lips, naughty black eyes and glossy black ringlets, were a continual source of aesthetic pleasure. Sometimes in the dingy schoolroom the Frenchwoman, brought up amongst the great European galleries, would look up from her desk and see her against a background of cherries and pineapples, cherubs and golden flagons, surrounded by elegant young men in velvets and satins. ... 'Tais-toi, Irma ... Miss McCraw vient d'arriver.' A gaunt female figure in a puce-coloured pelisse was emerging from the outdoor 'dunnie', an earth-closet reached by a secluded path edged with begonias. The governess walked at her usual measured pace, uninhibited as Royalty, and with an almost royal dignity. Nobody had ever seen her in a hurry, or without her steel rimmed spectacles.

Greta McCraw had undertaken to take on picnic duty today, assisted by Mademoiselle, purely as a matter of conscience. A brilliant mathematician – far too brilliant for her poorly paid job at the College – she would have given a five pound note to have spent this precious holiday, no matter how fine, shut up in her room with that fascinating new treatise on the Calculus. A tall woman with dry ochre skin and coarse greying hair perched like an untidy bird's nest on top of her head, she had remained oblivious to the vagaries of the Australian scene despite a residence of thirty years. Climate meant nothing, nor fashion, nor the never ending miles of gum trees and dry yellow grass, of which she was hardly more aware than of the mists and mountains of her native Scotland, as a girl. The boarders, used to her outlandish wardrobe, were no longer amused, and her choice for today's picnic went without comment – the well known church-going toque and black laced boots, together with the puce-coloured pelisse, in which her bony frame took on the proportions of one of her own Euclidian triangles, and a pair of rather shabby puce kid gloves.

Mademoiselle, on the other hand, as an admired arbiter of fashion, was minutely examined and passed with honours, down to the turquoise ring and white silk gloves. 'Although,' said Blanche, 'I'm surprised at her letting Edith go out in those larky blue ribbons. Whatever is Edith looking at over there?' A pasty-faced fourteen-year-old with the contours of an overstuffed bolster was standing a few feet away, staring up at the window of a room on the first floor. Miranda tossed back her straight corn-coloured hair, smiling and waving at a pale little pointed face looking dejectedly down at the animated scene below. 'It's not fair,' said Irma, waving and smiling too, 'after all the child is only thirteen. I never thought Mrs A. would be so mean.'

Miranda sighed : 'Poor little Sara – she wanted so much to go to the picnic.'

Failure to recite 'The Wreck of the Hesperus' yesterday had condemned the child Sara Waybourne to solitary confinement upstairs. Later, she would pass the sweet summer afternoon in the empty schoolroom, committing the hated masterpiece to memory. The College was already, despite its brief existence, quite famed for its discipline, deportment and mastery of English literature.

Now an immense purposeful figure was swimming and billowing in grey silk taffeta on to the tiled and colonnaded verandah, like a galleon in full sail. On the gently heaving bosom, a cameo portrait of a gentleman in side whiskers, framed in garnets and gold, rose and fell in tune with the pumping of the powerful lungs encased in a fortress of steel busks and stiff grey calico. 'Good morning, girls,' boomed the gracious plummy voice, specially imported from Kensington.

'Good morning, Mrs Appleyard,' chorused the curtseying half-circle drawn up before the hall door.

'Are we all present, Mademoiselle? Good. Well, young ladies, we are indeed fortunate in the weather for our picnic to Hanging Rock. I have instructed Mademoiselle that as the day is likely to be warm, you may remove your gloves after the drag has passed through Woodend. You will partake of luncheon at the Picnic Grounds near the Rock. Once again let me remind you that the Rock itself is extremely dangerous and you are therefore forbidden to engage in any tomboy foolishness in the matter of exploration, even on the lower slopes. It is, however, a geological marvel on which you will be required to write a brief essay on Monday morning. I also wish to remind you that the vicinity is renowned for its venomous snakes and poisonous ants of various species. I think that is all. Have a pleasant day and try to behave yourselves in a manner to bring credit to the College. I shall expect you back, Miss McCraw and Mademoiselle, at about eight o'clock for a light supper.'

The covered drag from Hussey's Livery stables at Lower Macedon, drawn by five splendid bay horses, was already drawn up at the College gates with Mr Hussey on the box. Mr Hussey had personally driven 'The College' on all important occasions ever since the grand opening day when the parents had come up by train from Melbourne to drink champagne on the lawns. With his kindly shrewd blue eyes and cheeks perpetually blooming like the Mount Macedon rose gardens, he was a prime favourite with everyone in the district; even Mrs Appleyard called him her 'good man' and enjoyed graciously inviting him into her study for a glass of sherry...

'Steady there Sailor ... Woa Duchess ... Belmonte, I'll give you such a lathering ...' The five well-trained horses were actually standing like statues, but it was all part of the fun; Mr Hussey like all good coachmen having a nice sense of style and timing. 'Mind your gloves on the wheel Miss McCraw, it's dusty ...' He had long ago given up attempting to teach this basic truth to lady passengers about to enter one of his cabs. At last everyone was seated to the satisfaction of special friends and enemies and the two governesses. The three senior girls, Miranda, Irma and Marion Quade, inseparable companions, were allotted the coveted box seat in front beside the driver, an arrangement with which Mr Hussey was well pleased. Nice high-spirited girls, all three of 'em ...

'Thank you Mr Hussey – you may go now,' Miss McCraw ordered somewhere from the rear, suddenly aware of non-mathematical responsibilities and in full command.

They were off; the College already out of sight except for the tower through the trees as they bowled along the level Melbourne-Bendigo road, vibrating with particles of fine red dust. 'Get up Sailor, you lazy brute ... Prince, Belmonte, get back in your collars ...' For the first mile or two the scenery was familiar through the daily perambulation of the College crocodile. The passengers knew only too well, without bothering to look out, how the scraggy stringy bark forest lined the road on either side, now and then opening out onto a lighter patch of cleared land. The Comptons' whitewashed cottage whose sprawling quince trees supplied the College with jellies and jams, the clump of wayside willows at which the governess in charge would invariably call a halt and head for home. It was the same in Longman's *Highroads of History*, where the class were forever turning back for recapitulation at the death of King George the Fourth before starting off again with Edward the Third next term ... Now the willows in rich summer green were gaily passed and a sense of adventure ahead took over as heads began to peer through the buttoned tarpaulin flaps of the drag. The road took a slight turn, there was a fresher green amongst the dun coloured foliage and now and then a stand of blue-black pines, a glimpse of Mount Macedon tufted as usual with fluffy white clouds above the southern slopes, where the romantic summer villas hinted at far off adult delights.

At Appleyard College SILENCE WAS GOLDEN, written up in the corridors and often imposed. There was a delicious freedom about the swift steady motion of the drag and even in the warm dusty air blowing up in their faces that set the passengers chirping and chattering like budgerigars.

On the box seat, the three senior girls perched beside Mr Hussey were talking in blissful inconsequence of dreams, embroidery, warts, fireworks, the coming Easter Vacation. Mr Hussey, who spent a large part of his working day in listening to miscellaneous conversation, kept his eyes on the road ahead and said nothing.

'Mr Hussey,' said Miranda, 'did you know today is Saint Valentine's Day?'

'Well, Miss Miranda, I can't say I did. Don't know much about Saints. What's this one's particular job?'

'Mam'selle says he's the Patron Saint of Lovers,' Irma explained. 'He's a darling – sends people gorgeous cards with tinsel and real lace – have a caramel?'

'Not while I'm driving, thanks all the same.' At last Mr Hussey had a conversational innings. He had been to the Races last Saturday and seen a horse belonging to Irma's father come in first. 'What was the name of the horse and the distance?' Marion Quade wanted to know. She wasn't specially interested in horses but liked to store up snippets of useful information, like her late Father, an eminent Q.C.

Edith Horton, hating to be left out of anything and anxious to show off her ribbons, now leaned forward over Miranda's shoulder to ask why Mr Hussey called his big brown horse Duchess? Mr Hussey, who had his favourites amongst the passengers, was uncommunicative. 'Comes to that, Miss, why are *you* called Edith?'

'Because Edith is my Grandmother's name,' she said primly. 'Only horses don't have grandmothers like we do.'

'Oh don't they just!' Mr Hussey turned his square shoulders away from the silly child.

The morning grew steadily hotter. The sun bore down on the shiny black roof of the drag, now covered with fine red dust that seeped through the loosely buttoned curtains into eyes and hair. 'And this we do for pleasure,' Greta McCraw muttered from the shadows, 'so that we may shortly be at the mercy of venomous snakes and poisonous ants ... how foolish can human creatures be!' Useless, too, to open the book in her satchel with all this schoolgirl chatter in one's ears.

The road to Hanging Rock turns sharply away to the right a little way out of the township of Woodend. Here Mr Hussey pulled up outside the leading hotel to rest and water his horses before starting on the last lap of the drive. Already the heat inside the vehicle was oppressive and there was a wholesale peeling off of the obligatory gloves. 'Can't we take our hats off too. Mam'selle?' asked Irma whose ink-black curls were flowing out in a warm tide under the brim of her stiff school sailor. Mademoiselle smiled and looked across at Miss McCraw, sitting opposite, awake and vertical, but with closed eyes, two puce kid hands locked together on her lap. 'Certainly not. Because we are on an excursion, there is no necessity to look like a wagon load of gypsies.' And re-entered the world of pure uncluttered reason.

The rhythmic beat of the horses' hooves combined with the close air of the drag was making them drowsy. As it was still only eleven o'clock, with plenty of time in which to reach the picnic grounds for lunch, the governesses conferred and Mr Hussey was requested to let down the steps of the drag at a suitable spot off the road. In the shade of an old white gum the zinc-lined wicker basket that kept the milk and lemonade deliciously cool was taken out and unpacked, hats were removed without further comment and biscuits handed round.

'It's a long time since I tasted this stuff,' said Mr Hussey sipping at his lemonade. 'I don't take any hard liquor though, when I've got a big day on my hands like this.'

Miranda had risen to her feet, a mug of lemonade raised high above her head. 'To Saint Valentine!' 'Saint Valentine!' Everyone including Mr Hussey raised their mugs and sent the lovely name ringing down the dusty road. Even Greta McCraw, who wouldn't have cared if they were drinking to Tom of Bedlam or the Shah of Persia and was listening exclusively to the Music of the Spheres in her own head, absently raised an empty mug to her pale lips. 'And now,' said Mr Hussey, 'if your saint has no objections, Miss Miranda, I think we had better be on our way.'

'Humans,' Miss McCraw confided to a magpie picking up crumbs of shortbread at her feet, 'are obsessed with the notion of perfectly useless movement. Nobody but an idiot ever seems to want to sit still for a change !' And she climbed reluctantly back into her seat.

The basket was re-packed, the passengers counted in case anyone should be left behind, the steps of the drag pulled up under the floorboards and once again they were on the road, moving through the scattered silvery shade of straight young trees, where the horses pressed forward through ripples of golden light that broke on straining shoulders and dark sweating rumps. The five sets of hooves were almost soundless on the soft unmade surface of the country road. No traveller passed by, no bird song splintered the sunflecked silence, the grey pointed leaves of the saplings hung lifeless in the noonday heat. The laughing chattering girls in the warm shadowed vehicle unconsciously fell silent until they were out again in full sunlight. 'It must be nearly twelve o'clock,' Mr Hussey told his passengers, looking not at his watch but at the sun. 'We haven't done too badly so far, ladies ... I swore black and blue to your boss I'd have you back at the College by eight o'clock.' The word 'College' sent a chill into the warmth of the drag and nobody answered.

For once Greta McCraw must have been attending to general conversation, which she seldom did in the teachers' sitting-room. 'There is no reason why we should be late, even if we linger for an extra hour at the Rock. Mr Hussey knows as well as I do that two sides of a triangle are together greater than the third. This morning we have driven along two sides of a triangle ... am I correct, Mr Hussey?' The driver nodded in rather dazed agreement. Miss McCraw was a queer fish all right. 'Very well, then – you have only to change your route this afternoon and return by the third side. In this case, since we entered this road at Woodend at right angles the return journey will be along the hypotenuse.'

This was really too much for Mr Hussey's practical intelligence. 'I don't know about a hippopotamus, ma'am, but if you're thinking of the Camel's Hump,' he pointed with his whip to the Macedon ranges, where the Hump stood out against the sky, 'it's a blooming sight longer road than the one we came by, arithmetic or not. You might be interested to know there isn't even a made road – only a sort of rough track over the back of the Mount.'

'I was *not* referring to the Camel's Hump, Mr Hussey. Thank you for your explanation all the same. Knowing little of horses and roads I tend to become theoretical. Marion, can you hear me up there in front? You understand what I mean, I hope?' Marion Quade, the only member of the class to take Pythagoras in her stride, was a favourite pupil, in the sense that a savage who understands a few words of the language of a shipwrecked sailor is a favourite savage.

While they were talking the angle of vision had gradually altered to bring the Hanging Rock into sudden startling view. Directly ahead, the grey volcanic mass rose up slabbed and pinnacled like a fortress from the empty yellow plain. The three girls on the box seat could see the vertical lines of the rocky walls, now and then gashed with indigo shade, patches of grey green dogwood, outcrops of boulders even at this distance immense and formidable. At the summit, apparently bare of living vegetation, a jagged line of rock cut across the serene blue of the sky. The driver was casually flicking at the amazing thing with his long handled whip. 'There she is ladies ... only about a mile and a half to go!'

Mr Hussey was full of comfortable facts and figures. 'Over five hundred feet in height ... volcanic ... several monoliths ... thousands of years old. Pardon me, Miss McCraw, I should say millions.' 'The mountain comes to Mahommed. The Hanging Rock comes to Mr Hussey.' The very peculiar governess was smiling up at him : a secret crooked smile that seemed to Mr Hussey to have even less sense than the words. Mademoiselle, catching his eye, only just stopped herself from winking at the dear bewildered man. Really, poor Greta was getting more eccentric every day!

The drag turned sharply to the right, the pace quickened

and the voice of practical sanity boomed from the box seat. 'I reckon you ladies will be wanting your lunches. I know I'll be ready for that chicken pie I've been hearing so much about.' The girls were all chattering again and Edith was not the only one with thoughts centred on chicken pie. Heads craned out between the flaps for another sight of the Rock, appearing and disappearing with every turn of the road; sometimes close enough for the three girls in front to make out the two great balancing boulders near the summit, sometimes almost obscured by the foreground of scrub and tall forest trees.

The so-called Picnic Grounds at the base of the Hanging Rock were entered through a sagging wooden gate, now closed. Miranda, an experienced gate opener on the family property at home, had climbed down unasked from the box seat and was expertly manipulating the warped wooden latch under the admiring eye of Mr Hussey, who noted the sure touch of the slender hands, the dragging weight of the gate neatly supported on one hip. As soon as it was opened wide enough on its rusty hinges to allow the safe passage of the drag, a flock of parrots flew out screeching from an overhanging tree, winging away across the sunlit grassy flats towards Mount Macedon, rising up all blue and green to the south.

'Come up Sailor ... Duchess, get over you ... Belmonte, what d'you think you're doing ...? Cripes Miss Miranda, you'd think they'd never set eyes on a blooming parrot before.' So Mr Hussey, in the best of holiday tempers, guided the five bay horses out of the known dependable present and into the unknown future, with the same happy confidence with which he daily negotiated the narrow gates of the Macedon Livery Stables and his own backyard.

2

Manmade improvements on Nature at the Picnic Grounds consisted of several circles of flat stones to serve as fireplaces and a wooden privy in the shape of a Japanese pagoda. The creek at the close of summer ran sluggishly through long dry grass, now and then almost disappearing to re-appear as a shallow pool. Lunch had been set out on large white tablecloths close by, shaded from the heat of the sun by two or three spreading gums. In addition to the chicken pie, angel cake, jellies and the tepid bananas inseparable from an Australian picnic, Cook had provided a handsome iced cake in the shape of a heart, for which Tom had obligingly cut a mould from a piece of tin. Mr Hussey had boiled up two immense billycans of tea on a fire of bark and leaves and was now enjoying a pipe in the shadow of the drag where he could keep a watchful eye on his horses tethered in the shade.

The only other occupants of the Picnic Grounds were a party of three or four people encamped some distance away under some blackwoods on the opposite side of the creek, where a large bay horse and a white Arab pony were lunching from two chaffbags beside an open wagonette. 'How dreadfully quiet it is out here,' observed Edith, helping herself lavishly to cream. 'How anyone can prefer to live in the country I can't imagine. Unless of course they are dreadfully poor.'

'If everyone else in Australia felt like that, you wouldn't be making yourself fat on rich cream,' Marion pointed out.

'Except for those people over there with the wagonette we might be the only living creatures in the whole world,' said Edith, airily dismissing the entire animal kingdom at one stroke.

The sunny slopes and shadowed forest, to Edith so still

and silent, were actually teeming with unheard rustlings and twitterings, scufflings, scratchings, the light brush of unseen wings. Leaves, flowers and grasses glowed and trembled under the canopy of light; cloud shadows gave way to golden motes dancing above the pool where water beetles skimmed and darted. On the rocks and grass the diligent ants were crossing miniature Saharas of dry sand, jungles of seeding grass, in the never ending task of collecting and storing food. Here, scattered about amongst the mountainous human shapes were Heaven-sent crumbs, caraway seeds, a shred of crystallized ginger – strange, exotic but recognizably edible loot. A battalion of sugar ants, almost bent in half with the effort, were laboriously dragging a piece of icing off the cake towards some subterranean larder dangerously situated within inches of Blanche's yellow head, pillowed on a rock. Lizards basked on the hottest stones, a lumbering armour-plated beetle rolled over in the dry leaves and lay helplessly kicking on its back; fat white grubs and flat grey woodlice preferred the dank security of layers of rotting bark. Torpid snakes lay coiled in their secret holes awaiting the twilight hour when they would come sliding from hollow logs to drink at the creek, while in the hidden depths of the scrub the birds waited for the heat of the day to pass…

Insulated from natural contacts with earth, air and sunlight, by corsets pressing on the solar plexus, by voluminous petticoats, cotton stockings and kid boots, the drowsy well-fed girls lounging in the shade were no more a part of their environment than figures in a photograph album, arbitrarily posed against a backcloth of cork rocks and cardboard trees.

Hunger satisfied and the unwonted delicacies enjoyed to the last morsel, the cups and plates rinsed at the pool, they settled down to amuse themselves for the remainder of the afternoon. Some wandered off in twos and threes, under strict injunctions not to stray out of sight of the drag; others, drugged with rich food and sunshine, dozed and dreamed. Rosamund produced some fancywork, Blanche was already asleep. Two industrious sisters from New Zealand were making pencil sketches of Miss McCraw, who had at last removed the kid gloves in which she had absently begun to eat a banana with disastrous results. Sitting upright on a fallen log with her knife of a nose in a book, and her steel-rimmed spectacles, she was almost too easy to caricature. Beside her Mademoiselle, her blond hair falling about her face, was relaxed at full length on the grass. Irma had borrowed her mother o'pearl penknife and was peeling a ripe apricot with a voluptuous delicacy worthy of Cleopatra's banquet. 'Why is it, Miranda,' she whispered, 'that such a sweet pretty creature is a schoolteacher – of all dreary things in the world . . .? Oh here comes Mr Hussey, it seems a shame to wake her.'

'I am not asleep, ma petite – only day-dreaming,' said the governess, propping her head on an elbow with a far-away smile. 'What is it, Mr Hussey?'

'I'm sorry to disturb you, Miss, but I want to make sure we get away no later than five. Sooner, if my horses are ready.'

'Of course. Whatever you say. I shall see that the young ladies are ready whenever you are. What time is it now?'

'I was just going to ask you, Miss. My old ticker seems to have stopped dead at twelve o'clock. Today of all days in the whole bloomin' year.'

It happened that Mademoiselle's little French clock was in Bendigo being repaired.

'At Moosoo Montpelier's, Miss?'

'I think that is the watchmaker's name.'

'In Golden Square? Then if I may say so, you've done real well for yourself.' A faint unmistakable blush belied the coolness of the French lady's 'Indeed?' However, Mr Hussey had got his teeth into Moosoo Montpelier and seemed unable to let him go, shaking him up and down like a dog with a bone. 'Let me tell you, Miss, Moosoo Montpelier and his father before him is one of the best men in his line in all Australia. And a fine gentleman, too. You couldn't have gone to a better man.'

'So I understand. Miranda – you have your pretty little diamond watch – can you tell us the time?'

'I'm sorry Mam'selle. I don't wear it any more. I can't stand hearing it ticking all day long just above my heart.'

'If it were mine,' said Irma, 'I would never take it off – not even in the bath. Would you, Mr Hussey?'

Jerked into reluctant action, Miss McCraw closed her book, sent an exploratory pair of bony fingers into the folds of the flat puce bosom and came out with an old-fashioned gold repeater on a chain. 'Stopped at twelve. Never stopped before. My papa's.' Mr Hussey was reduced to looking knowingly at the shadow of the Hanging Rock which ever since luncheon had been creeping down towards the Picnic Grounds on the flat. 'Shall I put the billy on again for a cup of tea before we go? Say about an hour from now?'

'An hour,' said Marion Quade, producing some squared paper and a ruler. 'I should like to make a few measurements at the base of the Rock if we have time.' As both Miranda and Irma wanted a closer view of the Rock they asked permission to take a walk as far as the lower slope before tea. It was granted after a moment's hesitation by Mademoiselle, Miss McCraw having disappeared again behind her book. 'How far is it as the cock crows, Miranda?'

'Only a few hundred yards,' said Marion Quade. 'We shall have to walk along by the creek which will take a little longer.'

'May I come too?' asked Edith, rising to her feet with a prodigious show of yawning. 'I ate so much pie at lunch I can hardly keep awake.' The other two looked enquiringly at Miranda and Edith was allowed to tag along behind.

'Don't worry about us, Mam'selle dear,' smiled Miranda. 'We shall only be gone a very little while.'

The governess stood and watched the four girls walking off towards the creek; Miranda a little ahead gliding through tall grasses that brushed her pale skirts, Marion and Irma following arm in arm with Edith bumbling along in the rear. When they reached the clump of rushes where the stream changed its course Miranda stopped, turned her shining head and gravely smiled at Mademoiselle who smiled back and waved, and stood there smiling and waving until they were out of sight round the bend. 'Mon Dieu!' she exclaimed to the empty blue, 'now I know . . .'

'What do you know?' asked Greta McCraw, suddenly peering up over the top of her book, alert and factual, as was her disconcerting way. The Frenchwoman, seldom at

23

loss for a word, even in English, found herself embarrassingly tongue-tied. It simply wasn't possible to explain to Miss McCraw of all people her exciting discovery that Miranda was a Botticelli angel from the Uffizi ... impossible to explain or even think clearly on a summer afternoon of things that really mattered. Love for instance, when only a few minutes ago the thought of Louis' hand expertly turning the key of the little Sèvres clock had made her feel almost ready to faint. She lay down again on the warm scented grass, watching the shadows of overhanging branches moving away from the hamper containing milk and lemonade. Soon it would be exposed to the full glare of the sun and she must rouse herself and carry it into the shade. Already the four girls must have been away for ten minutes, perhaps more. It was unnecessary to consult a watch. The exquisite languor of the afternoon told her that this was the hour when people weary of humdrum activities tend to doze and dream as she was doing now. At Appleyard College the pupils in the late afternoon classes had to be continually reminded to sit up straight and get on with their lessons. Opening one eye, she could see the two industrious sisters at the pool had put away their sketchbooks and fallen asleep. Rosamund nodded over her embroidery. By a sheer effort of will Mademoiselle made herself count over the nineteen girls under her care. All except Edith and the three seniors were visible and within easy call. Closing her eyes, she permitted herself the luxury of continuing an interrupted dream.

Meanwhile the four girls were still following the winding course of the creek upstream. From its hidden source somewhere in the tangle of bracken and dogwood at the base of the Rock it approached the level plain of the Picnic Grounds as an almost invisible trickle, then suddenly for a hundred yards or so became deeper and clearer, running quite swiftly over the smooth stones and presently opening out into a little pool ringed by grass of a brilliant watery green. Which no doubt had made this particular spot the choice of the party with the wagonette for their picnic. A stout bewhiskered elderly man with a solar topee tipped over a large scarlet face was lying fast asleep on his back with his hands crossed over a stomach swathed in a scarlet cummerbund. Nearby, a little woman in an elaborate silk dress sat with closed eyes propped against a tree and a pile of cushions from the wagonette, fanning herself with a palmleaf fan. A slender fair youth – or very young man – in English riding breeches was absorbed in a magazine, while another of about the same age, or a little older, as tough and sunburned as the other was tender and pink of cheek, was engaged in rinsing the champagne glasses at the edge of the pool. His coachman's cap and dark blue jacket with silver buttons were thrown carelessly over a clump of reeds, exposing a mop of thick dark hair and a pair of strong copper-coloured arms, heavily tattooed with mermaids.

Although the four girls following the endless loops and turns of the wayward creek were now almost abreast of the picnic party, the Hanging Rock remained tantalizingly hidden behind the screen of tall forest trees. 'We really must find a suitable place to cross over,' said Miranda, screwing up her eyes, 'or we shall see nothing at all before we have to turn back.' The creek was getting wider as it approached the pool. Marion Quade produced her ruler : 'At least four feet and no stepping stones.'

'I vote we take a flying leap and hope for the best.' said Irma, gathering up her skirts. 'Can you manage it, Edith?' Miranda asked.

'I don't know. I don't want to wet my feet.'

'Why not?' asked Marion Quade.

'I might get pneumonia and die and then you'd stop teasing me and be sorry.'

The bright fast-flowing water was crossed without mishap, to the obvious approval of the young coachman who had greeted their approach with a low penetrating whistle. As soon as the girls were out of earshot and walking away towards the southern slopes of the Rock, the youth in riding breeches threw down the *Illustrated London News* and strolled down towards the pool. 'Can I lend a hand with those glasses?'

'No, you can't. I'm only giving 'em a bit of a lick over so Cook won't rouse on me when I get home.'

'Oh ... I see ... I'm afraid I don't know much about washing up. ... Look here, Albert ... I hope you won't mind my saying so, but I wish you hadn't done that just now.'

'Done what, Mr Michael?'

'Whistled at those girls when they were going to jump over the creek.'

'It's a free country as far as I know. What's the harm in a whistle?'

'Only that you're such a good chap,' said the other, 'and nice girls don't like being whistled at by fellows they don't know.'

Albert grinned. 'Don't you believe it! The sheilas is all alike when it comes to the fellers. Do you reckon they come from Appleyard College?'

'Dash it all, Albert, I've only been in Australia a few weeks – how should *I* know who they are? As a matter of fact I only saw them for a moment when I heard you whistle and looked up.'

'Well you can take my word for it,' Albert said, 'and I've knocked about a fair bit – it's all the same if it's a bloody college they come from or the Ballarat Orphanage where me and my kid sister was dragged up.'

Michael said slowly, 'I'm sorry, I didn't know you were an orphan.'

'As good as. After me mum cleared out with a bloke from Sydney and me dad walked out on the two of us. That's when we was clapped into the bloody orphanage.'

'An orphanage?' repeated the other, who felt himself listening to a first hand account of life on Devil's Island. 'Tell me – if you don't mind talking about it – what's it like to be brought up in one of those places?'

'Lousy.' Albert had finished the glasses and was neatly putting away the Colonel's silver mugs in their leather case.

'Lord, how revolting!'

'Oh, it was clean enough in its way. No lice or anything except when some poor little bugger of a kid gets sent there with nits in its head and Matron gets out a bloody great scissors and cuts off its hair.' Michael appeared fascinated by the subject of the orphanage. 'Go on, tell me some more about it. . . . Did they let you see much of your sister?'

'Well, you see, there was bars on all the windows in my day – boys in one classroom, girls in another. Jeez, I haven't thought about that bloody dump for donkey's years.'

'Don't talk so loud. If my Aunt hears you swearing she'll try and make Uncle give you the sack.'

'Not him!' said the other, grinning. 'The Colonel knows I look after his horses damn well and don't drink his whisky. Well, hardly ever. Tell you the truth I can't stand the stink of the stuff. This 'ere French fizz of your Uncle's will do me. Nice and light on the stomach.' Albert's worldly wisdom was unending. Michael was filled with admiration.

'I say, Albert – I wish you'd cut out that Mr Michael stuff. It doesn't sound like Australia and anyway my name's Mike to you. Unless my Aunt's listening.'

'Have it your own way! Mike? Is that short for the Honourable Michael Fitzhubert what's on your letters? Jeez. What a mouthful! I wouldn't recognize mine if I was to see it written down in print.'

To the English youth whose own ancient name was a valued personal possession that travelled everywhere with him, like his pigskin valise and well-filled notecase, this somewhat startling observation needed several minutes of silence to digest, while the coachman surprisingly went on, 'My Dad used to change his name now and then when he got in a tight corner. I forget what they signed us up at the orphanage. Not that I bloody well care. As far as I'm concerned one bloody name's the same as another.'

'I like talking to you, Albert. Somehow you always get me thinking.'

'Thinking's all right if you have the time for it,' replied the other, reaching for his jacket. 'I'd better be harnessing up Old Glory or your Auntie's fur will be flying. She wants to get off early.'

'Right-o. I'll just stretch my legs a bit before we go.' Albert stood looking after the slim boyish figure gracefully clearing the creek and striding off towards the Rock. 'Stretch his legs is it? I don't mind betting he wants another look at them sheilas . . . That little beaut with the black curls.' He went back to his horses and began stacking the cups and plates into the Indian straw basket.

The four girls were already out of sight when Mike came out of the first belt of trees. He looked up at the vertical face of the Rock and wondered how far they would go before turning back. The Hanging Rock, according to Albert, was a tough proposition even for experienced climbers. If Albert was right and they were only schoolgirls about the same age as his sisters in England, how was it they were allowed to set out alone, at the end of a summer afternoon? He reminded himself that he was in Australia now : Australia, where anything might happen. In England everything had been done before : quite often by one's own ancestors, over and over again. He sat down on a fallen log, heard Albert calling him through the trees, and knew that this was the country where he, Michael Fitzhubert, was going to live. What was her name, the tall pale girl with straight yellow hair, who had gone skimming over the water like one of the white swans on his Uncle's lake?

3

The creek had hardly been crossed before the Hanging Rock had risen up directly ahead of the four girls, clearly visible beyond a short grassy slope. Miranda had been the first to see it. 'No, no, Edith! Not down at your boots! Away up there – in the sky.' Mike remembered afterwards how she had stopped and called back over her shoulder to the little fat one trudging behind.

The immediate impact of its soaring peaks induced a silence so impregnated with its powerful presence that even Edith was struck dumb. The splendid spectacle, as if by special arrangement between Heaven and the Head Mistress of Appleyard College, was brilliantly illuminated for their inspection. On the steep southern façade the play of golden light and deep violet shade revealed the intricate construction of long vertical slabs; some smooth as giant tombstones, others grooved and fluted by prehistoric architecture of wind and water, ice and fire. Huge boulders, originally spewed red hot from the boiling bowels of the earth, now come to rest, cooled and rounded in forest shade.

Confronted by such monumental configurations of nature the human eye is woefully inadequate. Who can say how many or how few of its unfolding marvels are actually seen, selected and recorded by the four pairs of eyes now fixed in staring wonder at the Hanging Rock? Does Marion Quade note the horizontal ledges crisscrossing the verticals of the main pattern whose geological formation must be memorized for next Monday's essay? Is Edith aware of the hundreds of frail starlike flowers crushed under her tramping boots, while Irma catches the scarlet flash of a parrot's wing and thinks it a flame amongst the leaves? And Miranda, whose feet appear to be choosing their own way through the ferns as she tilts her head towards the glittering peaks, does she already feel herself more than a spectator agape at a holiday panto-mime? So they walk silently towards the lower slopes, in single file, each locked in the private world of her own per-ceptions, unconscious of the strains and tensions of the molten mass that hold it anchored to the groaning earth : of the creakings and shudderings, the wandering airs and cur-rents known only to the wise little bats, hanging upside down in its clammy caves. None of them see or hear the snake dragging its copper coils over the stones ahead. Nor the panic exodus of spiders, grubs and woodlice from rotting leaves and bark. There are no tracks on this part of the Rock. Or if there ever *have* been tracks, they are long since obliter-ated. It is a long long time since any living creature other than an occasional rabbit or wallaby trespassed upon its arid breast.

Marion was the first to break through the web of silence. 'Those peaks . . . they must be a million years old.'

'A million. Oh, how horrible!' Edith exclaimed. 'Miranda! Did you hear that?' At fourteen, millions of years can be almost indecent. Miranda, illumined by a calm wordless joy, merely smiled back. Edith persisted. 'Miranda! It's not true, is it?'

'My Papa made a million out of a mine once – in Brazil,' Irma said. 'He bought Mama a ruby ring.'

'Money's quite different,' Edith rightly observed.

'Whether Edith likes it or not,' Marion pointed out, 'that fat little body of hers is made up of millions and millions of cells.' Edith put her hands over her ears, 'Stop it, Marion! I don't want to hear about such things.'

'And what's more, you little goose, you have already lived for millions and millions of seconds.'

Edith had gone quite white in the face. 'Stop it! You're making me feel giddy.'

'Ah, don't tease her, Marion,' Miranda soothed, seeing the usually unsnubbable Edith for once deflated. 'The poor child's overtired.' 'Yes,' said Edith, 'and those nasty ferns are pricking my legs. Why can't we all sit down on that log and look at the ugly old Rock from here?'

'Because,' said Marion Quade, 'You insisted on coming with us, and we three seniors want a closer view of the Hanging Rock before we go home.'

Edith had begun to whimper. 'It's nasty here ... I never thought it would be so nasty or I wouldn't have come ...'

'I always thought she was a stupid child and now I know,' Marion reflected out loud. Precisely as she would have stated a proven truth about an isosceles triangle. There was no real rancour in Marion – only a burning desire for truth in all departments.

'Never mind, Edith,' Irma comforted. 'You can go home soon and have some more of Saint Valentine's lovely cake and be happy.' An uncomplicated solution not only to Edith's present woe but to the sorrows of all mankind. Even as a little girl, Irma Leopold had wanted above all things to see everyone happy with the cake of their choice. Sometimes it became an almost unbearable longing, as when she had looked down at Mademoiselle asleep on the grass this afternoon. Later it would find expression in fantastic handouts from an overflowing heart and purse, no doubt acceptable to Heaven, if not to her legal advisers : handsome donations to a thousand lost causes – lepers, sinking theatrical companies, missionaries, priests, tubercular prostitutes, saints, lame dogs and deadbeats all over the world.

'I have a feeling there used to be a track somewhere up there,' said Miranda. 'I remember my father showing me a picture of people in old-fashioned dresses having a picnic at the Rock. I wish I knew where it was painted.'*

'They may have approached it from the opposite side,' said Marion, producing her pencil. 'In those days they probably drove from Mount Macedon. The thing I should like to see are those queer balancing boulders we noticed this morning, from the drag.'

'We can't go much further,' said Miranda. 'Remember, girls, I promised Mademoiselle we wouldn't be long away.'

At every step the prospect ahead grew more enchanting

*The picture Miranda remembered was 'Picnic at Hanging Rock, 1875' by William Ford, now hanging in the National Gallery of Victoria.

with added detail of crenellated crags and lichen-patterned stone. Now a mountain laurel glossy above the dogwood's dusty silver leaves, now a dark slit between two rocks where maidenhair fern trembled like green lace. 'Well, at least let us see what it looks like over this first little rise,' said Irma, gathering up her voluminous skirts. 'Whoever invented female fashions for nineteen hundred should be made to walk through bracken fern in three layers of petticoats.' The bracken soon gave way to a belt of dense scratchy scrub ending in a waist-high shelf of rock. Miranda was first out of the scrub and kneeling on the rock to pull up the others with the expert assurance that Ben Hussey had admired this morning when she opened the gate. ('At the age of five,' her father loved to remember, 'our Miranda threw a leg over a horse like a boundary rider.' 'Yes,' her mother would add, 'and entered my drawing-room with her head thrown back, like a little queen.')

They found themselves on an almost circular platform enclosed by rocks and boulders and a few straight saplings. Irma at once discovered a sort of porthole in one of the rocks and was gazing down fascinated at the Picnic Grounds below. As if magnified by a powerful telescope, the little bustling scene stood out with stereoscopic clarity between the groups of trees : the drag with Mr Hussey busy amongst his horses, smoke rising from a small fire, the girls moving about in their light dresses and Mademoiselle's parasol open like a pale blue flower beside the pool.

It was agreed to rest a few minutes in the shade of some rocks before retracing their steps to the creek. 'If only we could stay out all night and watch the moon rise,' Irma said. 'Now don't look so serious, Miranda, darling – we don't often have a chance to enjoy ourselves out of school.'

'And without being watched and spied on by that little rat of a Lumley,' Marion said.

'Blanche says she knows for a fact Miss Lumley only cleans her teeth on Sundays,' put in Edith.

'Blanche is a disgusting little know-all,' Marion said, 'and so are you.' Edith went on unperturbed, 'Blanche says Sara writes poetry. In the dunnie, you know. She found one on the floor all about Miranda.'

'Poor little Sara,' Irma said. 'I don't believe she loves anyone in the world except you, Miranda.'

'I can't think why,' Marion said.

'She's an orphan,' Miranda said gently.

Irma said, 'Sara reminds me of a little deer Papa brought home once. The same big frightened eyes. I looked after it for weeks but Mama said it would never survive in captivity.'

'And did it?' they asked.

'It died. Mama always said it was *doomed*.'

Edith echoed, '*Doomed?* What's that mean, Irma?'

'Doomed to die, of course! Like that boy who "stood on the burning deck, whence all but he had fled, tra ... la la ..." I forget the rest of it.'

'Oh, how nasty! Do you think I'm *doomed*, girls? I'm not feeling at all well, myself. Do you think that boy felt sick in the stomach like me?'

'Certainly – if he'd eaten too much chicken pie for his lunch,' Marion said. 'Edith, I do wish you would stop talking for once.'

A few tears were trickling down Edith's pudgy cheek. Why was it, Irma wondered, that God made some people so plain and disagreeable and others beautiful and kind like Miranda; dear Miranda, bending down to stroke the child's burning forehead with a cool hand. An unreasoning tender love, of the kind sometimes engendered by Papa's best French champagne or the melancholy cooing of pigeons on a Spring afternoon, filled her heart to overflowing. A love that included Marion, waiting with a flinty smile for Miranda to have done with Edith's nonsense. Tears sprang to her eyes, but not of sorrow. She had no desire to weep. Only to love, and shaking out her ringlets she got up off the rock where she had been lying in the shade and began to dance. Or rather to float away, over the warm smooth stones. All except Edith had taken off their stockings and shoes. She danced barefoot, the little pink toes barely skimming the surface like a ballerina with curls and ribbons flying and bright unseeing eyes. She was at Covent Garden where she had been taken by her grandmother at the age of six, blowing kisses to admirers in the wings, tossing a flower from her bouquet into the stalls. At last she sank into a full-blown curtsey to the Royal Box, half way up a gum tree. Edith, leaning against a boulder, was pointing at Miranda and Marion, making their way up the next little rise. 'Irma. Just look at them. Where in the world do they think they're going without their shoes?' To her annoyance Irma only laughed. Edith said crossly, 'They must be mad.' Such abandoned folly would always be beyond the understanding of Edith and her kind, who early in life take to woollen bedsocks and galoshes. Looking towards Irma for moral support, she was horrified to see that she too had picked up her shoes and stockings and was slinging them at her waist.

Miranda was a little ahead as all four girls pushed on through the dogwoods with Edith trudging in the rear. They could see her straight yellow hair swinging loose above her thrusting shoulders, cleaving wave after wave of dusty green. Until at last the bushes began thinning out before the face of a little cliff that held the last light of the sun. So on a million summer evenings would the shadows lengthen upon the crags and pinnacles of the Hanging Rock.

The semi-circular shelf on which they presently came out had much the same conformation as the one lower down, ringed with boulders and loose stones. Clumps of rubbery ferns motionless in the pale light cast no shadows upon the carpet of dry grey moss. The plain below was just visible; infinitely vague and distant. Peering down between the boulders Irma could see the glint of water and tiny figures coming and going through drifts of rosy smoke, or mist. 'Whatever can those people be doing down there like a lot of ants?' Marion looked out over her shoulder. 'A surprising number of human beings are without purpose. Although it's probable, of course, that they are performing some necessary function unknown to themselves.' Irma was in no mood for one of Marion's lectures. The ants and their business were dismissed without further comment. Although Irma was aware, for a little while, of a rather curious sound coming up from the plain. Like the beating of far-off drums.

Miranda was the first to see the monolith rising up ahead, a single outcrop of pock-marked stone, something like a monstrous egg perched above a precipitous drop to the plain. Marion, who had immediately produced a pencil and notebook, tossed them into the ferns and yawned. Suddenly overcome by an overpowering lassitude, all four girls flung themselves down on the gently sloping rock in the shelter of the monolith, and there fell into a sleep so deep that a horned lizard emerged from a crack to lie without fear in the hollow of Marion's outflung arm.

A procession of queer looking beetles in bronze armour were making a leisurely crossing of Miranda's ankle when she awoke and watched them hurrying to safety under some loose bark. In the colourless twilight every detail stood out, clearly defined and separate. A huge untidy nest wedged in the fork of a stunted tree, its every twig and feather intricately laced and woven by tireless beak and claw. Everything if only you could see it clearly enough, is beautiful and complete – the ragged nest, Marion's torn muslin skirts fluted like a nautilus shell, Irma's ringlets framing her face in exquisite wiry spirals – even Edith, flushed and childishly vulnerable in sleep. She awoke, whimpering and rubbing red-rimmed eyes. 'Where am I? Oh, Miranda, I feel awful!' The others were wide awake now and on their feet. 'Miranda,' Edith said again, 'I feel perfectly awful! When are we going home?' Miranda was looking at her so strangely, almost as if she wasn't seeing her. When Edith repeated the question more loudly, she simply turned her back and began walking away up the rise, the other two following a little way behind. Well, hardly walking – sliding over the stones on their bare feet as if they were on a drawing-room carpet, Edith thought, instead of those nasty old stones. 'Miranda,' she called again. 'Miranda!' In the breathless silence her voice seemed to belong to somebody else, a long way off, a harsh little croak fading out amongst the rocky walls. 'Come back, all of you! Don't go up there – come back!' She felt herself choking and tore at her frilled lace collar. 'Miranda!' The strangled cry came out as a whisper. To her horror all three girls were fast moving out of sight behind the monolith. 'Miranda! Come back!' She took a few unsteady steps towards the rise and saw the last of a white sleeve parting the bushes ahead.

'Miranda ...!' There was no answering voice. The awful silence closed in and Edith began, quite loudly now, to scream. If her terrified cries had been heard by anyone but a wallaby squatting in a clump of bracken a few feet away, the picnic at Hanging Rock might yet have been just another picnic on a summer's day. Nobody *did* hear them. The wallaby sprang up in alarm and bounded away, as Edith turned back, plunged blindly into the scrub and ran, stumbling and screaming, towards the plain.

4

About four o'clock in the afternoon of the Picnic, Mrs Appleyard awoke from a long luxurious nap on the drawing-room sofa. She had been dreaming, as she often did, of her late husband. This time they were walking along the Pier at Bournemouth, where a number of pleasure craft and fishing boats were tied up. 'Let us go for a sail, my dear,' said Arthur. A fourposter bed with an old-fashioned box mattress was bobbing about on the waves. 'Let us swim for it,' said Arthur, and taking her arm dived into the sea. To her surprise and pleasure she found herself swimming beautifully, cutting through the water like a fish, without using her legs or arms. They had just reached the fourposter and were climbing on board when the sound of Whitehead running the lawnmower under the window put an end to the delightful dream. How Arthur would have revelled in the respectable luxuries of life at Appleyard College! He had always, she remembered complacently, called her his financial genius. Already the College was paying handsome dividends ... A few minutes later, still in the best of tempers, and determined to be gracious on this pleasant holiday afternoon, she appeared at the schoolroom door. '*Well*, Sara, I hope you have learned your poetry so that you can go into the garden for the rest of the afternoon. Minnie shall bring you some tea and cake.'

The scraggy, big-eyed child who had automatically risen from the desk when the Headmistress entered, was shifting uneasily from one black stockinged spindle-shank to another. '*Well?* Stand up straight when you answer me, please, and put your shoulders back. You are getting a dreadful stoop. Now then. Have you got your lines by heart?'

'It's no use, Mrs Appleyard. I can't learn them.'

'How do you mean you *can't*? Considering you have

been alone in here with your Reader ever since luncheon?'

'I *have* tried,' said the child, passing her hand over her eyes. 'But it's so silly. I mean if there was any sense in it I could learn it ever so much better.'

'Sense? You little ignoramus! Evidently you don't know that Mrs Felicia Hemans is considered one of the finest of our English poets.'

Sara scowled her disbelief of Mrs Hemans' genius. An obstinate difficult child. 'I know another bit of poetry by heart. It has ever so many verses. Much more than "The Hesperus". Would that do?'

'Hhm ... What is this poem called?'

' "An Ode to Saint Valentine".' For a moment the little pointed face brightened; looked almost pretty.

'I am not acquainted with it,' said the Headmistress, with due caution. (One couldn't in her position be too careful; so many quotations turned out to be Tennyson or Shakespeare.) 'Where did you find it, Sara – this, er, Ode?'

'I didn't find it. I wrote it.'

'You *wrote* it? No, I don't wish to hear it, thank you. Strange as it may seem, I prefer Mrs Hemans'. Give me your book and proceed to recite to me as far as you have gone.'

'I tell you, I can't learn that silly stuff if I sit here for a week.'

'Then you must go on trying a little longer,' said the Head, handing over the Reader, outwardly calm and reasonable, and sick to death of the sullen tight-lipped child. 'I shall leave you now, Sara, and expect you to be word perfect when I send Miss Lumley in half an hour. Otherwise, I am afraid I shall have to send you to bed instead of sitting up until the others return for supper after the picnic.' The schoolroom door closed, the key turned in the lock, the hateful presence swept from the room.

Out in the gay green garden beyond the schoolroom the bed of dahlias glowed as if they were on fire, caught by the late afternoon sun. At the Hanging Rock, Mademoiselle and Miranda would be pouring out tea under the trees ... Resting her heavy head on the inkstained lid of the desk the child

Sara burst into wild angry sobs. 'I hate her ... I hate her ... Oh, Bertie, Bertie, where are you? Jesus, where are you? If you are really watching the sparrows fall like it says in the Bible, why don't you come down and take me away? Miranda says I mustn't hate people even if they are wicked. I can't help it, darling Miranda ... I hate her! I hate her!' There was a scrape of the desk on the floorboards as Mrs Hemans went hurtling towards the locked door.

The sun had gone down in a blaze of theatrical pink and orange behind the College tower. Mrs Appleyard had eaten a substantial supper on a tray in her study: cold chicken, Stilton cheese and chocolate mousse. Meals at the College were unfailingly excellent. Sara had been sent to bed dry-eyed and unrepentant with a plate of cold mutton and a glass of milk. In the lamp-lit kitchen Cook and a couple of the maids were playing cards at the scrubbed wooden table, capped and aproned ready for the imminent return of the picnickers.

The night gradually darkened and thickened. The tall almost empty house for once had fallen silent, filled with shadows, even after Minnie had lighted the lamps on the cedar staircase where Venus, with one hand strategically placed upon her marble belly, gazed through the landing window at her namesake pendant above the dim lawns. It was a few minutes past eight o'clock. Mrs Appleyard, playing patience in her study, with one ear cocked for the sound of the drag coming up the gravel drive, decided to ask Mr Hussey to step inside for a glass of brandy ... there was still enough left in the decanter since the Bishop of Bendigo had lunched at the College.

Mr Hussey, over several years of experience, had proved himself so punctual and entirely reliable that at half past eight by the grandfather clock on the stairs, the Headmistress rose from the card table and pulled the velvet cord of her private bell, that jangled with authority in the kitchen. It was immediately answered by Minnie, rather red in the face. Mrs Appleyard, from whom the housemaid stood at a respectful distance in the doorway, noted with disapproval the crooked cap. 'Is Tom about still, Minnie?'

'I don't know, Mum, I'll ask Cook,' said Minnie, who had last seen her adored Tom half an hour ago, stretched out in his underpants on the truckle bed in her attic room.

'Well, see if you can find him and send him to me as soon as you do.'

After two or three more rounds of Miss Milligan, Mrs Appleyard, who normally despised the luxury of cheating at patience, deliberately dealt herself a necessary Knave of Hearts and went out on to the gravel sweep before the porch, where a lighted kerosene lantern swung from a metal chain. Against a cloudless dark blue sky the slate roofs of the College glimmered like silver. In one of the upstairs rooms a solitary light was burning behind a drawn blind : Dora Lumley, off duty and reading in bed.

The scent of stocks and sundrenched petunias was overpowering on the windless air. At least the night was fine and Mr Hussey a driver of high renown. All the same she wished young Tom could be found, if only to agree with his Irish commonsense that there was nothing to worry about in the drag being nearly an hour late. She went back to the study and began another game of patience, getting up almost at once to compare her gold watch with the clock in the hall. When it struck for half past nine she rang for Minnie again, and was informed that Tom was taking a hot bath in the coach house and would be there 'directly'. Another ten minutes dragged by.

At last came the beat of hooves on the highroad, perhaps half a mile away ... now they were crossing over the culvert ... she could see lights moving on the dark trees. A chorus of drunken voices as the vehicle gathered speed on the flat road and passed the College gates at a fast trot – a dragload of revellers returning from Woodend. At the same moment Tom, who had heard them too, presented himself in carpet slippers and a clean shirt at the open door. If Mrs Appleyard had a liking for anyone in her immediate orbit it was surely merry-eyed Irish Tom. No matter what was asked of him, from emptying the pig bucket to playing a tune on the mouthorgan for the maids, or driving the drawing mistress to the Woodend Station, it was all the same to Tom. 'Yes,

Ma'am? You were after wanting me, so Minnie was saying?'

Under the unshaded light of the porch the heavy folded cheeks were the colour of tallow. 'Tom,' said Mrs Appleyard, looking him full in the face as if to screw an answer out of him with her gimlet eyes, 'do you realize that Mr Hussey is shockingly late?'

'Is that a fact, Ma'am?'

'He promised me faithfully this morning to have them back here by eight o'clock. It is now half past ten. How long would you say it takes to drive from the Hanging Rock?'

'Well, it's a fair step from here . . .'

'Think carefully, please. You are familiar with the roads.'

'Say three to three and a half hours and you wouldn't be far out.'

'Exactly. Hussey intended to leave the Picnic Grounds soon after four o'clock. Directly after tea.' The carefully modulated College voice became suddenly raucous. 'Don't stand there gaping at me like an idiot! What do you think has happened?'

In the lilting Irish singsong that fluttered many a female heart beside his Minnie's, Tom was soothing at her side. If the distraught face had been reasonably kissable, he might even have dared a conciliatory peck on the flaccid cheek, unpleasantly close to his well scrubbed nose. 'Now don't you be distressing yourself, Ma'am. It's five grand horses he's driving and him the best coachman this side of Bendigo.'

'Do you think I don't know all that? The point is – have they had an accident?'

'An accident, Ma'am? Well, now, I never so much as gave it a thought, such a fine night and all . . .'

'Then you're a bigger fool than I thought! I know nothing of horses but they can *bolt*. Do you hear me, Tom? Horses can bolt. For God's sake, *say* something!' It was one thing for Tom to stall and cajole in the kitchen. Quite another here in the front porch with the Headmistress standing over him twice as large as life with her tall black shadow behind her on the wall . . . 'Ready to eat me she looked,' he told Minnie afterwards, 'and the devil of it was I knew in my bones the poor creature was right.' Greatly daring he put a hand on one grey silk wrist encircled by a heavy bracelet from which hung a blood red heart. 'If you'd come inside and sit down for a wee while, Minnie can bring you a cup of tea . . .'

'Listen ! What's that? God be praised, I can hear them now !'

It was the truth, at last : hooves on the highroad, two advancing lights, the blessed scrape of wheels as the drag came slowly to a halt at the College gates. 'Woa there Sailor . . . Duchess get over . . .' Mr Hussey talking to his horses in a voice almost unrecognizably hoarse. From the dark mouth of the drag the passengers came straggling out one by one into the light of the carriage lamps fanning out on to the gravel drive. Some crying, some sodden with sleep, all hatless, dishevelled, incoherent. Tom had gone bounding off down the drive at the first hint of the drag's approach, leaving the Headmistress to dragoon her trembling limbs into a commanding stance on the porch. First to come stumbling towards her up the shallow steps was the Frenchwoman, ashen under the light.

'Mademoiselle ! What is the meaning of all this ?'

'Mrs Appleyard – something terrible has happened.'

'An accident? Speak up ! I want the truth.'

'It's all so dreadful . . . I don't know how to begin.'

'Compose yourself. A fit of hysterics will get us nowhere. . . . And where in Heaven's name is Miss McCraw ?'

'We left her behind . . . at the Rock.'

'Left her behind? Has Miss McCraw taken leave of her senses ?'

Mr Hussey was pushing through the sobbing wild-eyed girls. 'Mrs Appleyard, may I speak to you alone? . . . I think the French lady is going to faint.' He was right. Mademoiselle, exhausted with the strains and stresses of the day, had passed out on the hall carpet. From the servants' quarters Minnie and Cook, who had long since removed caps and aprons for a fitful sleep, had come running through the baize door under the staircase, which Miss Lumley in a purple dressing gown and curl papers was descending with a lighted candle. Smelling salts were produced for Mademoiselle, and brandy, and with Tom's help the governess was carried off to her room. 'Oh, the poor things,' said Cook, 'they look worn out – whatever can have happened at the picnic? Quick, Minnie, don't bother asking the Madam, we'll give them some of my hot soup.'

'Miss Lumley ... get these girls to bed immediately. Minnie will help you. ... Now, Mr Hussey.' The door of Mrs Appleyard's sitting-room closed behind the broad still magnificently upright weary back. 'If I might have a drop of spirits, Ma'am, before I begin.'

'You may – I see you are exhausted. ... Now then, tell me as briefly and plainly as you can, exactly what has happened.'

'My God, Ma'am, if only I *could* tell you ... you see, that's the worst of it. ... Nobody *knows* what's happened. Three of your young ladies and Miss McCraw are missing at the Rock.'

Extract from Ben Hussey's story as given to Constable Bumpher of Woodend, on the morning of Sunday, February the fifteenth, at the Police Station.

After the two teachers and myself realized that nobody in our party had the correct time, both my own watch and Miss McCraw's having stopped during the drive out, it was agreed that we should leave the Picnic Grounds as soon as convenient after lunch, as Mrs Appleyard was expecting us back at the College no later than eight o'clock. The French lady arranged we should have some tea and cake after I had harnessed up my horses as we had a fairly long drive ahead of us. I should say it was then about half past three, judging by the way the shadows were moving on the Rock.

As soon as my billies were boiling I went over to tell the two ladies in charge that tea was ready. The elderly teacher who had been sitting reading under a tree when I had last seen her, was not there. In fact, I never saw her again. The French lady seemed very upset and asked me if I had noticed Miss McCraw walking away from the camp, which I had not. She told me: 'None of the girls saw which way she went. I can't understand her not being back here on time – Miss McCraw is such a punctual lady.' I asked if all the rest of my passengers were present and ready to leave. She told me: 'All but four. With my permission they went for a short walk along the creek so as to get a closer view of the Hanging Rock. All except Edith Horton are senior girls and very reliable.' The three missing girls had travelled with me to the Picnic Grounds on the box seat. I knew them quite well. They were Miss Miranda (I never heard her surname), Miss Irma Leopold and Miss Marion Quade.

I wasn't particularly worried so far, only a bit put out by the delay in getting away. I know that part of the country pretty well and I soon had the girls organized to look for them, in pairs, round about the creek on the flat, cooeeing and calling out as they went. About an hour must have gone by when the girl Edith Horton came running out of the scrub near the South Western base of the Rock, crying and laughing and with her dress torn to ribbons. I thought she was going to have a fit of hysterics. She said she had left the other three girls 'somewhere up there', pointing to the Rock, but seemed to have no idea in which direction. We asked her over and over again to try and remember which way they had gone, but all we could get out of her was that she had got frightened and had run back downhill all the way. Luckily, I always carry some emergency brandy in my flask. We gave her some and wrapped her up in my driving coat and Miss Rosamund (one of the senior girls) took her off to lie down in the drag while we went on with the search. I called all the girls back and counted them and this time we went further afield — right up to the base of the Rock on the southern elevation, trying to find Edith Horton's tracks but they had petered out almost at once on stony ground. Without a magnifying glass it was impossible to see anything in the way of a footprint. None of the scrub seemed to be disturbed except for a few yards where she had come out on to the open ground and started to run back towards our camp at the creek. For further reference, we marked the opening between these trees with some sticks. Meanwhile two of the senior girls had gone off along the creek intending to make some enquiries from another picnic party who were there when we arrived, before lunch, but they had put out their

fire and left – probably while I was attending to my horses.
Four people and a wagonette. I think it was Colonel Fitzhubert's but did not actually see any of them to speak to.
Several of the girls said they had seen this wagonette driving
away earlier in the afternoon with the young fellow on the
white Arab pony riding behind. We must have gone on
calling and searching for several hours. I couldn't believe my
senses that three or four sensible people could disappear so
quickly in such a comparatively small area without some
kind of tracks. I am still just as mystified as I was yesterday
afternoon.

As even the lowest and most accessible levels of the Rock
are exceedingly treacherous, especially for inexperienced girls
in long summer dresses, I was afraid of letting them out of
my sight in case they got lost themselves what with the holes
and precipices and to my knowledge only one over-grown
track leading towards the summit, which presumably the
missing persons did not take, as I made a point of looking
there very thoroughly at the point where it starts. There were
no signs of crushed undergrowth, footprints, etc., either here
or anywhere else.

As it grew later and darker – we had no means of knowing
the time except by the sinking sun – we lit a number of fires
along the creek in such a way that they could be seen from
various angles by anyone on this side of the Rock. We also
kept on cooeeing as loudly as we could singly and all together.
I got the two billies and beat on them with the crowbar I
always keep in the drag for emergencies.

By this time the French lady and I were at our wits' end
to decide whether to drive back to Woodend with the news
or to go on looking. We had only the two oil lamps on the
drag and my hurricane lamp lit up a few square yards at a
time. If the missing persons were still somewhere on the
Rock, which I had begun to doubt, without matches they
would be in real danger after dark unless they had the sense
to sit tight in a cave until daylight. The French lady and
some of the girls were getting a bit hysterical and no wonder.
None of us had had so much as a cup of tea since lunchtime.
We were too worried to think of making it. We had some

45

lemonade and biscuits and I decided to take the party back to the College without looking any more that night.

I don't honestly know if I did right to act as I did but I take full responsibility for the decision. I am pretty well acquainted with the three missing girls and I reckoned that unless they had all three met with an accident which seemed unlikely, Miss Miranda who is well used to the Bush would have kept her head and found some safe place to shelter for the night. As for the teacher, I hope for her own sake she didn't wander off on her own. A knowledge of arithmetic don't help much in the Bush.

After calling in at the police station at Woodend, on the way home, and briefly informing the officer on duty what had occurred at the Hanging Rock, we drove to Appleyard College without further delay. I forgot to mention that I made a careful investigation of the public lavatories (Ladies and Gents) situated at the Picnic Grounds about half way between the creek and the base of the Rock. There were no footprints or any other signs of recent use.

5

For the inmates of Appleyard College, Sunday the fifteenth of February was a day of nightmare indecision : half dream, half reality; alternating, according to temperament, between wildly rocketing hopes and sinking fears.

The Headmistress, after a night passed in staring at the wall of her bedroom interminably whitening to the new day, was on deck at her usual hour with not a hair of the pompadour out of place. Her first concern this morning was to ensure that nothing of yesterday's happenings should be so much as whispered beyond the College walls. The three wagonettes that ordinarily took the boarders and governesses to the various churches had been countermanded before Mr Hussey had taken his leave last night, churches in Mrs Appleyard's opinion being hot beds of gossip on a fine Sunday morning. Thank Heaven Ben Hussey was a sensible creature who could be trusted to keep his mouth shut except for the confidential report already in the hands of the local police. At the College absolute silence until further notice was the rule. It may be fairly assumed that it was obeyed by those of the staff and pupils still on their legs and able to communicate after last night's ordeal, at least half of the picnickers being confined to their rooms with shock and exhaustion. However, we may have our suspicions that Tom and Minnie, as natural news-spreaders, and possibly Cook, all of whom had unofficial visitors during Sunday afternoon, were not quite so conscientious, and that Miss Dora Lumley may have exchanged a few words at the back door with Tommy Compton who delivered the Sunday cream. Doctor McKenzie of Woodend had been sent for and turned up in his gig soon after breakfast : an elderly G.P. of infinite wisdom who, taking in the situation with one shrewd gold-spectacled glance, prescribed a whole holiday on Monday, light nourishing food and some mild sedative. Mademoiselle was confined to her room with a migraine. The old doctor patted the pretty hand on the coverlet, sprinkled a few drops of eau de cologne on the patient's burning forehead and observed mildly, 'By the by, my dear young lady, I hope you're not so foolish as to blame yourself in any way for this unfortunate affair? It may very well turn out to be a storm in a tea-cup, you know.'

'Mon Dieu, Doctor – I pray that you are right.'

'Nobody,' said the old man, 'can be held responsible for the pranks of destiny.'

Edith Horton, for once in her life something of a heroine, was pronounced by Doctor McKenzie to be in good physical trim thanks to the prolonged fit of screaming – in a girl of her age Nature's answer to hysteria – although he was a little disturbed by her remembering nothing whatever of the thing that had sent her running back alone and terrified from the Rock. Edith liked Doctor McKenzie – who didn't? – and appeared to be trying, as far as her limited intelligence allowed, to co-operate. It was possible, he decided as he drove home, that the child hit her head on a rock – easily done in that rough country – and was suffering from a mild form of concussion.

Mrs Appleyard had spent the greater part of Sunday alone in her study, following a conversation with Constable Bumpher of Woodend, who had brought with him a none too bright young policeman for the purpose of taking notes on a relatively unimportant matter which Bumpher expected to be satisfactorily cleared up before Sunday evening. City people were forever getting themselves lost in the tall timber and getting Christians off their beds on Sunday mornings to find them. It appeared, however, that the facts concerning the three missing schoolgirls and their governess were more than ordinarily vague, apart from Ben Hussey's story which did no more than sum up events already known and confirmed. Bumpher had arranged for the two young men picnicking at the Hanging Rock on Saturday – so far the last people to see the missing girls crossing the creek – to give the police any further information which might be required, if they had not already been found, on Monday. The only other person that Bumpher would like to speak to this morning for a few minutes, if convenient, was the girl Edith Horton, who had actually been with three of the missing persons, possibly for several hours, before she had returned panic-stricken to the luncheon camp. Accordingly, Edith, red eyed in a cashmere dressing gown to match, was brought down to the study only to prove an inarticulate and utterly useless source of information. Neither the Constable nor the Head could extract anything more constructive than a sniff or two and sulky negatives. Perhaps the young policeman might have done better but he was not given a chance and Edith was escorted back to bed. 'It doesn't signify,' said Bumpher, accepting a glass of brandy and water. 'In my private opinion, Ma'am, the whole affair will be cleared up within a few hours. You've no idea how many people get themselves lost if they stray a few yards off the beaten track.' 'I wish, Mr Bumpher,' said Mrs Appleyard, 'I could agree with you. My head girl, Miranda, was born and bred in the Bush ... with regard to the governess, Miss McCraw ...'

It had already been established that nobody had seen Miss McCraw leaving the picnic party after lunch. Although for some unknown reason she must have suddenly decided to get up from under the tree where she had been reading and followed the four girls towards the Rock. 'Unless,' said the policeman, 'the lady had some private arrangements of her own? To meet a friend or friends, for instance, outside the gates?'

'Definitely no. Miss Greta McCraw, whom I have employed for several years, to my knowledge has not a single friend, or acquaintance even, on this side of the world.'

Her book had already been found with her kid gloves exactly where she had been sitting, by Rosamund, one of the senior girls. Both Mrs Appleyard and the policeman were agreed that a mathematics mistress, no matter how 'smart at figures' as Bumpher put it, could be fool enough to lose her way like anyone else, although the point was rather more delicately made. Even Archimedes, it was suggested, might have taken a wrong turning with his thoughts on higher things. All this the young policeman took down with much hard breathing and pencil licking. (Later, when the passengers in the drag on its outward journey were briefly questioned, it would be recalled by several witnesses, including Mademoiselle, that Miss McCraw had been talking rather wildly of triangles and short cuts, and had even suggested to the driver that they should go home by a different and quite impractical route.)

A continuous search of the Picnic Grounds and as much of the Hanging Rock as could be clambered over and observed at close quarters, had already been set in motion by the local police. One of the most baffling features, as already reported by Mr Hussey, was the absence of any kind of tracks other than some crushed bracken and the bruised leaves of a few bushes on the lower slopes of the eastern face of the rock. On Monday, unless the mystery had been solved, a black tracker was being brought from Gippsland, and – at the instigation of Colonel Fitzhubert – a bloodhound, for whom certain articles of the missing persons' clothing were labelled by Miss Lumley and handed over at the constable's request. A number of locals, including Michael Fitzhubert and Albert Crundall, were already assisting the police in the careful toothcombing of the surrounding scrub. News travels as fast in the Australian Bush as it does in a city, and by Sunday evening there was hardly a house within fifty miles of Hanging Rock where Saturday's mysterious disappearance was not being discussed over the evening meal. As always, in matters of surpassing human interest, those who knew nothing whatever either at first or even second hand were the most emphatic in expressing their opinions; which are well known to have a way of turning into established facts overnight.

If Sunday the fifteenth had been a nightmare at the College, Monday the sixteenth was, if anything, worse; beginning with a ring at the hall door at six a.m. by a young reporter from a Melbourne newspaper on a flat-tyred bicycle, who had to be restored by Cook with breakfast in the kitchen and sent back newsless on the Melbourne Express.

This unhappy youth was the first unwelcome caller of many, many more. The massive cedar door, rarely used except on ceremonial occasions, was opening and shutting from morning till night on a variety of callers, some well intentioned, others merely inquisitive, including a few male and female hyenas drawn quite frankly and openly by the smell of blood and scandal. None of these people were admitted. Even the curate from Macedon and his kind little wife, both dreadfully embarrassed, but imbued with a genuine desire to help in time of trouble, were dismissed like everyone else with a curt 'not at home' on the porch.

Meals were served with their customary clockwork precision, but only a few of the usually ravenous young women who sat down to the mid-day dinner did more than trifle with the roast mutton and apple pie. The seniors gathered together in little whispering groups. Edith and Blanche sniffed and slouched arm in arm for once uncorrected; the New Zealand sisters endlessly embroidered, murmuring of remembered earthquakes and other horrors. Sara Waybourne, who had lain awake all Saturday night waiting for Miranda to return from the picnic and kiss her good night as she always did, no matter how late the hour, flitted restlessly from room to room like a little ghost until Miss Lumley, whose head was pounding like a sledge hammer, produced some linen to be hemmed before tea. Miss Lumley herself, and the junior sewing mistress, when not engaged in running messages for the Head and other unrewarding duties, complained to their mutual satisfaction of being 'put upon' – a handy phrase which covered everyone in authority from the Almighty down. The essay on the Hanging Rock, still chalked up on the blackboard as the major exercise in English Literature for Monday, February the sixteenth, at eleven thirty a.m., was never so much as mentioned again. At last the sun sank behind the glowing dahlia bed; the hydrangeas shone like sapphires in the dusk; the statues on the staircase held aloft their pallid torches to the warm blue night. So ended the second dreary day.

By the morning of Tuesday the seventeenth, the two young men who had been the last to see the missing girls on Saturday afternoon had dictated their respective statements to the local police. Albert Crundall at the Woodend Station, and the Hon. Michael Fitzhubert in his Uncle's study at Lake View. Both had affirmed their complete ignorance as to the subsequent movements of the four girls after they had crossed the creek near the pool and walked away in the direction of the lower slopes of the Hanging Rock. Michael with faltering tones and downcast eyes which seemed to have receded into his head since Sunday morning, when Albert had come galloping back from Manassa's store with the news of the girls' disappearance. Constable Bumpher had seated himself at the Colonel's writing table with Michael opposite stiff on a highbacked chair.

After the usual formalities were completed, 'I think, sir,' said the policeman, 'we had better start off with a few questions, just to get the general picture, so to speak.' Young Mr Fitzhubert, with his shy charming smile and English good manners, was obviously the uncommunicative type. 'Now then, when you saw the girls crossing the creek, did you recognize any of them?'

'How could I? I have only been in Australia about three weeks and haven't met any young girls.'

'I see. Did you have any conversation with any of these girls – either before or after they crossed to the opposite bank?'

'Certainly not! I've just told you, Constable, I didn't even know any of them by sight.' At which guileless reply the Constable permitted himself a dry grin, adding mentally, 'Stone the crows! With that face and all that money?' He asked, 'How about Crundall? Did *he* speak to any of these girls?'

'No. Only stared and whistled at them.'

'What were your Uncle and Aunt doing while this was going on?'

'As far as I can remember they were both dozing. We had champagne for lunch and I suppose it made them sleepy.'

'What effect does champagne have on *you*?' asked the policeman, pencil in air.

'None as far as I know. I don't drink much at any time and when I do it's usually wine, you know, at home.'

'Well then, you were perfectly clear in the head and sitting with a book under a tree when you saw them crossing the creek. Now suppose you go on from there. Just try and remember any little detail even if it seems unimportant now. You understand of course this is an entirely voluntary statement on your part?'

'I watched them crossing the creek ...' He swallowed and went on again in an almost inaudible voice. 'They all did it differently.'

'Speak up, please. How do you mean differently? Ropes? Vaulting poles?'

'Heavens no! I only meant some of them were more agile, you know – more graceful.'

Bumpher, however, was not at this moment concerned with grace. The young man continued: 'Anyway, as soon as we were out of earshot I got up and went over to speak to Albert who was washing some glasses at the creek. We had a bit of a talk – oh, perhaps ten minutes, and I said I would take a little stroll before it was time to go home.'

'What time was it then?'

'I didn't look at my watch but I knew my uncle wanted to leave not later than four o'clock. I began walking towards the Hanging Rock. By the time it began to go uphill there was some bracken fern and bushes and the girls were already out of sight. I remember thinking the scrub looked pretty thick for girls to tackle in light summer dresses, and expected to see them coming down any minute. I sat down for a few minutes on a fallen tree. When Albert called out I came back to the pool immediately, mounted the Arab pony and rode home, most of the way behind my Uncle's wagonette. I can't think of anything else. Will that do?'

'Nicely, thank you, Mr Fitzhubert. We may get you to help us again later.' Michael groaned inwardly. The brief interview had been a fairly close imitation of a dentist's drill boring into a sensitive cavity. 'Only one more thing I'd like to check up on before we get it written down,' the policeman

53

was saying. 'You mentioned seeing *three* girls crossing the creek. Is that correct?'

'I'm sorry. You're right of course, there were four girls.'

Bumpher's pencil was hovering again. 'What made you forget there were four of 'em, do you think?'

'Because I forgot the little fat one, I suppose.'

'So you looked pretty closely at the other three, did you?'

'No I didn't.' (God help me it's the truth. I only looked at *her*.) 'I suppose you would have remembered if there was an elderly lady with them?'

Michael, looking irritated, said, 'Of course I would. There was no one else. Only the four girls.'

While this was going on Albert at the Woodend police station was giving his statement to one Jim Grant – the young policeman who had been out to Appleyard College with Bumpher on Sunday morning. Unlike Michael, Albert, fairly well used to the twists and turns which a policeman can give to the most innocent remark, was rather enjoying himself, being officially acquainted with young Grant through the trifling matter of a Sunday cockfight.

'I've told you, Jim,' he was saying, 'I only seen them sheilas the once.' 'I'll trouble you not to call me Jim when I'm on duty,' said the other, who had reached the perspiring stage of exasperation. 'It don't smell good in the Force. Now then. How many girls did you see crossing that creek?' 'All right Mr Bloody Grant. Four.'

'There's no call for swearing neither. I'm only performing my duty.'

'I suppose you know,' said the coachman, producing a small bag of caramels and ostentatiously sucking one in a hollow tooth, 'that this is a statement what I give to the police free, gratis, and for nothing. I'm only doing it to oblige and don't you forget it, Mr Grant.'

Jim resisted the peace offering of a caramel and continued. 'What did you do after Mr Fitzhubert started to walk towards the Rock?'

'The Colonel wakes up and starts hollering it's time to go home and I goes after Mr Michael and blow me if he isn't sitting down on a log and the sheilas out of sight.'

'About how far from the pool would this log be?'

'Look, Jim, you know as well as I do. The bloody police and everyone else know the exact spot. I showed it to Mr Bumpher himself last Sunday.'

'All right, I'm only ascertaining the facts – go on.'

'Anyway, Michael gets on that Arab pony what his Uncle lets him ride and rides home to Lake View.'

'The little beaut! I'll say some people are lucky! Gee, Albert, you couldn't get the Hon. Who's This to give me a loan of it to show at Gisborne? Nothing to beat that pony for fifty miles round here. Mind you, I wouldn't be wanting the saddle and bridle ... just the mount for the afternoon. The Colonel knows I haven't bad hands on a horse.'

'If you think I've come all the way down here from Lake View to scrounge a ride on the Arab for you ...' said Albert, rising. 'No more questions? Then I'll be off. Ta-ta.'

'Hi, wait a moment. There *is* one more,' cried Jim, making a pass at the other's coat tails. 'When Mr Fitzhubert mounted this pony of his you say he rode home to Lake View with the wagonette? Did you actually see him all the way?'

'I haven't got eyes in the back of me bloody head. He rode behind us some of the way so as we wouldn't get his dust and some of the way he was ahead, according to the road. I didn't take that much notice except that we all arrived at the front gates of Lake View at the same time.'

'What time was that, do you think?'

'Round about half past seven it must have been. I remember Cook had my dinner waiting in the oven.'

'Thank you, Mr Crundall.' The young policeman closed his notebook with some formality. 'This interview will be written out in full and shown to you later for your approval. You may go now.' The permission was superfluous. Albert was already slipping the bridle over the head of a strawberry cob tethered in a patch of clover on the opposite side of the road.

For three consecutive mornings the Australian public had been devouring, along with its bacon and eggs, the luscious details of the College Mystery as it was now known to the

55

Press. Although no further information had been unearthed and nothing resembling a clue, so that the situation remained unchanged since the girls and their governess had been reported missing by Ben Hussey late on Saturday night, the public must be fed. To this end, some additional spice had been added to Wednesday's columns' photographs of the Hon. Michael's ancestral home, Haddingham Hall (inset of sisters playing with spaniel on the terrace) and of course Irma Leopold's beauty and reputed millions on coming of age. Bumpher, however, was far from satisfied with all this. After consultation with his friend, Detective Lugg, based at Russell Street, he had decided to make yet another attempt to extract something in the way of concrete evidence from the schoolgirl Edith Horton. Accordingly, at eight o'clock on the morning of Wednesday the eighteenth, another glorious day lightened by a gay little breeze, he had arrived at Appleyard College in a buggy and pair, with young Jim in attendance, for the purpose of driving Edith Horton and the French Governess to the Picnic Grounds at Hanging Rock.

Mrs Appleyard, although the arrangement smacked vaguely of frivolity, could hardly object. The police, said Bumpher, were doing their utmost to clear up the mystery and in his opinion and that of Detective Lugg, it was essential that Edith as a key witness should be confronted with the actual scene as a spur to memory. The Headmistress, aware of Edith's limited intelligence and unlimited obstinacy, plus a possible mild concussion, thought the expedition a waste of time and said so to Bumpher, who bluntly disagreed. Despite a rather unprepossessing manner, Bumpher was no fool at his job and had a great deal of experience in the way different people react under police questioning. He told her : 'All of us trying to make this girl remember may have got her more bamboozled than ever. I've known people with shocking memories turn into quite useful witnesses once they get back to where they started, so to speak. We'll try and take it easy this time ...' And so, with a relaxing atmosphere in mind, the Constable had allowed himself to enjoy the drive with Mademoiselle sitting up beside him smart and pretty in a shady hat, and had even shouted her a brandy and soda and

Edith and young Jim a lemonade, while they were changing horses at the hotel in Woodend.

Now they were standing at the exact spot on the Picnic Grounds where Edith and the three other girls had crossed the creek by the pool on the afternoon of Saint Valentine's Day. Straight ahead, on the sunlit face of the Hanging Rock, the forest branches threw faintly stirring patterns of shade. 'Like blue lace,' thought Mademoiselle, wondering how anything so beautiful could be the instrument of evil ... 'Now then, Miss Edith!' The policeman was well away, all smiles and fatherly patience. 'In which direction do you say you began walking the other day when you started off from this very spot?'

'I don't say. I told you before, one gum tree's the same as another to me.'

'Edith chérie,' put in Mademoiselle, 'perhaps you could tell the Sergeant what you four girls were chattering of just then ...? I am sure they *were* chattering, Mr Bumpher ...'

'That's right,' said the policeman. 'That's the idea. Miss Edith, did anyone suggest which way they wanted to go?'

'Marion Quade was teasing me ... Marion can be very disagreeable sometimes. She said those peaky things up there were a million years old.'

'The Peaks. So you were walking towards the Peaks?'

'I suppose so. My feet were hurting and I didn't pay much attention. I wanted to sit down on a fallen tree instead of going on but the others wouldn't let me.'

Bumpher threw a hopeful glance at Mademoiselle. There were a number of logs and fallen branches scattered about but at least a fallen tree was something concrete to work from. 'Now that you've remembered about the log, Miss Edith, perhaps you will think of something else? Just take a look around from here and see if there's anything at all that you can recognize. Stumps, ferns, queer-shaped stones ...?'

'No,' said Edith. 'There isn't.'

'Oh, well, never mind,' said the policeman, resolving to renew the attack after lunch. 'Where would you like to eat our sandwiches, Mademoiselle?'

Jim was sent back to the buggy for the lunch boxes and

they had just made themselves comfortable on the grass when Edith volunteered, apropos of nothing, 'Mr Bumpher! There *is* one thing I seem to remember.'

'Fine. What was it?'

'A cloud. A funny sort of cloud.'

'A cloud? Fine! Except that clouds unfortunately have a way of moving from one place to another in the sky, you know.'

'I am quite aware of that,' said Edith all at once prim and grown up. 'Only this one was a nasty red colour and I remember it because I looked up and saw it through some branches ...' Slowly she took a large bite of ham sandwich ... 'It was just after I passed Miss McCraw.'

Bumpher's own sandwich fell unnoticed on to the grass. 'Miss McCraw? Stone the crows! You never told us you saw Miss McCraw! Jim, get your notebook. I don't know if you realize, Miss Edith, that what you have just told me is very important.'

'That's why I'm telling you,' said Edith smugly.

'When did your teacher join up with you and the other three girls? Think very hard please.'

'She's not my teacher,' said Edith, taking another bite of the sandwich. 'My mamma didn't want me to do senior mathematics. She says a girl's place is in the home.'

Bumpher had somehow produced an ingratiating grin.

'Quite so. Very sensible lady, your mother ... now go on please, about Miss McCraw. Where was she when you suddenly looked up and saw her? Close by? A long way off?'

'She seemed to be quite a long way off.'

'A hundred yards, fifty yards?'

'I don't know, I'm not much good at sums. I told you, I only saw her in the distance through the trees as I was running back to the creek.'

'You were running downhill, of course?'

'Of course.'

'And Miss McCraw was walking uphill, in the opposite direction. Is that correct?'

To his dismay the witness had begun to wriggle and giggle. 'Oh mercy! She did look so funny.'

'Why?' asked Bumpher. 'Get this down, Jim. Why did she look so funny?' 'I'd rather not say.'

'Please tell us, Edith,' Mademoiselle coaxed. 'You're giving Mr Bumpher such valuable help.'

'Her skirt,' said Edith, stuffing the corner of her handkerchief into her mouth.

'What about her skirt?'

Edith was giggling again. 'It's too rude to say out loud in mixed company.' Bumpher was leaning towards her as if his keen blue eyes could bore a hole in her brain tissues. 'You don't need to mind about me. I'm old enough to be your Dad! ... that's the idea.' Edith was whispering something into Mademoiselle's attentive little pink ear. 'She says, Constable, that Miss McCraw was not wearing a skirt – only les pantalons.'

'Drawers,' the constable instructed young Jim. 'Now then, Miss Edith. You are positive this woman you saw in the distance walking uphill through the trees was really Miss McCraw?'

'Positive.'

'Wasn't it a bit hard to recognize her without her dress?'

'Not at all. None of the other teachers are such a peculiar shape. Irma Leopold once told me "The McCraw is exactly the same shape as a flat iron!" '

And that was the last and only piece of factual information to be extracted from Edith Horton, either on Wednesday, February the eighteenth, or on any subsequent occasion.

As soon as the police buggy had turned out of the drive on to the highroad, Mrs Appleyard had sat down resolutely at her desk and locked the study door. It was becoming a habit. As she went about her business, erect, uncommunicative, outwardly unperturbed, she was increasingly aware of a rising murmur of questioning voices from the outside world. Voices of cranks, clergymen, clairvoyants, journalists, friends, relations, parents. Parents of course were the worst. One could hardly toss their letters into the wastepaper basket as one could the offer, with stamped envelope enclosed, to find the missing girls with a patent magnet. A hard core of commonsense told her that it was reasonable enough, even for a parent whose daughter had returned from the picnic safe and well, to write for further information and reassurance. These were the letters that kept her chained and chafing at her desk for hours at a time. An indiscreet word addressed to an overwrought mother might easily at this stage set off a conflagration of lies and rumours that no amount of hosing down with the icy waters of truth could extinguish.

Mrs Appleyard's task this morning was the odious and infinitely more dangerous one of writing to inform the parents of Miranda and Irma Leopold and the legal guardian of Marion Quade that all three girls and a governess had mysteriously disappeared from the Hanging Rock. Fortunately – or perhaps unfortunately – none of the three letters would reach their destination without considerable delay. Nor would any of the recipients have had access to the published reports of the College Mystery, for reasons to be presently disclosed. Again her thoughts reverted to the morning of the picnic. Again she saw the orderly rows of girls in hats and gloves, the two mistresses in perfect control. Again she heard her own brief words of farewell on the porch, warning of dangerous snakes and insects. Insects! What in the name of Heaven had happened on Saturday afternoon? And why, why, why had it happened to three senior girls so valuable to the prestige and social standing of Appleyard College? Marion Quade, a brilliant scholar, though not wealthy like the other two, could be counted on for academic laurels, almost equally important in their way. Why couldn't it have been Edith who had disappeared, or that little nobody Blanche, or Sara Waybourne? As usual, the very thought of Sara Waybourne was an irritant. Those great saucer eyes, holding a perpetual unspoken criticism intolerable in a child of thirteen. However, Sara's fees were always promptly paid by an elderly guardian whose private address was never divulged. Discreet, elegant, 'Obviously a gentleman,' as her Arthur would have put it.

The memory of Arthur standing at her elbow as he often did while she struggled with a difficult piece of correspondence wiped the elegant guardian from her mind. All this was getting her nowhere. With something like a groan she took up a thin steel-nibbed pen and began to write. First to the Leopolds, undoubtedly the most impressive parents on the College register : fabulously rich and moving in the best international society, but now in India where Mr Leopold was buying polo ponies from a Rajah in Bengal. According to Irma's last letter, her parents would at this moment be somewhere in the Himalayas, on a frantic expedition with elephants and palanquins and silk embroidered tents; address, for at least a fortnight, unknown. At last the letter was completed to the writer's satisfaction – a judicious blend of sympathy and practical commonsense. Not too much sympathy in case by the time it was received the whole damnable business had been satisfactorily cleared up and Irma back at school. A problem, too, whether or not to touch on the black tracker and the bloodhound. . . . She could almost hear Arthur's 'Masterly, my dear, masterly.' And so, according to its purpose, we may be sure it was.

Next in order of precedence came Miranda's mother and father, owners of vast cattle stations in the backblocks of Northern Queensland. Not quite in the millionaire class but entrenched in a setting of solid wealth and well-being as members of one of Australia's best known pioneer families. Exemplary parents who could be relied on not to fuss over trifles of missed trains or an epidemic of measles at the College; but in this preposterous situation as unpredictable as anyone else. Miranda was the only girl, the eldest of five children, and, well Mrs Appleyard knew it, the apple of her parents' eyes. The whole family had been staying at St Kilda during the Christmas holidays, but had returned last month to the luxurious isolation of Goonawingi. Only a few days ago Miranda had happened to mention that the Goonawingi mail arrived with the stores, sometimes only once in four or five weeks. However, one could never be sure, thought the Headmistress, sucking on the nib, that some busybody of a visitor wouldn't come riding over with the newspapers and let the cat out of the mail bag. As will have been noted Mrs Appleyard was not prone to sentiment, yet this was the hardest letter she had ever been obliged to write in her whole life. As she gummed down the flap of the envelope the closely written pages proclaimed themselves the messengers of doom. She shrugged : 'I am becoming fanciful', and took a nip or two of brandy from the cupboard behind the desk.

Marion Quade's lawful guardian was a family solicitor, very much in the background except for the payment of Marion's fees. By good fortune he was at present in New Zealand, on a fishing trip at some inaccessible lake. In Mrs Appleyard's hearing, her guardian had lately been referred to by Marion as a 'dodderer'. With the fervent hope that the solicitor would live up to his reputation and let sleeping dogs lie until further information came to hand, the letter was signed and sealed. And finally, another to the octogenarian father of Greta McCraw, living alone with his dog and his Bible on a remote island in the Hebrides. The old man was unlikely to make trouble or even communicate, having never penned his daughter a line since her arrival in Australia as a girl of eighteen. All four letters were stamped and laid on the hall table for Tom to post on tonight's train.

6

On the afternoon of Thursday, February the nineteenth, Michael Fitzhubert and Albert Crundall were seated in amicable silence before a bottle of Ballarat Bitter in the little rustic boathouse fronting Colonel Fitzhubert's ornamental lake. Albert was off duty for an hour or two and Mike was taking a temporary respite from assisting at his aunt's annual garden party. The Lake was deep and dark, icy cold despite the languorous summer heat, overgrown at one end with waterlilies whose creamy cups caught and held the rays of the late afternoon sun. On a patch of lily pads a single white swan was standing on one coral leg, now and then sending out showers of concentric ripples across the surface of the lake. On the opposite side, banks of treeferns and blue hydrangea mingled with the natural forest rising steeply behind the low verandahed house on whose lawns the guests were strolling under the elms and oaks. Two maids behind a trestle table were serving strawberries and cream : it was rather a smart party, including guests from nearby Government Cottage, the summer residence of the State Governor, with a hired footman, three musicians from Melbourne and plenty of French champagne. There had earlier been talk of putting the coachman into a tight black jacket for service at the champagne bar to which Albert had replied that he was hired to look after the horses. 'As I said to your Uncle, "I'm a coachman, sir, not a bloody waiter".' Mike laughed. 'You look like a sailor, with those mermaids and things tattooed all over your arms.'

'A sailor done them for me, in Sydney. Wanted to do me chest, too, but I ran out of cash. Pity. I was only fifteen . . .'

Transported to a world where boys of fifteen cheerfully spent their last shilling on being thus disfigured for life, Mike

63

gazed at his friend with something like awe. He himself at fifteen had been hardly more than a child with a shilling a week pocket money and another for 'the plate' on Sunday mornings ... Since the afternoon of the picnic a comfortable non-demanding friendship had developed between the two young men. To see them now – Albert loose of limb in rolled-up shirt sleeves and moleskin trousers. Michael stiff in garden party attire with a carnation in his buttonhole – they looked an ill-assorted pair. 'Mike's all right,' Albert had told his friend the cook. 'Him and me are mates.' And so in the finest sense of that much abused word, they were. The fact that Albert, who had just tried his friend's grey topper on his own tousled bullet head, looked like a music hall turn; and that Mike in Albert's wide brimmed greasy sundowner might have stepped from the pages of *The Magnet* or the *Boys Own Paper*, meant less than nothing. As did the accident of birth that had rendered one of them almost illiterate, and the other barely articulate, at the age of twenty – a Public School education being by no means a guarantee of adult expression. In each other's presence, neither young man was conscious of his shortcomings, if such they were.

There was a cosy sense of mutual understanding, and not too much talk. Topics of conversation were mainly of local interest, when they arose; the mare's off hind leg which Albert was painting with Stockholm tar, or the Colonel's obstinate enthusiasm for the time-wasting rose garden that called for more bloody weeding than an acre of spuds and anyway what was the good of all them roses? Neither had anything much in the way of embarrassing political, or for that matter any other kind of convictions, which they would have recognized as their own if shown them written down in cold print. Which in friendship makes everything simpler. There was no obstructive nonsense, for instance, in Mike's father being a Conservative member of the English House of Lords, while Albert's, when last heard of, was an itinerant rouse-about, in perpetual strife with the Boss of the Shed. For Albert, young Fitzhubert was the ideal companion, sitting silently for hours on an upturned chaff box in the stable yard, drinking in the other's native wisdom and wit. Some of Albert's more hair-raising anecdotes were true, others not. It made no odds. For Mike, the coachman's free-roving conversation was a continual source of pleasurable instruction, not only about life in general but Australia. In the Lake View kitchen, the Honorable Michael, a member of one of the oldest and richest families in the United Kingdom, was commonly referred to as 'that poor English bastard': an expression of genuine compassion for one who obviously had so much to learn. 'Cripes,' said Cook, whose wages were considered good at twenty-five shillings a week, 'I wouldn't be him, not for a cartload of nuggets.' Meanwhile, in the drawing-room Mike was telling his Uncle and Aunt, 'Albert's such a jolly good chap. And so clever. I can't tell you what a lot he knows about all sorts of things.'

'Hmm. I don't doubt it,' the Colonel agreed with a wink. 'Rough as bags, young Crundall, but no fool and a first-rate man with the horses.' His wife sniffed, almost breathing in the hay and horse dung. 'I can't imagine that Crundall's conversation would be exactly edifying.'

In the cool peace of the boathouse this afternoon there was precious little conversation, edifying or otherwise, what with the bottle of cold beer and the lake to look out upon, placid under its pattern of slowly lengthening shadows. In the distance 'The Blue Danube' drifted over the water from the rose garden as the party grew ever duller and cooler. The roses, admired to excess, were no longer conversationally adequate. The Colonel, with two or three chosen males, had retreated under the weeping elm armed with tumblers of Scotch and soda, while Mrs Fitzhubert held the rest of the party together as best she could on lemonade.

'Confound it – it's gone five already.' Michael was reluctantly unwinding his long legs under the table. 'I promised my Aunt I'd show Miss Stack the rose garden before they go.'

'Stack? That the one with a pair of legs on her like champagne bottles?'

Mike had no idea, the unknown Miss Stack's legs being of no moment whatsoever.

'I seen her getting out of the Government Cottage dog-cart this afternoon. Jeez, that reminds me – the groom was telling me the cops had the bloodhounds out at Hanging Rock again today.'

'Good God!' exclaimed the other sitting down again. 'What for? Have they found anything new?'

'No bloody fear! What I say is this : if them Russell Street blokes and the abo tracker and the bloody dog can't find 'em, what's the sense of you and me worrying our guts out? (We may as well finish the bottle.) Plenty of other people have got themselves bushed before today and as far as I'm concerned that's the stone end of it.'

Mike was staring out at the shining disc of the lake. He said slowly : 'As far as *I'm* concerned, it's *not* the end of it. I wake up in a cold sweat every night wondering if they're still alive dying of thirst somewhere on that infernal Rock at this very minute ... while you and I are sitting here drinking cold beer.' If Michael's young sisters had heard the low impassioned voice, so different to his usual clipped and breezy utterance, they would hardly have recognized the brother whose confidences at home, if any, were reserved for an elderly cocker spaniel.

'That's where you and me is different,' Albert was saying. 'If you take my advice, the sooner you forget the whole thing the better.'

'I can't forget it, I never will.'

The white swan, poised all this time on the lily pads, now chose to stretch one pink leg and then the other and go flapping away across the lake towards the opposite bank. The two young men watched its flight in silence until it disappeared amongst the reeds.

'Ah, they're pretty birds all right, them swans,' Albert breathed. 'Beautiful,' Mike said, miserably aware of the strange young woman awaiting him in the rose garden. Painfully he unwound his long pin-striped legs from under the rustic seat, stood up, blew his nose, lit a cigarette, got as far as the door of the boathouse, stopped and turned round again.

'Listen,' Albert said. 'I'm no great shakes on music but isn't that "God Save the Queen"? The Gov. must be leaving.'

'I don't care if he is ... there's something I must say to you but I don't know how to begin.' Albert had never seen him look so serious. 'As a matter of fact ... I've been working out a plan –'

'It'll keep,' Albert said, lighting a cigarette. 'Better hop it, hadn't you? Your Auntie'll raise Hell if you're not on show.'

'Confound my Aunt. The point is, it *won't* keep. It's now or never to be any use. You know that bridle track you were telling me about yesterday?' Albert nodded. 'You mean the one takes you down to the plains on our side of the Mount?'

'I daresay it sounds a wild goose chase to you and maybe it is but I don't care. I've decided to make a search of the Rock on my own, in my own way. No police. No blood-hounds. Just you and me. That is if you'll come along and show me the ropes. We could take the Arab and Lancer, get off to an early start, and be home here for dinner without any awkward questions. Now then – I've got it off my chest. How about it?'

'Barmy. Nuts. You run along and show Miss Bottle Legs them roses and you and me have a yarn about it some other time.'

'Oh, I know what you're thinking,' said the other with such bitterness that Albert was quite shaken. 'Hi, wait a bit, Mike! I was only meaning –'

'You're thinking : poor bastard's a new chum in the Bush and so on. Hell, I know all that but it doesn't matter. I lied to you just now about a plan. It's really not so much a *plan* as a *feeling*.' Albert's eyebrows flew up but he said nothing. 'All my life I've been doing things because other people said they were the right things to do. This time I'm going to do something because *I* say so – even if you and everyone else thinks I'm mad.'

'It's like this,' Albert said, 'feelings is all very well but every inch of that bloody Rock has been gone over with a tooth-comb. What the Hell do you think *you* can do?'

'Then I'll be going alone,' Mike said.

'Who says you're going alone. We're mates, aren't we?'

'Then you will?'

'Of course I will, you big dope – Aw, cut it out. It won't

take much fixing. We don't want nothing but a bit of tucker for you and me and a feed for the two horses. When do you reckon we go?'

'Tomorrow if you can get away.'

Tomorrow was Friday and Albert's day off, long dedicated to a cockfight in Woodend. 'No, never you mind about that. . . . How early can you start?'

Mrs Fitzhubert's lace parasol could be seen wobbling towards them above the hydrangea hedge and it was hastily agreed to meet at the stable tomorrow morning at half past five.

Now at last the Lake View lawns were deserted, the marquee dismantled, the trestle tables carried away into storage for another year. A few sleepy starlings were still gossiping in the tallest trees as the pink silk-shaded lamps of Mrs Fitzhubert's drawing-room broke into a rosy glow.

Out at the Hanging Rock the long violet shadows were tracing their million-year-old pattern of summer evenings across its secret face. Turning their weary blue serge backs upon its magnificent spectacle of gilded peaks slowly darkening upon a turquoise sky, the police party climbed into the waiting vehicle and was driven swiftly towards the familiar comforts of the Woodend Hotel. Constable Bumpher for one had had a bellyful of the Rock and its mysteries and was looking forward with understandable pleasure to a couple of beers and a nice juicy steak.

In spite of glorious weather and congenial company, it had proved a thoroughly unrewarding day. In view of the belated evidence of the girl Horton – if evidence it could be called – the search had been immediately intensified, including the recall of the bloodhound, who had been furnished with a piece of calico from Miss McCraw's underwear. There seemed no reason to doubt that Edith had actually seen and passed the mathematics teacher making her way up the Rock in white calico drawers. The vague wordless encounter, however, remained unsubstantiated; nor was it ever established if Miss McCraw had experienced an equally fleeting vision of the terrified girl. Some slight disturbance of the bushes and bracken towards the western end of the rock face had been noted as early as last Sunday morning. It was now thought possible they might have been part of the track taken by Miss McCraw after leaving the rest of the party after lunch. It petered out almost at once; strangely enough, at much the same level of striated rock as certain other faint scratchings and bruisings of the undergrowth at the eastern end where the four girls may have begun their perilous ascent. All day long the bloodhound had sniffed and fossicked its delicate way through thick dusty scrub and sunbaked rocks and stones. The dog, who had proved equally unsuccessful at picking up the scent of the three missing girls earlier in the week, was greatly hampered by the well-meaning army of voluntary searchers having effaced the first elusive imprints where a hand had rested perhaps on a dusty boulder, a foot on springy moss. The animal, however, did raise some false hopes during Thursday afternoon, by standing for nearly ten minutes growling and bristling on an almost circular platform of flat rock considerably further towards the summit, whereon the magnifying glass disclosed absolutely no signs of any disturbance more recent than the ravages of Nature over some hundreds or thousands of years. Bumpher, scanning his meagre notes in the failing light of the cab, had hoped that part or all of the teacher's purple silk cape would have been found stuffed into a hollow log, maybe, or under a loose rock. 'Beats me what the old girl could have done with it! Considering hundreds of people have been traipsing about in the scrub ever since Sunday last. Let alone the dog.'

Meanwhile, like most other dwellers on the Mount this evening, Colonel Fitzhubert and his nephew were discussing the recall of the bloodhound. Mrs Fitzhubert, worn out with the rigours of hospitality, had retired to bed. The Colonel was bitterly disappointed about the bloodhound. He had pinned his faith on it from the beginning and felt almost personally let down by its failure to come up with a clue. ''Pon my word,' he remarked to his nephew over the dinner table, 'I'm beginning to think this thing's gone too far for dogs or anything else. Be a week this coming Saturday since those poor girls disappeared. Have a glass of port? Most likely dead as mutton by now at the bottom of one of those infernal precipices.' The old boy appeared so genuinely concerned that Mike was tempted to confide his plans for tomorrow's expedition to the Hanging Rock. Aunt, however, would be sure to raise a thousand objections. After fiddling in silence with the walnuts he asked if he could have the Arab for the day on Friday? 'It's Albert's day off, you know, and he says he wants to take me for a fairly long ride.'

'By all means. Where do you think of going?'

Always a half-hearted liar, even in trifles, Mike muttered something about the Camel's Hump. 'Splendid! Crundall knows this country like the back of his hand. He'll see you get some good soft going for a gallop. If it wasn't for my Rose Show Committee tomorrow afternoon I might have joined you myself.' (God bless the Rose Show!) 'And don't be late for dinner,' the Colonel added. 'You know how your Aunt fusses.' Mike did know and promised faithfully to be back at Lake View by seven at least.

'Which reminds me,' said his Uncle, 'you and I are expected for lunch and tennis at Government Cottage on Saturday.'

'Lunch and tennis,' the nephew repeated, wondering inwardly how long it would take himself and Albert to get as far as the pool at the Picnic Grounds.

'Have a peach, my boy? Or some of this infernal jelly stuff? Women have no idea of household organization.'

Mike, who had been wandering on the Rock under the moon, was jerked back to the concrete reality of the lamplit dining table. 'It's the same thing every summer ... on the night of your Aunt's garden party ... these confounded leftovers – scraps of cold turkey ... jelly ... masquerading as dinner. High Tea more like. ... Now when we used to go camping at Bombala, I made it my personal responsibility to arrange for the servants to –'

'If you'll excuse me, Uncle,' said Mike, rising, 'I think I'll turn in without waiting for coffee. We're making an early start in the morning.'

'All right, my boy – enjoy yourself. Better ask cook to fix you an early breakfast. Nothing like bacon and eggs before a gallop. Good night!'

'Good night, sir.' ... Eggs. Porridge ... according to Albert there wasn't even fresh water on the Hanging Rock.

7

A restless windy night on the Mount was followed by a calm windless dawn with residents still asleep in brass bedsteads under silken coverlets waking to the tinkle of fern-fringed streams and the scent of late flowering petunias. On the Colonel's lake the waterlilies were just beginning to open as Mike let himself out of the French windows of his room and crossed the croquet lawn, heavy with dew, where his Aunt's peacock was taking an early breakfast. For the first time since the events of last Saturday he felt almost light-hearted. In such an exquisitely ordered world the Hanging Rock and its sinister implications were a nightmare, thrust aside. In the avenue of chestnuts birds were awake and calling, hens cackling from a fowl yard. A puppy barked with joyous insistence on rousing the entire neighbourhood to greet the new day. A thin curl of smoke rose from the Fitzhubert kitchen where a servant was already making up the fire.

Michael, suddenly aware that he had gone without breakfast, hoped that Albert had remembered to fix up some lunch. Arrived at the stables he found the coachman tightening up the girth of the white pony. 'Good morning,' said Michael in his pleasant English voice : the upper class Englishman's ritual good morning to any human being encountered before nine a.m. from Bond Street to the Blue Nile. Albert's response was equally characteristic of his class and country. 'Hi! You! Hope you had the sense to get yourself a cuppa?'

'It doesn't matter,' said Michael, whose knowledge of tea making was limited to a spirit lamp and silver tea strainer in his Cambridge rooms. 'I've brought my flask filled with brandy, and matches. You see, I *am* beginning to know something about the Bush. Was there anything else?'

Albert gave him a fatherly grin. 'Only our tucker in the billy with a couple of mugs and a clasp knife; some clean rags and a drop of iodine. You never know what we might find once we start looking. ... Jeez ... don't look so bloody miserable. It's your own idea. ... And two lots of chaff. You can tie this one on your saddle. Woa there, Lancer. He's a bit lively first thing in the morning, aren't you, old boy? Right? Let's get off.'

Out on the steep chocolate road several other households beside Lake View were astir, with smoke rising from the chimneys in preparation for brass hot water cans and trays of early morning tea. The Fitzhuberts and their friends were a smug little community, well served. A sprinkling of Collins Street doctors, two Supreme Court judges, an Anglican bishop, several lawyers with tennis-playing sons and daughters, enjoying good food, good horses and good wine. Pleasant comfortable people for whom the current Boer War was the most catastrophic event since the Flood, and Queen Victoria's approaching Jubilee a world-shattering occasion to be celebrated by champagne and fireworks on the lawns.

The two young men on horseback passed a groom sluicing himself at a pump before an ornate wooden stable, admired by Michael as 'artistic', dismissed by Albert as 'fancy crap'. A stubbly-faced milkman jogging along in a two-wheeled cart ('that poor cow was fined in Woodend last week for watering his milk'); a housemaid sweeping the steps of a trellised verandah; a gravelled drive bordered by six foot delphiniums; a chained invisible dog barking its lungs out behind a hedge of rambler roses.

The road wound its charming leisurely way between sleeping gardens still heavy with dew and shadowed by the upper mountain slopes. Swathes of virgin forest ran right down to an immaculate tennis lawn, an orchard, a row of raspberry canes. The lush luxuriant gardens were unlike anything Michael had seen in England. There was a heart-breaking innocence about them; a sort of casual gaiety that proclaimed them pleasure gardens, redeeming the undistinguished architecture of red roofed houses set amongst willow and maple, oak and elm. The rich volcanic soil on which roses glowed all summer long with an almost tropical brilliance was watered by innumerable mountain streams, cunningly deployed – here a ferny grotto, there a pool of goldfish spanned by a rustic bridge, a tea-house above a miniature waterfall. Mike was enchanted by this strangely favoured country where palms, delphiniums and raspberry canes grew side by side. No wonder his Uncle hated returning to Melbourne at the end of the summer.

'Costs a packet to live up here amongst the nobs,' Albert was saying. 'Look at the staff we keep at Lake View! Me at the stables. Mr and Mrs Cutler down at the gardener's lodge. Cook and a couple of girls in the house. To say nothing of the bloody rose garden and four or five damn good horses eating their heads off all the year round.' Mike, who had never troubled to enquire into his Australian relations' finances, was more interested in looking over a trim privet hedge at a flower bed ablaze with purple and yellow pansies. Their scent drifting out on to the road was somehow the perfect accompaniment to the swimming colour and light of the waking day.

'What's the name of them thingummy-bobs?' Albert asked. 'Smell good, don't they? Pansies, that's right. They was my kid sister's favourite flowers.'

'Poor little thing! I hope she has a garden of her own now.'

'As far as I know, some old geezer took a fancy to her a few years ago and that's all I ever heard. Tell you the truth, I only seen her the once after she left the orphanage. She was a good kid though, a bit like me – wouldn't stand no nonsense from nobody.'

While they were talking Albert had pulled Lancer over to the right into a narrow lane bordered on one side by a stretch of forest, on the other by an old moss-encrusted orchard where ducks in the long grass made the horses shy. Here the homely sights and sounds of village life were left behind. They entered the green gloom of the forest. 'Cuts off a good five miles this way. There's a rough sort of track somewhere along here that takes us right down over the other side of the Mount.' The remainder of the journey was travelled without further conversation, the track turning and twisting amongst fallen logs and running streams. Except for an occasional bird or rabbit, the only living creature encountered was a little wallaby bounding out of a clump of fishferns almost under Lancer's feet. Albert's two tin mugs clattered like cymbals as the big black horse rose up on his hind legs, almost bringing down the pony a few inches in the rear. Albert grinned over his shoulder. 'Scare the daylights out of the little bugger, wallabies do. You all right? I thought you would have went a sugar-doodle!'

'It would have been worth a spill to see my first kangaroo.'

'I'll say this for you, Mike. You may be a bloody fool at times, but you can handle that pony all right.' A somewhat backhanded compliment, none the less appreciated.

When they came out of the forest and on to the more thinly-wooded country on the other side, the morning was well advanced under a sky hazy with heat. They pulled up their horses in the shade and looked down across the plain below. Directly ahead, the Hanging Rock floated in splendid isolation on a sea of pale grass, in full sunlight its jagged peaks and pinnacles even more sinister than the hideous caves of Mike's recurring nightmares. 'You're not looking too good on it, Mike. No good riding this far on a empty stomach. Get a move on and we'll have some tucker as soon as we get down to the creek.'

So much had happened since last Saturday that it was a shock to find everything exactly the same at the spot where they had lunched and Albert had rinsed out the glasses at the pool. The ashes of their picnic fire still filled the blackened ring of the fireplace, the creek gurgled as it had been gurgling ever since over the smooth stones. The horses were tethered and fed under the same group of blackwoods, the same sunlight filtered through the leaves on to the lunch laid out on a piece of newspaper on the grass : slices of cold meat and bread, a bottle of tomato sauce, a billy of sweet milkless tea. 'Hop into it, Mike, you said you was hungry.'

Far from hungry now, from the first sight of the Rock this morning he had been stricken by an aching emptiness of the spirit beyond the power of cold lamb to fill. Lying back in the tepid shade, he drank mug after mug of scalding tea. As soon as Albert had finished a hearty meal and stamped out the ashes of their fire with the toe of his boot, he rolled over on the grass with a request to be kicked on the backside in ten minutes' time by Mike's watch. Within seconds he was sound asleep and snoring. Mike went over and stood beside the creek at the place where the four girls each after her fashion had crossed it on Saturday afternoon. Here the little dark one with the ringlets had stood for a moment looking down at the water before she jumped, laughing and shaking out her curls : the thin one in the middle had cleared it without an instant's hesitation and never looked back : the dumpy fat one had nearly missed her footing on a loose stone. Miranda, tall and fair, skimmed it like a white swan. The three other girls had been talking and laughing together as they walked off towards the Rock, but not Miranda, lingering for a moment on the opposite bank to push back a lock of straight yellow hair fallen over one cheek, so that he saw, for the first time, her grave and lovely face. Where were they going? What strange feminine secrets did they share in that last gay fateful hour?

Albert in his short life had slept in a variety of places where Mike would never have closed an eye : under dubious bridges, in hollow logs, empty houses and even the bug-infested cell of a small town lock-up. He slept deep and fitfully anywhere, like a dog, and was even now standing up refreshed and tousling his hair. 'What sort of a bump of thingummy-bob have you got?' he wanted to know, producing a stub of pencil. 'If I make a bit of a plan can you follow it? Where do you want to start?'

Where indeed? As a child Mike used to play hide and seek with his sisters in a little civilized wood, crouching in the dark shelter of rhododendrons or a hollow oak. Once in sudden panic after too long waiting to be found he had come running out to find the seekers, who, fearing him dead or lost forever, had sobbed and blubbered all the way home. For some reason he found himself remembering it all now. Perhaps the end of the Hanging Rock affair would be something like that. The thought, uncommunicable even to Albert, would not be denied : a search with dogs and trackers and policemen was only one way of looking, perhaps not even the right way. It might even end, if it ever did end, in a sudden unexpected finding that had nothing to do with all this purposeful seeking.

It was arranged that each of the young men should take a given area on Albert's plan, searching with a special regard for caves, overhanging rocks, fallen logs or anything capable of affording the slightest shelter to the missing girls.

As a particular opening in a clump of trees at the southwest end of the Rock had been identified by several witnesses present when the girl Edith had come running towards them, crying and dishevelled, on the afternoon of February the fourteenth, Albert now elected to take over his part of the search from this point, and accordingly set out whistling to make a careful examination of the lower slopes where it was rumoured there had once been a forest track long overgrown with bracken and blackberries. No sooner was his faded blue shirt out of sight between the trees than Michael had stopped walking. Albert chancing to look back over his shoulder wondered if the poor bugger was feeling crook. A wild bloody goose chase if ever there was one . . .

Actually, his friend was listening to the murmuring life of the forest welling up out of the warm green depth. In the noonday stillness all living creatures except man, who long ago renounced the god-given sense of balance between rest and action, had slowed down their normal pace.

Fronds of curled brown velvet snapped under his touch, his boots trod down the neat abodes of ants and spiders : his hand brushing against a streamer of bark dislodged a writhing colony of caterpillars in thick fur coats, brutally exposed to midday light. From a loose stone, a sleeping lizard awoke and darted to safety at the clumping monster's approach. The rise grew steeper, the undergrowth denser. The gentle youth, hard breathing, his yellow crest damp on his glistening forehead, pushed on through the waist-high bracken, with every step cutting a swathe of death and destruction through the dusty green.

Behind him, perhaps fifty yards below, lay the pool :

directly ahead a thinly-wooded incline. Somewhere here, perhaps on this very spot, Miranda had led the way through the patch of bracken and plunged into the dogwood, as Mike himself was doing now. As the vertical façade of the Rock drew nearer, the massive slabs and soaring rectangles repudiated the easy charms of its fern-clad lower slopes. Now outcrops of prehistoric rock and giant boulders forced their way to the surface above layers of rotting vegetation and animal decay : bones, feathers, birdlime, the sloughed skins of snakes; some with jagged horns and jutting spikes, obscene knobs and scabby carbuncles; others smoothly humped and rounded by the passing of a million years. On any one of these awesome rocks, Miranda might have pillowed her bright weary head.

Mike was still stumbling and climbing with no particular plan in mind when he was halted by a faint but unmistakable cooee at his back. He had lost all count of time and looking over his shoulder was surprised to see the Picnic Grounds diminished to a patch of pink and gold light between the trees. Again he heard the cooee, louder and more insistent. For the first time since leaving Albert at midday he remembered his promise to rejoin him at the pool no later than four o'clock. It was already half past five. From a pigskin notebook in his pocket he tore out several leaves and carefully stuck them on to the twigs of a bush of mountain laurel, where he left them hanging in the calm evening air like little white flags, and retraced his steps down to the creek. Albert awaiting him with a mug of tea had nothing of any interest to report : had seen nothing out of the ordinary and was itching to get back to Lake View and his evening meal. 'Jeez, I began to think you was lost. What the hell was you doing up there all that long?'

'Just looking ... I put some little flags on a bush out of my pocket book so I could find it again.'

'Smart Alec, aren't you? Well, drink up your tea and we'll get a move on. I swore blind to Cookie I'd get you home for dinner at eight.'

Mike said slowly : 'I'm not going home. Not tonight.'

'Not going home?'

'You heard me, didn't you?'

'Stone the crows! Have you gone off your rocker?'

'You can tell them up at the house I'm staying the night in Woodend. Any bloody lie you like so long as there's no fussing.' Albert was looking at him with a new respect. Incidentally, it was the first time he had heard Mike using what he called 'language'. He glanced up at the pink and glowing sky and shrugged. 'Be dark soon. Have a bit of sense. What's the good of you stopping here all night on your Pat Malone?'

'That's my business.'

'Beats me what you're looking for but you won't find it in the dark, I can tell you that much.' Now Mike really *was* swearing, with passionate conviction. At Albert, the police, bloody so-and-so's who kept poking their noses into other people's affairs, bloody so-and-so's who knew damn all about every bloody thing just because they were Australians –

'You win,' Albert said, walking off towards the horses. 'I'll leave you the rest of the tucker, what there is of it, and the billy. There's a bit of feed for the pony still in your bag.'

Mike said awkwardly, 'I'm sorry I called you all those names just now.'

'Aw, you done right . . . if that's the way you was feeling . . . well, ta-ta, I'll be hitting the trail. And mind you put out the fire before you leave tomorrow. I don't fancy spending me week-end fighting bush fires at Hanging Rock.'

Lancer was impatient to be off and Albert cantered off over the flats towards the Mount. He knew exactly where to hit the turn off between two gum trees and was soon out of sight.

Across the level golden plain long shadows were crawling out of the forest, over the thin lines of post and rail fences, a few scattered sheep, a windmill with motionless silver sails catching the last of the sun. On the Rock, darkness stored all day in its fetid holes and caves seeped out into the twilight and it was night. Albert was right, of course. Mike knew perfectly well that he could do nothing until dawn came. At what hour in this strange land did the sun rise? He fetched some bark, rekindled the dying fire and by its fitful light reluctantly ate some of the meat and bread. Behind him, the Rock pressed unseen against the starless sky. A few yards away a shifting patch of white came and went as the Arab drank at the creek. A pile of bracken fern made a fairly comfortable bed although the night air had set him shivering the moment he lay down. He took off his jacket and folding it across his body lay on his back looking up at the sky. Only once in his life had he slept in the open – on the French Riviera with a party of Cambridge friends who had lost their way somewhere on the hills at the back of Cannes. There had been stars and vineyards and nearby lights, rugs for the girls and fruit and wine left over from the day's excursion. Remembering what had then seemed a pinnacle of high adventure he thought how ridiculously young he must have been for his eighteen years.

Presently he dropped off into a wakeful dream in which the ring of the Arab's hooves on a loose stone was the housemaid throwing back the shutters of his room at Haddingham Hall. Still only half awake he hoped Annie wouldn't pull up the blinds yet, and awoke to the black, closely-drawn curtains of the Australian night. He fumbled for the matches and saw for a flickering moment the face of his watch beside him on the ground. It was still only ten o'clock. Wide awake now and aching all over he threw a broken branch on to the fire and lay watching the crown of dry leaves flaring up in showers of sparks reflected in the pool.

When the first glimmer of daylight showed up he was already boiling the billy for tea. Gulping it down with a morsel of dry bread which some sugar ants were endeavouring to drag bodily into their hole, he gave the pony the last of the chaff and was ready to start. Many days later, when Bumpher was firing questions at him all over again, he realized that he had no definite plan of action when he had crossed the creek and begun walking towards the Rock. Only a compulsion to go back to the little bush with the flags and begin the search again from there.

It was another glorious morning, warm and windless as yesterday. After the endless wakeful night it was a positive relief to be forcing his chilled body through the waist-high bracken. The stunted laurel was easily located by the scraps of paper, now limp with dew. A parrot flashed through the trees ahead where magpies were gurgling in full-throated morning joy. Veiled in lacy green of fern and foliage, the formidable buttresses of the Hanging Rock were not yet in view. A few yards from where he had stopped to extricate one foot from an apparently bottomless cleft a little wallaby came hop-hopping out of the ferns on a zig-zag course that suggested some kind of natural track. There were certain things that animals knew more about than people – Mike's cocker spaniel for instance was aware of cats and other enemies half a mile away. What had the wallaby seen, what did it know? Perhaps it was trying to tell him something as it stood looking down at him from a ledge of rock. There was no fear in its gentle eyes. It was easy enough to hoist himself up on to the ledge but not to follow the little creature's leaping progress through the scrub where it disappeared. The ledge where he now found himself abutted on to a natural platform of striated rock ringed with stones, boulders and clumps of wiry fern, shaded by straggling eucalypts. Here he was forced to rest, if only for a moment, his leaden legs. His head on the contrary was less like a head than an air balloon, tethered somewhere above his aching shoulders. The well drilled body accustomed to its hearty British intake of eggs and bacon, coffee and porridge was loudly complaining, although its owner was not conscious of hunger – only beset with a windy longing for gallons of ice cold water. A sloping rock offered a meagre shade. He laid his head on a stone and fell instantly into the thin ragged sleep of exhaustion, waking with a sudden stab of pain over one eye. A trickle of blood was oozing on to the pillow. The pillow was as hard and sharp as a stone under his burning head. The rest of his body was deathly cold. Shivering, he reached out for the coverlet.

At first he thought it was the sound of birds in the oak tree outside his window. He opened his eyes and saw the eucalypts, their long pointed silver leaves hanging motionless on the heavy air. It seemed to be coming from all round him – a low wordless murmur, almost like the murmur of distant voices, with now and then a sort of trilling that might have been little spurts of laughter. But who would be laughing down here under the sea ...? He was forcing his way through viscous dark-green water, looking for the musical box whose sweet tinkling voice was sometimes behind, sometimes just ahead. If only he could move faster, trailing useless legs through the green, he might catch up with it. Suddenly it ceased. The water grew thicker and darker; he saw bubbles rising from his mouth, began to choke, thought, 'This is what it feels like to drown,' and woke coughing up the blood that was trickling down his cheek from the cut on his forehead.

He was wide awake and stumbling to his feet when he heard her laughing, a little way ahead. 'Miranda! Where are you? ... Miranda!' There was no answering voice. He began running as well as he could towards the belt of scrub. The prickly grey green dogwood tore at his fine English skin. 'Miranda!' Now huge rocks and boulders blocked his path on the rising ground, each a nightmare obstacle to be somehow walked around, clambered over, crawled under, according to size and contour. They grew larger and more fantastic. He cried out: 'Oh, my lost, lovely darling, where are you?' and raising his eyes for an instant from the treacherous ground saw the monolith, black against the sun. A scatter of pebbles went rolling down into the chasm below as he slipped on a jagged spur and fell. A spear of pain jabbed at his ankle, he got up again and started hauling himself up on to the next boulder. There was only one conscious thought in his head: *Go on.* A Fitzhubert ancestor hacking his way through bloody barricades at Agincourt had felt much the same way; and had, in fact, incorporated those very words, in Latin, in the family crest: *Go on.* Mike, some five centuries later, went on climbing.

8

It was a new sensation for Albert to be troubled by anything
beyond his own immediate affairs and he didn't care for it.
Riding home over the mountain on Friday evening his
thoughts kept reverting to his friend alone all night at the
creek. The poor bastard wouldn't even know how to make
himself comfortable on a bed of bracken by digging a hole
for his shoulders. Or how to light a fire with a handful of
bark when the night turned cold, as it did quite early on the
Macedon plains, even in summer. No doubt about it, something had got under Mike's skin. Just what, Albert didn't
understand, but there it was. Perhaps all the nobs like Mike's
family in England were on the barmy side. Or was there
really something in all this flamdoodle about looking for the
lost sheilas that made sense? Albert himself had once known
an unreasoning urge to go to the Ballarat Races and put a
whole five pounds on an outsider that came romping home
at forty to one. Perhaps Mike felt like that about finding
the sheilas. For his part he was bloody well sick of the
sheilas ... probably dead long ago, come to that. ... He
hoped Cook had kept something hot for his tea tonight. And
what in Hell was he going to say to the Boss? Thus uncomfortably musing Albert trotted slowly home on a loose rein.

Darkness was filling the avenue with fragrant glooms and
mysteries when he turned in at the gates of Lake View. After
unsaddling Lancer and hosing him down in the stable yard,
he made his way to the kitchen, there to be cheered by
generous helpings of warmed-up steak and kidney pudding
and apricot tart. 'Best go and see them inside,' Cook advised.
'The master's in a regular state with you being so late and all
– what have you done with young Michael?'

'He's all right. I'll go when I've finished me tea,' said the coachman, helping himself to more tart. It was after ten o'clock, and the Boss was alone in the study playing patience with the French windows open onto the verandah when Albert coughed loudly and knocked on the leaded pane.

'Come in, Crundall. For God's sake, where's Mr Michael?'

'I have a message from him, sir. I —'

'Message? Didn't you come home together? What the blazes has gone wrong?'

'Nothing, sir,' said the coachman, frantically seeking the appropriate fib which he had been concocting while he was eating the apricot tart, and now eluded him under the old boy's accusing blue eyes. 'How do you mean, nothing? My nephew never told us he intended to be out for dinner?' At Lake View being absent for a meal without due notice was almost worthy of capital punishment.

'He didn't intend to be out that long sir. The fact is, we left it a bit late starting for home and Mr Michael reckoned he'd stay the night at the Macedon Arms and ride home tomorrow.'

'Macedon Arms? That miserable little pub near the Woodend Station? Never heard such nonsense!'

'I think, sir,' said Albert, gaining confidence as all good liars do, 'he thought it'd save any inconvenience this end?'

The Colonel snorted. 'Considering Cook has been keeping his dinner hot for a good three hours.'

'Between you and me,' Albert said, 'Mr Michael was a bit done in after that long ride in the sun this morning.' 'Where did you go?' the Colonel asked. 'A fair way. It was really me put the idea into his head to take it easy and stop the night in Woodend.'

'So it was *your* brilliant idea, was it? The boy's all right, I suppose?'

'Right as rain.'

'Let's hope the Arab's properly stalled for the night – if they *have* a stable down there – very well, then, you may go. Good night.'

'Good night, sir. Will you be wanting Lancer tomorrow?'

'Yes. I mean no. Dammit. I can't make any arrangements

for Saturday until I've seen my nephew. We're expected to tennis at Government Cottage.'

Although he normally fell into instant dreamless sleep the moment his head touched the pillow, Albert passed the rest of the night in a succession of disturbing dreams in which the voice of Michael kept calling for help from regions always inaccessible. Sometimes it came drifting in through the tiny window from the lake, sometimes in moaning gusts from the avenue, sometimes almost beside him, close to his ear – 'Albert, where are you, Albert?' – so that he actually sat up in bed, sweating and wide awake. For once it was a positive relief when the sun rose, filling his little box of a room with orange light, and it was time to get up, put his head under the pump and see to the horses.

Directly after breakfast and without a word to anyone – not even his good friend Cookie – he pinned a note on the stable door, saddled up Lancer and set off over the Mount for the Picnic Grounds. '*Home soon*' he had written with deliberate intent to deceive and delay. No sense in getting everyone's fur flying up at the house when it might well be the truth that Mike at this moment was trotting quietly home within a few miles of the Lake View turn. Reason insisted there was no cause for alarm. Mike was an experienced rider who knew the track yet against all reason a nagging fear persisted.

Moving at an easy canter, Lancer was soon on the soft going between tall forest trees, where Albert's practised eye noted the damp red surface of the seldom-used track showed no hoofmarks other than their own of yesterday. At every turn he craned forward in the saddle expecting to see the pony's snow-white crest as the Arab came swinging towards him out of the ferns. On the highest point of the track where the forest thinned out he pulled up Lancer under the same tree where he and Michael had stopped yesterday morning. Across the plain the Hanging Rock rose up in violent contrasts of midday light and shade. Barely glancing at its now familiar splendours, his eye swept the empty shimmering plain for a patch of moving white. The descent on dry slippery grass and loose stones, even for an animal as surefooted as Lancer, was slow. As soon as he had finally slithered on to the plain and felt the level ground under his four feet he was off again like the wind. They had just entered the belt of light timber on the fringe of the Picnic Grounds when the big horse propped so violently that his rider nearly lost a stirrup, at the same time letting out a long rasping whinny that went echoing through the glade like the wail of a foghorn. It was answered by another, only fainter, and within seconds the white pony, without a saddle and trailing a rope halter on the ground, came trotting towards them out of the scrub. Albert was only too glad to sit comfortably back in the saddle and allow the two horses to lead the way back to the creek.

It was cool and pleasant in the shade of the blackwoods by the pool where at first glance everything looked much the same as when the two young men had parted there last night. The ashes of Mike's fire ringed the stones of the fireplace, his hat, with a parrot feather stuck in the brim, hung from the same overhanging branch. Nearby, the pony's admired English saddle rested on a smooth stump. ('Could've thrown a bag over it,' reflected Albert with professional concern, 'with all them magpie droppings. And why didn't the bugger have the sense to wear his hat? He's not all that used to the Australian sun in February . . .') For some unaccountable reason, Albert's doubts and fears of the last few hours now gave place to a sense of irritation, even of anger. 'Blast the bloody young fool! I wouldn't mind betting he's gone and lost himself somewhere up there on the bloody Rock. . . . Hell, I shouldn't have got meself mixed up with all this . . .' However, mixed up with it he was to the extent of crawling laboriously in and out of the scrub and bracken in search of fresh tracks leading towards the Rock.

There were any number of footprints to choose from, including Albert's own of yesterday. The narrow imprint of Michael's riding boots was easily picked up on the loose soil. Trouble was going to start when they faded out amongst the stones and rubble on the Rock. He had only been following Michael's trail for fifty yards or so, when he noticed another set of footprints, only a few feet away, almost parallel to the others, but coming downhill towards the pool. 'Funny thing that ... looks like he went up and come down again the same way.... Jeez, what's that over there?'

Mike was lying on his side, slumped over a tussock, with one leg doubled up under him. He was unconscious; deathly pale, but breathing. He must have tripped and fallen heavily over the tussock – perhaps broken some ribs or an ankle. There was nothing to account for the cut across the forehead, nor the scratches on his face and arms. Albert had enough practical experience of broken bones not to attempt to move him into a more comfortable position. He did, however, manage to pillow the head on some fresh bracken, fetch water from the creek and wipe the dried blood from the pale dusty face. The brandy flask was still in the jacket pocket – he withdrew it gingerly and forced a few drops between the other's lips. The boy moaned without opening his eyes as the liquid dribbled down his chin. How long had Mike been lying here on the ground, beset by ants and hovering flies? The skin felt clammy under Albert's hand and altogether the poor bugger looked in such a bad way he decided to waste no more time and go immediately for help.

Of the two horses, the Arab was the freshest. Lancer could be trusted to remain tied up and docile in the shade for several hours. In a few minutes he had the pony saddled and bridled and was out on the Woodend Road. He had only gone a few hundred yards when he caught sight of a young shepherd with a collie dog, strolling across a paddock on the other side of the fence. When the shepherd was close enough to hear what Albert was shouting at him, he shouted back that he had just said goodbye to Doctor McKenzie of Woodend, who had been delivering the shepherd's wife of a son. With large orange ears flapping against the light, the proud father cupped two red paws together and bawled into a rising cloud of dust, 'Nine pounds seven ounces on the kitchen scales and the blackest hair you ever did see.' Albert was already gathering up the Arab's reins. 'Where is he now?'

'In his cradle, I reckon,' said the shepherd, his simple mind centred exclusively on the lusty babe.

'Not the kid you fool – the Doctor !'

'Oh, him !' The shepherd grinned and waved vaguely towards a bend in the empty road. 'In his gig he is. You'll catch up with him easy with that pony of yours.' Whereupon the collie, to whom life and death were all one on this pleasant summer afternoon, took a playful nip at the Arab's off hind leg that sent him flying down the road in a cloud of dust.

Doctor McKenzie's gig was soon overtaken and heading back towards the Picnic Grounds. Michael was still lying exactly as Albert had left him. After a brisk professional appraisement the old man got to work on the cut forehead, producing dressings and disinfectant from a shiny black leather bag. Oh, those little black bags of hope and healing – how many weary miles were they carried under the seats of gigs and buggies, jolting over the paddocks and unmade roads. How many hours did his patient horse stand waiting under sun and moon for the doctor to come out of some stricken weatherboard cottage carrying his little black bag? 'No serious damage that I can see,' Doctor McKenzie was saying as he knelt over Mike on the tussock. 'The ankle's bady bruised. Probably he's had a fall somewhere up on the Rock. And a touch of the sun. The important thing is to get him home to bed as fast as we can.' On a makeshift stretcher contrived from the Doctor's all-purpose buggy rug (one side imitation leopard, the other shiny black waterproof) and two straight saplings Mike was expertly hoisted on to the gig. 'Leave it to me young man – I've had thirty years of experience fitting 'em in so they don't spill out on the road.' He was amazingly gruff and efficient, amazingly gentle for one who had been up half the night wrestling with the shepherd's wife's reluctant nine-pounder.

Albert mounted the pony and, leading Lancer on a halter, much to that splendid animal's disgust, rode on slowly ahead of the gig. It was close on midnight when the little procession turned into the avenue at Lake View. The Colonel, to whom a message had been despatched several hours ago from Woodend, was pacing up and down outside the gates with a hurricane lamp. His wife on learning that Mike was safely on his way home had allowed herself to retire to bed. Doctor McKenzie, an old family friend, leaned over the side of the gig. 'Nothing to be alarmed about, Colonel. Sprained ankle, cut forehead. Badly shocked.'

In the hall a housemaid hovered with cans of hot water and fresh linen. Michael was put to bed with an eiderdown and hot bottles and after a sip of warm milk had opened for a moment a pair of haunted eyes. 'The boy's been through hell,' the Doctor decided. Aloud he said : 'Now mind, Colonel, absolute rest, no visitors and no questions — at least not until he starts to talk himself.' The Colonel spluttered, 'What *I* want to know is why the Devil Mike was left at the Hanging Rock all night on his own?' After a day spent in alternating fits of rage and secret fears he was nearing explosion point. 'Damn you, Crundall, what was all that poppy-cock you told me last night about Mike staying at the pub in Woodend?'

'Now, then, Colonel, no good crying over spilt milk,' the Doctor interrupted. 'The boy's safe and sound in his bed and that's all that matters. As for Crundall here, you can thank your stars he didn't waste any time in going for help.'

Albert was stubbing the toe of his boot against the leg of the dining-room sideboard, with a face of stone. 'It was like this. Your nephew was set on going to the Picnic Grounds on Friday to have another look for them girls. No, I don't know *why* any more than you do. When it was time for us to go home he was still mooching about on the Rock and wouldn't come home. I done my best to make him change his mind. And if you don't bloody well take my word for it you can get yourself another coachman.' After a few seconds' pause in which Albert had said affectionate good-byes to the Arab and the cob, given Lancer a last rub down and was looking for a bit of horsebreaking in parts unknown, the Colonel held out his hand. With a stab of something like pity Albert saw that it was the shaking hand of a very tired old man. 'You believe what I been telling you?'

'I believe you, Crundall ... you gave us a devil of a fright, though. Better eat some of that chicken.'

'I'll see to my horses first and have a bite in the kitchen before I turn in.'

'Have a whisky then?'

'Not for me. I'll be off now. Good night, sir. Good night, Doc.'

'Good night, Crundall, and thanks for your help today.'

'You're right about Crundall, Doctor. He's a good boy, rough as bags, but I'd be damned sorry to lose him,' said the Colonel, pouring himself a drink. 'It's this hanging about all day waiting for news gets my goat. Rather be in the firing line any time. You'll join me in a whisky?'

'Thank you, no grog for me till I get home and into my dressing gown. My wife always leaves me a bit of supper.' He had picked up the little black bag and was pulling on his leather driving gloves. 'I know of a nurse just finishing a case near here. I'll send her up in the morning if Mrs Fitzhubert's agreeable? Good. I'll call in a day or two – sooner if you want me. Meanwhile I'll give all necessary instructions to the nurse.'

Colonel Fitzhubert stood in the hall watching the gig move off into the shadows and put out the light. Outside the open door of Mike's room a night light glimmered, where a housemaid with her shoes off nodded in a chair. He poured himself a nightcap and went into the study to perform the nightly ritual of altering the date of the calendar on his desk. *Saturday, 21 February.* Great Heavens! It was Sunday morning! *Sunday, 22 February.* Exactly eight days since that infernal business at the Hanging Rock.

As soon as Albert had attended to the horses he flung himself fully clothed on his unmade truckle bed and fell asleep. He seemed to have hardly laid his head on the pillow before he was wide awake and staring at the little square of grey light at the window, with the events of yesterday, no longer confused by physical exhaustion as they had been last night, falling neatly into place like the pieces of a fretwork puzzle. Except that one of the key pieces was missing. Which was it, and where exactly did it fit into the pattern? Better start at the beginning when he had found Mike slumped over the tussock on Saturday morning. How far had he wandered before he had fallen and injured his ankle? Had he gone back to the laurel bush and started again from there? Those silly little paper flags ...! The next minute Albert had sprung out of bed and was pulling on his boots.

The birds were asleep in the chestnuts as he crossed the lawn still heavy with dew and slipped silently into the dark shuttered house by the side door. The housemaid was snoring gently outside Michael's room, and from the Fitzhuberts' opposite issued the rhythmic trumpeting of male and female slumbers. Mike was lying on his back, drugged and faintly moaning. His riding breeches, badly torn and stained, were hanging over the back of a chair at the end of the bed. Albert lit a match and slid a cautious hand into the pockets. Thank God the pigskin notebook was still there! He took it over to the window and by its sickly light began slowly deciphering the scribbled entries, page by page. They appeared to begin in March of last year, starting off with an appointment at a Cambridge address, a cure for distemper, copied out from *Country Life*. Memo – Call for tennis racquet. At last, opposite a page bearing the sole item 'Worm Powders' he came upon the one he was looking for. A scrawl of crooked capitals, in pencil :

ALBERT ABOVE BUSH MY FLAGS
HURRY RING OF HIGH UP HIGH

HURRY FOUN

Here the writing petered out. When Albert had read it several times he tore out the page and put the notebook back in the breeches pocket. ABOVE BUSH. MY FLAGS. HURRY. He could feel Mike looking over his shoulder, trying to tell him that he had found an important clue high up on the Rock – so important he had been trying to write down instructions for Albert when he had passed out beside the creek. MY FLAGS. The thought of the little flags made him go over to the bed and gently stroke the limp blue-veined hand on the coverlet. 'Rough as bags, young Crundall,' so the Colonel was wont to label his coachman. There was nothing rough about young Crundall at this moment, tip-toeing on clumsy boots from Michael's room. Convinced that there was no time to lose, he had the Colonel roused by the sleep-sodden housemaid; the boy from Manassa's Store dragged from Sunday morning sleep and placed only half awake on the family bicycle to notify the Woodend Police Station. Meanwhile Albert himself on the strawberry cob had ridden off to join the police party at a given rendezvous on the road to the Rock. As neither Constable Bumpher nor Doctor McKenzie, who usually assisted the police, were available, Doctor Cooling of Lower Macedon had agreed to accompany young Jim (armed with a notebook and strict instructions from Bumpher to write everything down and keep his mouth shut) in a horse vehicle equipped with a stretcher and medical supplies.

The sun was high as they drove through the gates of the Picnic Grounds, Albert trotting ahead with the precious page from the notebook pinned in the pocket of his shirt. The two young men had soon picked up Michael's tracks where he had walked away from the creek early on Saturday morning. On the stunted laurel, the little white paper flags hung limp in the noonday stillness. For the hundredth time Albert took the scribbled page from his pocket. 'ABOVE BUSH MY ...' 'Ah ...' breathed the policeman, impressed despite his normal scorn of the laity. 'So he put them there, did he?'

'Jeez, did you think they was growing on it?'

In silence they plodded uphill, following the bruised and broken fern, the doctor a little way behind, picking his urban way in too tight boots of Sunday tan. 'Beats me,' said the policeman, 'how a new chum got himself up here at all.'

'Some of the English are all right in the Bush when they've been out here for some time,' Doctor Cooling conceded.

'This one has more bloody brains and guts than any of us three put together,' Albert said.

'All the same,' said the Doctor, whose temper was fraying in proportion to the rapid swelling of his feet, 'I have a feeling we're on a wild goose chase. Stands to reason, nothing of any importance could have been lying around on the Rock until yesterday, without someone having seen it long ago.' Albert rushed to the defence of his friend. 'You don't know Mike, Doctor. He wouldn't have wrote down what he did without he'd found something.' But the doctor, unimpressed, had already selected a smooth rock for a seat and was unlacing his boots. 'Just blow your whistle, Jim, if you come across anything and I'll follow you up.'

Albert and Jim were nosing about in the scrub like terriers. 'See that piece of bush where it's broke off? Still green. That's where Mike must've went into the scrub Saturday morning.' It was. They began climbing again, following the mounting trail and loudly cursing the hidden rocks and holes under foot. 'What's that he says in the note about a ring? Diamonds, would you think?'

Albert snorted. 'Ring of stones, more like.'

Jim, however, rather fancied the idea of diamonds. 'One of those college girls was an heiress and don't you forget it, Albert. We policemen are trained to look at every angle in a case of this kind.'

'You better look where you're going, young Jim, or you'll be over the edge – that rock ahead is the one they call the monolith.'

'I'm aware of that,' said the policeman, tripping over a loose stone, 'and those two big boulders up there are called the Balancing Boulders, for your information.' Level with the monolith, Mike had apparently struck off sharp to the left. High in the cloudless sky the saw-toothed ridge of the topmost peaks glittered like gold.

'Pretty, isn't it? Make a nice postcard – crikey, what's that over there, on the ground?'

Doctor Cooling had just dozed off when he awoke to the urgent shrilling of the police whistle, drew on his boots and began climbing towards the source. His progress was excruciatingly slow even with the help of Albert, who had come belting downhill white in the face and babbling incoherently of a body, and was now dragging him through the scrub and dreadful rocks. When they arrived at the Balancing Boulders, Jim was laboriously compiling his notes and measurements – 'Looks to me like we're too late, Doctor. Pity.'

'Aw, shut yer trap,' Albert growled. He would have given

a pound to go into the scrub and be sick. The little dark one with the curls was lying face downwards on a ledge of sloping rock directly underneath the lower of the two boulders, with one arm flung out over her head, like a little girl fallen asleep on a hot afternoon. Above the bloodstained muslin bodice swarms of tiny flies clustered. The much-publicized ringlets were matted with dust and blood. 'It's a miracle if she's still alive,' the doctor said, kneeling beside the body and laying firm professional fingers on the flaccid wrist. 'By Heaven, there's a pulse beat ... she's alive all right ... faint but unmistakable.' He rose stiffly to his feet. 'Crundall, you go down for the stretcher while Jim stops here with me and finishes his notes and I get her ready to move. ... You're certain you haven't touched her or shifted anything, Jim?' 'No, sir. Mr Bumpher's very particular about touching a corpse.' Doctor Cooling said sternly, 'Not a corpse, young man. A living, breathing girl, thank God! Better check up on your notes before we do anything.'

There were no signs of a struggle, or any violence. The girl, so far as the doctor could see without a thorough examination, was apparently uninjured. The feet, strange to say, were bare and perfectly clean, in no way scratched or bruised, although it was later established that Irma was last seen at the Picnic Grounds wearing white open-work stockings and strapped black kid shoes, none of which articles were ever recovered.

Jim Grant was dropped off at the Woodend Police Station to give in his report to Bumpher as soon as he returned. It was late on Sunday afternoon when the still unconscious girl was carried by Albert and Doctor Cooling into the gardener's lodge at the Lake View gates, and there installed in the best bedroom under the care of Mrs Cutler, the gardener's wife. In Mrs Cutler's long calico nightdress smelling of lavender and kitchen soap she lay with closed eyes on the vast double bed under a patchwork quilt, looking as Mrs Cutler remarked to her husband later, 'for all the world like a little doll.' The fine cambric petticoat drawers and camisole, 'all trimmed with real lace, poor lamb!' were so torn and dusty that the good woman took it upon herself to put them under the copper where they were burned on Monday morning. Greatly to Mrs Cutler's surprise the lamb had been brought in just as she had been lying on the Rock, without a corset. A modest woman, for whom the word corset was never uttered by a lady in the presence of a gent, she had made no comment to the doctor, who had simply assumed that the girl had very sensibly gone to a school picnic minus that tomfool garment responsible in his opinion for a thousand female complaints. Thus the valuable clue of the missing corset was never followed up nor communicated to the police. Nor to the inmates of Appleyard College where Irma Leopold, well known for her fastidious taste in matters of dress, had been seen by several of her classmates, on the morning of Saturday the fourteenth of February, wearing a pair of long, lightly boned, French satin stays.

The body was unblemished and virginal. After careful examination Doctor Cooling pronounced the girl to be suffering from nothing more serious than shock and exposure. No broken bones, and only a few minor cuts and bruises on the face and hands. On the hands, especially, the nails were badly torn and broken. There was a possibility of concussion, compatible with bruising in certain areas of the head; nothing much, but he would like another professional opinion. 'Well, thank God for that!' said Colonel Fitzhubert, on pins and needles in the tiny front passage. 'As far as my wife and I are concerned Miss Leopold can stay here until she's well enough to be moved. Mrs Cutler's a first-rate nurse.'

At sunset, when Doctor McKenzie dropped in to take a look at Michael on his way home, he went down to the Lodge for a consultation with Doctor Cooling, who was just taking his leave. 'I agree with you, Cooling,' said the old man. 'It's a miracle. By all ordinary text book standards, the patient should have been dead long ago.' 'I'd give my head to know what happened up there on the Rock,' Cooling said. 'And where the dickens are the other two girls? And the governess?' It was arranged that Doctor McKenzie should take over the patient along with Michael Fitzhubert, whose nurse would be available for any extra services that might be necessary. 'They *won't* be necessary,' Doctor

McKenzie smiled, 'I know your Mrs Cutler, Colonel. She'll do this job on her head. And enjoy it. Rest. That's the main thing. And if possible, when she regains consciousness, peace of mind.'

Doctor Cooling had driven off at dusk, well satisfied. 'All's well that ends well, Doctor, and thanks for your help. Sort of case that might easily have turned out a bit tricky. We'll soon be reading all about it in the papers, no doubt.'

Doctor McKenzie, however, was not so confident. He went back into the bedroom and stood there looking thoughtfully at the pale heart-shaped face on the pillow. There was no telling, especially with the young and tender, how the intricate mechanism of the brain would react to severe emotional shock. Instinct told him she must have suffered damnably, if not in body, in mind, no matter what had or had not occurred at the Hanging Rock. This wasn't, he was beginning to suspect, an ordinary case. Just how extraordinary, he didn't yet know.

For Mike, the timeless days melted imperciptibly into timeless nights. Sleeping or waking it made no difference in the dim grey regions where he was forever seeking some unknown nameless thing. Invariably it vanished just as he drew near. Sometimes he would wake and touch it as it brushed past, only to find himself clutching at the blanket on his bed. A burning pain in his foot came and went, gradually lessening as his head grew clearer. Sometimes he was conscious of the smell of disinfectant, sometimes of a drift of flowery scent from the garden. When he opened his eyes there was always somebody in the room, usually a strange young woman who seemed to be dressed in white paper that crackled when she moved. It might have been the third or fourth day when he fell at last into a deep dreamless sleep. When he woke up the room was in darkness except for a pale incandescent light given off by a white swan sitting on the brass rail at the end of his bed. Michael and the swan looked at each other without surprise until the beautiful creature slowly raised its wings and floated away through the open window. He slept again, awoke to sunshine and the scent of pansies. An elderly man with a clipped beard was standing beside the bed. 'You're a doctor,' said Mike in a voice for the first time recognizably his own, 'what's wrong with me?'

'You've had a pretty bad fall and hurt your ankle and knocked yourself about a bit. Looking better today though.'

'How long have I been ill?'

'Let's see. Must be five or six days now since they brought you back from the Hanging Rock.'

'Hanging Rock? What was I doing at Hanging Rock?'

'We'll talk about it later,' said Doctor McKenzie. 'Nothing to worry about, my boy. Worry never did a sick man any good. Now let's have a look at your ankle.'

While the ankle was being bandaged Mike said, 'The Arab. Did I fall off?' and fell asleep again.

When the nurse brought his breakfast next morning the patient was sitting up and asking loudly and clearly for Albert.

'My, we *are* getting better quickly! Now drink up your tea while it's nice and hot.'

'I want to see Albert Crundall.'

'Oh, you mean the coachman? He comes up here every morning to ask after you. Such devotion!'

'What time does he usually come?'

'Soon after breakfast. But you're not allowed visitors yet, you know, Mr Fitzhubert. Doctor McKenzie's orders.'

'I don't care what his orders are. I insist on seeing Albert, and if you won't deliver my message I'll jolly well get out of bed and go down to the stables myself.'

'Now, now,' said the nurse with a professional smile that turned her into an advertisement for toothpaste. 'Don't go getting yourself all worked up or I'll get the blame.' Something about the strangely glittering eyes of the devastatingly handsome youth made her add, 'Eat up your breakfast and I'll fetch your Uncle.' Colonel Fitzhubert, summoned to the bedside, came tip-toeing in on eggshells with a face suitably lugubrious for a sickroom and was overjoyed at seeing the patient actually sitting up, and with quite a high colour. 'Splendid! Looking almost yourself this morning, isn't he nurse? Now then, what's all this I hear about wanting visitors?'

'Not visitors. Only Albert. I want Albert.' His head fell back against the pillows.

'Over-tired – that's what we are,' said the nurse. 'If my patient gets talking to that coachman his temperature will go up for certain and I'll be getting what-for from Doctor McKenzie.'

'The girl's not only a plain Jane but an ass,' the Colonel decided, aware of currents beyond his understanding. 'Don't worry, Mike, I'll tell Crundall to come up and see you for ten minutes. If there's any trouble, nurse, I'll take the blame.'

At last Albert was here beside him, smelling of Capstan cigarettes and fresh hay and settling himself into the bedside chair as if it were a restive colt ready to turn and bolt under his weight. He had never before been an official visitor to a sickroom and was at a loss how to begin a conversation with a disembodied face cut off at the chin by the rigidly folded sheet. 'That bloody nurse of yours .. Went for her life soon as she saw me coming.' It was as good a kick-off as any. Mike even gave a faint grin. The tide of friendship flowed between them. 'Good for you.'

'Mind if I smoke?'

'Go ahead. They won't let you stay long.' The old comfortable silence settled down between them like a cat on a communal hearth and they were at one. 'Look,' Mike said, 'there's a lot I have to know. Until last night my head was in such a muddle I couldn't think properly. My Aunt came in here and started talking to the nurse – I think they thought I was asleep. Suddenly it all began to sort itself out. It seems that I went back to the Hanging Rock on my own, without telling anyone but you. Is that right?'

'That's right. To look for the sheilas ... Take it easy, Mike, you don't look too good on it yet.'

'I found one of them. Is that right?'

'That's right,' Albert said again. 'You found her and she's up here at the Lodge, alive and kicking.'

'Which one?' Michael asked in a voice so low Albert could hardly hear. The lovely face – lovely even on the stretcher as they had carried her down the Rock, was always in his mind now. 'Irma Leopold. The little dark one, with the curls.'

The room was so quiet that Albert could hear Mike's heavy breathing as he lay with his face turned to the wall. 'So you've nothing to worry about,' Albert said. 'Only to hurry up and get well. . . . Stone the crows! He's passed out! Where's that bloody nurse got to . . . ?' The ten minutes had expired and she was here at the bedside, doing something with a bottle and spoon. Albert slipped past her through the French windows and made his way to the stables with a heavy heart.

9

GIRL'S BODY ON ROCK — MISSING HEIRESS FOUND. Once
again the College Mystery was front page news, embellished
with the wildest flights of imagination, public and private.
The rescued girl was still unconscious at Lake View, and the
Hon. Michael Fitzhubert was not well enough to be questioned. Which added fuel to the flame of gossip and
rumoured horrors to be later disclosed. The police search of
likely and unlikely places in the locality had been resumed
with extra men from Melbourne, the dog and tracker
brought back on the remote possibility of unearthing a clue
to the fate of the other three victims. Drains, hollow logs,
culverts, waterholes : an abandoned pigsty where someone
had seen a light moving last Sunday. At the bottom of an old
mineshaft in the Black Forest a terrified schoolboy swore he
had seen a body; and so he had — the carcass of a decom-
posed heifer. And so it went on. Constable Bumpher, still
conscientiously sweating over notebooks filled with un-
answerable questions, would almost have welcomed a brand
new murder.

At Appleyard College the news of Irma's rescue was
briefly and formally announced by the Headmistress directly
after prayers on the following Monday morning; a carefully considered procedure that allowed a full hour for its
assimilation before the first classes of the day. After a
moment of stunned silence it was received with outbursts of
hysterical joy, tears, fond embraces between people barely
on speaking terms. On the staircase, where loitering was
strictly forbidden, Mademoiselle had come upon Blanche
and Rosamund locked in tearful embrace — 'Alors, mes
enfants, this is no moment for tears' — and felt her own, long
unshed, rising to her eyes. In the kitchen, Cook and Minnie

rejoiced over a glass of stout, while on the other side of the baize door Dora Lumley clutched the cheap lace at her throat as if she too had been rescued upon the Rock. Tom and Mr Whitehead, at first jubilant in the potting shed, had soon passed on to murder in general, winding up with Jack the Ripper and the gardener gloomily supposing he must be getting back to his lawns. By midday the inevitable reaction from the rapturous relief of the morning was general. Afternoon classes assembled to an undercurrent of whisperings and mutterings. In the governesses' sitting-room the subject of Irma's discovery was barely touched on. As if by common consent the thin veils of make-believe obscuring the ugly realities were left intact, and only the headmistress, behind the closed doors of her study, permitted herself a cold-blooded scrutiny of this new turn of affairs. With the finding of only one of the four missing persons, the situation as it affected the College had actually deteriorated.

Strong-minded persons in authority can ordinarily grapple with practical problems of facts. Facts, no matter how outrageous, can be dealt with by other facts. The problems of mood and atmosphere known to the Press as 'Situations' are infinitely more sinister. A 'situation' cannot be pigeonholed for reference and the appropriate answer pulled out of a filing cabinet. An atmosphere can be generated overnight out of nothing or everything, anywhere that human beings are congregated in unnatural conditions. At the Court of Versailles, at Pentridge Gaol, at a select College for Young Ladies where the miasma of hidden fears deepened and darkened with every hour.

Waking next morning from uneasy sleep, the Headmistress could feel its pressure on a head already heavy under a hedgehog assortment of steel curling pins. In the dragging hours between midnight and dawn she had resolved, not without certain misgivings, on a change of policy: a mild relaxation of discipline and variation of the daily scene. To this end, the boarders' sitting-room was hastily re-papered in a ghastly shade of strawberry pink, and a grand piano was installed in the long drawing-room. The Reverend Lawrence and his wife were invited to drive out one evening from the

Vicarage at Woodend with lantern slides of the Holy Land to be shown in the drawing-room, where Mr Whitehead's choicest hydrangeas were banked up in the fireplaces and coffee, sandwiches and fruit salad were served by the maids in long-tailed caps and frilled aprons. The whole thing presented the perfect picture of a fashionable boarding school at the height of material prosperity and educational wellbeing. Yet little Mrs Lawrence drove away with a migraine, unaccountably depressed. In vain were the senior girls sent into Bendigo by train with a governess to witness a matinée of *The Mikado*. They returned if anything in lower spirits : people in the audience had stared and whispered as they took their seats in the front row. They felt themselves a part of the spectacle – the cast of the College Mystery – and were thankful to climb into the waiting wagonettes.

Conscious of a tactical blunder, the Headmistress decided on other and harsher means; a tighter rein on the always too talkative staff and enforcement of the rule forbidding confidential chattering of groups unattended by a governess. Henceforth the daily crocodile of girls in their summer uniforms and ugly straw hats wound its way two and two along the Bendigo high road in the prescribed and grudging silence of a female chain gang.

Easter was approaching and with it the end of the term. Already the summer flowers were fading and one morning splashes of gold appeared amongst the willows fringing the creek behind the house. The garden held no autumn delights for the Headmistress to whom well kept beds and lawns were no more than a symbol of prestige. Neatness was all – and a continuous array of showy blooms to be admired beyond the stone walls by passers-by on the high road. The leaves fluttering down from the little tree outside her study window were an unnecessary reminder of the passing of time. It was now nearly a month since the day of the picnic. Mrs Appleyard had lately spent a few days in Melbourne, largely at police headquarters in Russell Street. Here the first thing to catch an eye continually on the alert was a notice pinned on an official board : MISSING. PRESUMED DEAD above a detailed description and three extremely bad photographs of

Miranda, Marion and Greta McCraw. The word DEAD leaped obscenely from the printed page. Yes, it was possible, but highly unlikely, said the Senior Detective with whom she was closeted for two hours in a stuffy room, that the girls had been abducted, lured away, robbed – or worse. 'And what,' asked the Headmistress, tightlipped and clammy with fear and the insufferable heat of the room, 'could be worse, may I ask, than that?' It appeared that they might yet be found in a Sydney brothel : such things happened now and then in Sydney when girls of respectable background disappeared without a trace. Not often in Melbourne. Mrs Appleyard could only shudder. 'They were exceptionally intelligent and well-behaved girls who would never have allowed any familiarity from strangers.'

'As far as that goes,' said the detective blandly, 'most young girls would object to being raped by a drunken seaman, if that's what you have in mind.'

'I did *not* have it in mind. My knowledge of such things is necessarily limited.' The detective drummed squat tobacco-stained fingers on the top of his desk. These perfect ladies were the Devil. Dirty minded as they come, he wouldn't mind betting. Aloud he said mildly, 'Exactly. Most unlikely under the circumstances. However, we policemen have to consider every possible avenue in a case of this kind where not a single clue has come to light since the day it was reported. February the fourteenth, if I remember without looking it up.'

'That is so. Saint Valentine's Day.'

For a moment he wondered if the old girl was going off her head. Her face was an unpleasant mottled red. He didn't want her fainting on him and rose, declaring the abortive interview at an end. For Mrs Appleyard, staggering out into the glaring heat of the street, the interview was over, but the nightmare remained and would not be exorcised by a sleeping pill, nor a glass or two of brandy at her city hotel.

Back at the College, a series of setbacks and disturbing happenings had been accumulating. During her absence a father had called with a seemingly reasonable excuse for taking his daughter away with him then and there. Without the support of Greta McCraw, who in times of crisis could be unexpectedly shrewd, even practical, Mademoiselle had felt obliged to comply, and Miss Lumley was requested to arrange for the packing and despatch of Muriel's boxes to Melbourne. Worse still, the French Governess had handed in her resignation, 'on account of my approaching marriage to M. Louis Montpelier, shortly after Easter,' as soon as Mrs Appleyard had taken off her hat in the hall. The Headmistress knew a lady when she saw one, and Mademoiselle de Poitiers was definitely a social asset on the staff, not to be easily replaced. Miss McCraw's position had already been filled by a breezy young graduate with prominent teeth and the unhappy name of Buck, to whom the boarders had taken an instant dislike. Greta McCraw for all her impersonal barking had never been known to bite an individual wrongdoer.

There was a pile of correspondence on Mrs Appleyard's desk this evening, which had to be read through, weary as she was, before she could allow herself to go to bed. Thank Heaven, nothing with a Queensland postmark! First to be opened was a request from a South Australian mother, that her daughter 'for urgent family reasons' be sent home immediately on the Adelaide Express. The girl's people were well off, highly respected citizens. What irresponsible talk had they been listening to, smug in their suburban mansion? Family reasons! Pah! She took the brandy bottle from the cupboard and had opened two more letters before noticing Mr Leopold's telegram at the bottom of the pile. Sent a few days ago, from some God-forsaken address in Bengal, the peremptory wording was utterly unlike the usual extravagant Leopold technique. UNDER NO CIRCUMSTANCES IS MY DAUGHTER TO RETURN TO APPLEYARD COLLEGE. LETTER FOLLOWS. To lose in such a manner her richest and most admired pupil made her feel physically faint, almost sick. The implications of this new catastrophe were dangerous and unending. Only a few weeks ago the Headmistress had been telling the Bishop's wife: 'Irma Leopold is such a charming girl. Worth half a million when she turns twenty-one, so I understand ... her mother was a Rothschild, you know.'

Two enormous bills from butcher and grocer completed the day's tally of woe.

Late as it was, she felt impelled to take out the College Ledger. Several of the boarders' fees were outstanding. Although commonsense told her that prompt payment in advance of next term's fees could hardly be expected, under the circumstances, from Miranda's parents or the legal guardian of Marion Quade, she had been relying on the Leopold cheque with its numerous extras – dancing, drawing, monthly matinées in Melbourne, all of which showed a handsome profit to the College. On the neatly ruled page another name stood out : Sara Waybourne. Sara's elusive guardian had failed to show himself at her study door for several months, his usual fee-paying procedure, with the amount taken from his pocket book in cash. At the present moment, a whole term of Sara's extras was still unpaid for. For Mr Cosgrove, always expensively dressed, who left behind him in the study the tang of eau de Cologne and morocco leather, there was no excuse for delay.

Nowadays the very sight of the child Sara slumped over a book in the garden was enough to send a flush of irritation crawling up the Head's neck under the boned net collar. The small pointed face was somehow the symbol of the nameless malady from which every inmate of the College was suffering in varying degrees. If it had been a weak rounded childish face it might have aroused an answering pity instead of a sense of resentment that one so puny and pale possessed a core of secret strength – a will as steely as her own. Sometimes, catching sight of Sara's bent head in the schoolroom, where the Headmistress occasionally descended from Olympus to deliver a Scripture lesson, the sour taste of an unmentionable passion had momentarily choked her utterance. Yet the wretched child had remained outwardly docile, polite and diligent : only the secret pain in the absurdly large eyes. It was long past midnight. She rose, put the ledger back in its drawer and climbed heavily upstairs.

The following morning as Sara Waybourne was getting ready her drawing materials for Mrs Valange's art class, she was summoned to the Headmistress's desk.

'I have sent for you, Sara, because of a serious matter I have to explain to you. Stand up straight and listen very carefully to what I have to say.'

'Yes, Mrs Appleyard.'

'I don't know if you are aware that your guardian has failed to pay for your education here for several months? I have written to him at the usual bank address but my letters have been returned from the Dead Letter Office in every case.'

'Oh,' said the child without a change of expression.

'When did you last have a letter from Mr Cosgrove? Think most carefully.'

'I remember quite well. At Christmas – when he asked if I could stay at school over the holidays.'

'I remember. It was most inconvenient.'

'Was it? I wonder why he hasn't written for such a long time? I want some books and some more crayons.'

'Crayons? That reminds me, since you can give me no help in this unfortunate matter I shall have to tell Mrs Valange to discontinue your drawing lessons – as from this morning. Please note that any drawing materials in your locker are the property of the College and must be returned to Miss Lumley. Is that a hole in your stocking? You would be better employed learning to darn than playing about with books and coloured pencils.'

Sara had just reached the door when she was called back. 'I omitted to mention that if I have not heard from your guardian by Easter I shall be obliged to make other arrangements for your education.'

For the first time a change of expression flickered behind the great eyes. 'What arrangements?'

'That will have to be decided. There are Institutions.'

'Oh, no. No. Not that. Not again.'

'One must learn to face up to facts, Sara. After all, you are thirteen years old. You may go.'

While the above conversation was taking place in the study, Mrs Valange, the visiting art mistress from Melbourne, was being hoisted into the dog-cart outside the Woodend Station by the nimble Tom, to whom the little lady clung like a drowning sailor, weighed down as usual by a sketching pad, umbrella and bulging valise. The contents of the valise were invariably the same : for the senior pupils, a plaster cast of Cicero's head wrapped in a flannelette nightgown in case his beak of a nose got chipped in the rattling of the Melbourne train; a plaster foot for the juniors; a roll of Michalet paper; and for herself a pair of easy slippers with woollen pompoms and flask of cognac. (A taste for French brandy, had it ever come up for discussion, was about the only subject on which Mrs Valange and Mrs Appleyard were of the same mind.)

'Well now, Tom,' began the voluble and always agreeable art mistress as they turned into the highway under the shade of the eucalypts. 'How's your sweetheart ?'

'To tell you the truth, Ma'am, me and Minnie are both giving the Madam notice at Easter. We don't seem to fancy it here any more if you know what I mean.'

'I *do* know, Tom, and I'm sorry to hear it. You can't think what horrible things people are saying about all this in the city, though I tell everyone it's best forgotten.'

'You're right there, Ma'am,' Tom agreed. 'All the same Minnie and me will remember Miss Miranda and the other poor creatures till our dying day.'

As the dog-cart turned in at the College gates his passenger caught sight of her favourite pupil Sara Waybourne on the front lawn, and briskly waved her umbrella. 'Good morning, Sara – no thank you, Tom, I prefer to carry the valise myself – come here, child – I've brought you a lovely new box of pastels from Melbourne. Rather expensive I'm afraid but it can go down on your account . . . you're looking rather doleful this morning.'

Mrs Valange's reception of Sara's depressing news was characteristic. 'Not go on with your art classes? Nonsense ! I am not in the least worried about your fees considering you are the only one with an ounce of talent. I shall go straight to Mrs Appleyard and tell her so – we have ten minutes before the class begins.'

The interview which now took place behind the closed door of the study is unnecessary to record in detail. For the first and last time the two ladies stood face to face with the gloves off. After a few perfunctory civilities on both sides, the fight was on, warmhearted little Mrs Valange lashing out with colourful accusations emphasized by a dangerously waving umbrella, Mrs Appleyard shaken out of her usual public calm growing even more immense and purple. At last the door of the study was actually heard to slam and the art mistress, a moral victor, though beaten on a point of professional procedure, stood with heaving bosom in the hall. Tom was summoned, and Mrs Valange, clutching the umbrella and the valise with Cicero still wrapped in the nightdress, was hoisted into the dog-cart and driven away to the station for the last time.

After a brief unwonted silence in which his passenger scribbled on scraps of paper with a piece of coloured chalk, Tom was handed a half crown and an envelope addressed to Sara Waybourne, with instructions to deliver it as soon as possible without Mrs Appleyard's knowledge. Tom had been only too happy to oblige. He had a soft spot for little Mrs Valange as he had for Sara, and had every intention of handing her the letter next morning when the boarders congregated for half an hour after breakfast in the garden. However, he was unexpectedly sent off on an errand for the Head, and the letter went out of his mind.

Weeks later, when he came across it crumpled at the back of the drawer, and Minnie read it out to him by the light of her candle, it kept both of them awake half the night. Although as Minnie very sensibly pointed out, what was the use of worrying their soul cases out? It was hardly Tom's fault, under the circumstances, that the letter had never been delivered. *Dear child*, she had written, *Mrs A. has told me everything – what a ridiculous fuss about nothing! This is to tell you I want you to come and stay with me for as long as you like at my home in East Melbourne – address enclosed – if your guardian doesn't come for you by Good Friday. Just let me know and I will arrange to meet the train. Don't worry about the art lessons and keep on drawing whenever you get a spare minute, like Leonardo da Vinci. Fond love. Your friend, Henrietta Valange.*

Mrs Valange's dramatic exit from the College intensified the strains and tensions of the last few days. Despite frustrating rules of silence and the ban on talking in twos and threes without a governess in attendance, it had been conveyed before nightfall, by the passing of scraps of paper and other news-carrying devices, that a Scene had occurred in the study and that the child Sara was somehow to blame. Sara, as usual, had nothing to communicate. 'Creeping about like an oyster,' as Edith, never strong on natural history, pointed out. 'If we don't get a handsome young drawing master,' said Blanche, 'I'm going to give up Art. I'm sick of coloured chalk in my nails.' Dora Lumley came bustling up : 'Girls, didn't you hear the dressing bells? Go upstairs at once and take an order mark each for talking in the passage.'

A few minutes later, still on the prowl, Miss Lumley came upon Sara Waybourne curled up behind the little door of the circular staircase leading to the tower. The governess thought she had been crying, but it was too dark to see her face properly. When they came out on to the landing under the light from the hanging lamp the child looked like a stray half-starved kitten. 'What's the matter, Sara? Are you feeling ill?'

'I'm all right. Please go away.'

'People don't sit down on cold stone in the dark just before tea time, unless they're weak in the head,' Miss Lumley said.

'I don't want any tea. I don't want anything.' The governess sniffed. 'Lucky you! I only wish *I* could say the same.' She thought : 'This wretched snivelling child. This horrible house . . .' and decided to write to her brother this very night asking him to look out for a position. 'Not a boarding school. I tell you – I can't stand much more of it, Reg . . .' It was as much as she could do not to scream as the tea bell clanged through the empty rooms below. The mice frisking in the long dark drawing-room had heard it too and scampered off under the shrouded sofas and chairs. 'You heard the bell, Sara? You can't go down like that with cobwebs all over you. If you aren't hungry, you had better go to bed.'

It was the same room that Sara had formerly shared with Miranda – the most coveted room in the house, with long windows overlooking the garden, and rose-patterned curtains. Nothing had been changed since the day of the picnic, by Mrs Appleyard's express instructions. Miranda's soft pretty dresses still hung in orderly rows in the cedar cupboard from which the child invariably averted her eyes. Miranda's tennis racquet still leaned against the wall exactly as it did when its owner, flushed and radiant, came running upstairs after a game with Marion on a summer evening. The treasured photograph of Miranda in an oval silver frame on the mantelpiece, the bureau drawer still stuffed with Miranda's Valentines, the dressing table where she had always put a flower in Miranda's little crystal vase. Often, pretending sleep, she had lain awake watching Miranda brushing out her shining hair by the light of a candle.

'Sara, are you still awake, you naughty Puss?' smiling into the dark pool of the mirror. And sometimes Miranda would sing, in a special tuneless voice that only Sara knew, strange little songs about her family : a favourite horse, her brother's cockatoo. 'Some day, Sara, you shall come home with me to the station and see my sweet funny family for yourself. Would you like that Pussy?' Oh, Miranda, Miranda ... darling Miranda, where are you?

At last night came down upon the silent wakeful house. In the south wing Tom and Minnie, locked in each other's arms, murmured endlessly of love. Mrs Appleyard tossed in her curling pins. Dora Lumley sucked peppermints and wrote interminable letters to her brother in her fevered head. The New Zealand sisters had crept into the same bed for company and were lying side by side, taut and fearful of an impending earthquake. A light was still burning in Mademoiselle's room, where a stiff dose of Racine, by the light of a solitary candle, had so far failed as a soporific. The child Sara was also wide awake, staring into the dreadful dark.

Presently the possums came prancing out on to the dim moonlit slates of the roof. With squeals and grunts they wove obscenely about the squat base of the tower, dark against the paling sky.

10

The reader taking a bird's eye view of events since the picnic
will have noted how various individuals on its outer circum-
ference have somehow become involved in the spreading pattern: Mrs Valange, Reg Lumley, Monsieur Louis Montpelier, Minnie and Tom – all of whose lives have already
been disrupted, sometimes violently. So too have the lives
of innumerable lesser fry – spiders, mice, beetles – whose
scuttlings, burrowings and terrified retreats are comparable,
if on a smaller scale. At Appleyard College, out of a clear
sky, from the moment the first rays of light had fired the
dahlias on the morning of Saint Valentine's Day, and the
boarders, waking early, had begun the innocent interchange
of cards and favours, the pattern had begun to form. Until
now, on the evening of Friday the thirteenth of March, it
was still spreading; still fanning out in depth and intensity,
still incomplete. On the lower levels of Mount Macedon it
continued to spread, though in gayer colours, to the upper
slopes, where the inhabitants of Lake View, unaware of their
allotted places in the general scheme of joy and sorrow, light
and shade, went about their personal affairs as usual, unconsciously weaving and interweaving the individual threads
of their private lives into the complex tapestry of the whole.

Both the invalids were now progressing favourably. Mike
was breakfasting on bacon and eggs and Irma had been
pronounced by Doctor McKenzie well enough for some
gentle questioning by Constable Bumpher, already advised
that the girl so far had remembered nothing of her experiences on the Rock; nor, in Doctor McKenzie's opinion or
that of the two eminent specialists from Sydney and Melbourne, would she *ever* remember. A portion of the delicate
mechanism of the brain appeared to be irrevocably damaged.

'Like a clock, you know,' the doctor explained. 'A clock that stops under a certain set of unusual conditions and refuses ever to go again beyond a particular point. I had one at home. Never got beyond three o'clock on an afternoon ...' Bumpher, however, was prepared to call on Irma at the Lodge and in his own words 'give it a go'.

The interview had begun at ten a.m. with the policeman in the bedside chair, nicely shaven, pencil and notebook at the ready. By midday he was sitting back with a cup of tea and expressing his gratitude for an abortive two hours that had yielded precisely nothing. At least nothing in the official sense, although he had appreciated being sadly smiled at now and then by one so young and beautiful. 'Well, I'll be off now, Miss Leopold, and if anything *does* happen to pop into your mind just send me a message and I'll be up here in two flicks of a duck's tail.' He rose to go, replaced the rubber band round the blank pages of his notebook with a reluctance not entirely official, mounted his tall grey horse and trotted slowly down the drive towards his one o'clock dinner in low spirits that even his favourite plum pie did nothing to dispel.

On the following Saturday afternoon, the Macedon grapevine reported the arrival of another visitor at the Lodge : a lady, pretty as a picture in lilac silk, in a buggy and pair driven by a foreign gentleman with a black moustache who had asked the way to Lake View at Manassa's store. Everyone on the Mount knew that Mrs Cutler was caring for the heroine of the College Mystery, rescued on Hanging Rock by Colonel Fitzhubert's handsome young nephew from England. The latest turn of events was juicy enough to set the village of Upper Macedon gossiping and guessing all over again. It was rumoured that the nephew had broken all his front teeth scaling a sixty-foot precipice. That he was madly in love with the girl. That the lovely little heiress had sent to Melbourne for two dozen chiffon nightdresses and wore three strings of pearls in bed at the Lodge.

In point of fact the heiress's formidable pile of morocco leather luggage stood as yet unopened in Mrs Cutler's vestibule. And who but la petite, thought Mademoiselle fondly, could look so beautiful, so chic, wrapped in a faded Japanese kimono? The venetian blinds were drawn against the green garden light that rippled on the whitewashed walls of the bare little room and on the immense double bed with its patchwork quilt, seemingly afloat in a sea cave. The soft summer air caressed and healed like water. They wept a little, embraced long and tenderly, abandoning themselves after the first impassioned greetings to the silent luxury of sorrow shared. There was so much to be said, so little that ever could or would be said. The shadow of the Rock lay with an almost physical weight upon their hearts. The thing was beyond words; almost beyond emotion. Mademoiselle was the first to return to the tranquil reality of the summer afternoon, drawing up the blinds with a reassuring click, of the present peace of the garden beyond. The weeping elm at the window was murmurous with gossiping doves.

'Let me look at you, chérie.' The wan little face framed by a fan of ringlets loosely tied by a scarlet ribbon was almost as white as Mrs Cutler's calico pillows. 'Too pale – but so pretty – do you remember how I scolded you for rubbing geranium petals on your lips? But see! I have the wonderful news for you!' On Dianne's outstretched hand an antique French ring flashed a million rainbows on the patchwork quilt and Irma's dimple came out like a star. 'Darling Mam'-selle! I'm so glad! Your Louis is a lovely man!'

'Tiens! You have guessed it already, my secret?'

'I didn't guess, dear Dianne – I knew. Miranda used to say I guessed with my head and knew with my heart.'

'Ah, Miranda,' the governess sighed. 'Only eighteen and such wisdom ...' They fell silent again as Miranda floated towards them over the lawn with shining hair. Mrs Cutler, who had taken an immediate fancy to the elegant French lady, now appeared with a tray of strawberries and cream. 'Dear Mrs Cutler! What would I have done without her? And the Fitzhuberts – how kind everyone is!'

'And the handsome nephew?' Mademoiselle wanted to know. 'Is he also kind? Oh, what a profile in the news-papers!'

Irma had nothing to say of the nephew, reported still

too weak to leave his room. 'You forget, Dianne, I only saw Michael Fitzhubert once, in the distance, on the day of the picnic.'

'A woman can see everything necessary in the wink of the eye,' Mademoiselle observed. 'Tiens! When I first see the back of my Louis' head I say to myself : "Dianne, that man he is yours".'

As it happened, Mike was at this moment reclining on the lawn in a deck chair with his Aunt's carriage rug wrapped about his long legs. Beyond the sloping lawn the lake studded with open lily cups lay like burnished pewter reflecting the afternoon light. From it came the lusty cries and grunts of Albert and Mr Cutler guiding a punt through the lilypads in search of tangling water weeds. In the light blue sky that he would always associate with his Macedon summer, little woolly white clouds were sailing across the dark spikes of the pine plantation on the mountain's crest. For the first time since his illness, he was conscious of a faint stirring of pleasure in his surroundings.

'Ah, there you are, Michael! In the fresh air at last !' Mrs Fitzhubert, weighed down with parasol, cushions and needlework, had appeared on the verandah. 'Tomorrow you shall have a visitor to brighten you up. You remember Miss Angela Sprack from Government Cottage?' The nephew however showed no enthusiasm at the prospect of a tête-a-tête with the Sprack girl, of whom he remembered nothing but the ninepin legs and a pink and white face that had reminded him of a simpering Reynolds portrait in the dining-room at Haddingham Hall.

'I can't imagine why you're so critical of poor Angela.'

'I don't mean to be critical. It's entirely my fault that I find Miss Sprack – how can I express it – too English.'

'What's all this poppycock about being too English?' asked the Colonel, emerging from the shrubbery with the spaniels. 'How the deuce *can* a person be too English?'

Mike however felt unequal to carrying on the argument on an international level. The visit from Government Cottage was got through somehow on the following afternoon.

The Sprack girl was just what Mike had expected – the kind he was implored by his mother to make a point of waltzing with at a county ball. 'Damn it, Angie,' the Major complained as they drove down the avenue in the Vice-Regal dog-cart, 'you're a regular nincompoop. Don't you realize that young man is one of the best matches in the whole of England? Fine old family. Title any day . . . plenty of cash.'

'I can't help it if he's not interested in talking to me,' sniffed the wretched girl. 'You could see for yourself how it was this afternoon. I'm positive he dislikes me, and that's the end of it.'

'You cast-iron goose! Have you no crumb of social sense? I've no doubt the little beauty up at the Lake View Lodge will have a try for the Honourable Michael, heiress or no.'

As soon as Michael had dutifully assisted those ghastly legs to clamber up into the dog-cart he had decided to take a stroll down to the lake before dinner. The Spracks, like all boring guests, had stayed far too long, and already the sky was flecked with sunset clouds, the lake calm and lovely in the fading light. He had just turned his back on the retreating dog-cart and was walking rather unsteadily across the lawn when his ear caught the splash of water coming from the direction of the lake, where a girl in a white dress was standing beside a giant clamshell that served as a birds' bath, under an oak. The face was turned away, but he knew her at once by the poise of the fair tilted head, and began running towards her with the sickening fear that she would be gone before he could reach her, as invariably happened in his troubled dreams. He was almost within touching distance of her muslin skirts when they became the faintly quivering wings of a white swan, attracted by the sparkling jet from the tap. When Mike sank down on the grass a few feet away, the swan rose almost vertically above the shell, and scattering showers of rainbow drops in its wake flew off over the willows on the other side of the lake.

Mike was feeling stronger every day, and more certain of his legs taking the direction he chose for them. 'I do think,' said his Aunt, 'that Michael should at least pay a courtesy call on Miss Leopold. After all, Michael, you *did* save her life. It's merely a question of good manners.'

'A deuced pretty girl, too,' the Colonel said. 'At your age my boy I'd have been knocking on her door long ago with a bottle of fizz and a bouquet!'

Mike knew they were right about calling. The visit could no longer be delayed, and Albert was sent over with a note suggesting the following afternoon, to which Miss Leopold had replied, in a bold sprawling hand, on Mrs Cutler's best pink notepaper, that she would be delighted to see him and hoped he would come to tea.

It is one thing to make a calm and reasonable decision overnight – quite another to implement it in the light of day. With dragging footsteps Michael approached the Lodge. What the devil was he going to talk about to a strange girl? Mrs Cutler was beaming in the porch. 'I have Miss Irma in the garden so she can get a bit of fresh air, poor lamb.' In a little trellised arbour there was a tea table set out with a white crochet cloth and a deck chair with a heart-shaped red velvet cushion for the visitor. The lamb was sitting up in a froth of muslin and lace and scarlet ribbons under a canopy of crimson rambler roses, which somehow reminded the young man of his sisters' Valentines.

Although Mike had been told often enough that Irma Leopold was a 'raving beauty' he found himself unprepared for the exquisite reality of the sweet serious face turned towards his own. She appeared younger than he had expected – almost childlike – until she smiled, and with an easy adult grace held out a hand adorned with a breathtaking bracelet of emeralds. 'It's so nice of you to come and see me. I do hope you don't mind tea out here in the garden? Do you like marrons glacés – the real French ones – I adore them. Deck chairs usually collapse but Mrs Cutler says this one is all right.' Delighted at not being obliged to take an active part in the conversation – in his limited experience raving beauties were alarmingly dumb – Mike lowered himself into the sagging canvas chair and said truthfully that there was nothing he liked better than tea in the garden. It reminded him of home. Irma smiled again and this time the dimple, soon to become internationally famous, came out. 'My Papa is a darling but he refuses to eat out of doors. Calls it "barbarous".' Michael grinned back, 'So does mine,' wriggled into a more comfortable position and helped himself unasked to another marron glacé. 'My sisters love anything in the way of a picnic. ... Oh, Heavens ... what a tactless idiot I am ... the last thing I meant to talk about was a picnic – oh, confound it, there I go again.'

'Oh, please – don't look so unhappy. Whether we talk of it or not, that awful thing is always in my mind ... always and always.'

'And in mine,' Mike said very low, as the Hanging Rock in its dark glittering beauty rose between them. 'I'm glad, really,' Irma said at last, 'that you mentioned the picnic just now. It makes it easier to say thank you for what you did on the Rock ...'

'It was nothing, nothing at all,' the young man mumbled into his faultless English boots. 'Besides, it was really my friend Albert, you know.'

'But Michael, I don't know – Doctor McKenzie wouldn't let me see the newspapers ... who *is* this Albert?' Michael launched into a description of the rescue on the Rock, in which Albert figured as the hero, the master mind, ending with : 'My Uncle's coachman. Wonderful chap!'

'When can I meet him? He must think me a monster of ingratitude.' Michael laughed. 'Not Albert.' Albert was so modest, so brave, so clever ... 'Ah, but you must get to know him ...' Irma, however, was aware of nothing but the face of the young man opposite, flushed and charmingly earnest in praise of his friend. She was becoming a little tired of the unknown Albert when Mrs Cutler came out of the Lodge with the tea tray and the conversation turned to chocolate cake. 'When I was six years old,' Michael said, 'I ate the whole of my little sister's birthday cake at one go.' 'You hear that Mrs Cutler? You had better cut me a slice before Mr Michael gobbles it all up.' A good laugh, that's what they needed, the poor young things ...

As soon as he could escape from his Aunt's dinner table

that evening, Michael went out to the stables with a kerosene lantern and two cold bottles of beer. The coachman was lying naked on his bed reading the racing tips in the *Hawklet* by the light of a candle whose wavering flame sent ripples of light across his powerful chest, tufted with coarse black hair. Dragons and mermaids writhed and wriggled with every movement of the muscular arm pointing to a broken rocking chair under the tiny window.

'It's bloody hot in here even after dark but I'm used to it. Take your coat off. There's a coupla mugs on that shelf.' The mugs were filled and at once provided swimming pools for sundry insects attracted by the candle. 'It's real good to see you on your pins again, Mike.' The old comfortable silence took over, broken presently by Albert. 'I seen you out on the lawn today with Miss Thingummy-bob.'

'By Jove! That reminds me! She wants me to take her out in the punt tomorrow.'

'I'll tie her up in front of the boathouse and leave the pole on the table. And mind out for them lily roots at the shallow end.'

'I'll be careful. I don't want to tip the poor girl into the mud.' Albert grinned. 'Now if it was Miss Bottle-legs, I reckon a ducking wouldn't do her no harm. Them quiet ones, Mike, is the worst. ...' He winked and took a pull at his beer. 'By the way,' Mike said laughing, 'Irma Leopold particularly wants to meet you.'

'Oh, she does, does she? Cripes, this cold beer hits the spot.'

'Until I told her about you today she had no idea who found her on the Rock. How about coming down to the boathouse tomorrow afternoon?'

'Not on your life!' and after taking another pull at his mug he began to whistle 'Two Little Girls in Blue'. As soon as he paused for breath, Mike said, 'Well what day *can* you make it?' But Albert, having changed into a more convenient key, had started again at the beginning with exasperating flourishes of his own invention. When at last he stopped, deflated, Mike repeated, 'Well? *What* day?'

'Never. You can count me out on that one, Mike.'

'Then what the devil am I to say to the girl?'

'That's your business.' He began whistling again, and Mike, now really annoyed, left his beer unfinished, opened the trap door in the floorboards and descended the ladder into the darkness of the feed room below. Confound Albert! What the blazes has got under his skin?

On the following day Irma was waiting for Mike on the rustic seat in the boathouse when she heard the scrape of wheels on gravel and looking up saw a broad-shouldered youth in a faded blue shirt trundling a barrow along the path skirting the lake He was moving so quickly that when she stood up and called from the boathouse door he was already half way to the shrubbery and out of earshot. Or might have been. She called again, this time so loudly that he stopped, turned round and slowly retraced his steps. At last he stood facing her, near enough for her to see the square brick red peasant face under a thatch of tumbled hair, the deep set eyes apparently focussed on some invisible object of interest above her head. 'Was you calling me, Miss?'

'I was shouting at you, Albert! You *are* Albert Crundall?'

'That's me,' he said, not looking at her.

'You know who *I* am, don't you?'

'Yes,' he said, 'I know who you are all right. Was you wanting me for anything, like?' The sunburned arms lay along the barrow handles, the indigo mermaids crinkled ready for flight.

'Only to say thank you for having rescued me up there on the Rock.'

'Oh, that ...'

'Aren't we going to shake hands? You saved my life, you know.' The strange creature was plunging backwards between the shafts of his barrow like an unbroken colt. Reluctantly he lowered his skyward gaze level with her own. 'Tell you the truth, I never give it another thought once the Doc and young Jim had you safe on the stretcher.' He might have handed her a lost umbrella or a brown paper parcel instead of her life. 'You just ought to hear what Mr Michael says about it!' The brick red features stretched to a near grin. 'Now there's a wonderful bloke, if you like!'

'Exactly what he says about *you*, Albert.'

'He does? Well, I'll be buggered. Excuse my language, Miss – I don't often get talking to toffs like you. Well, I'd better be getting on with me job. Ta-ta.' With a decisive flick of powerful wrists the mermaids sprang into action. He was gone, and Irma found herself almost royally dismissed.

It was exactly three o'clock. There is no single instant on this spinning globe that is not, for millions of individuals, immeasurable by ordinary standards of time : a fragment of eternity forever unrelated to the calendar or the striking clock. For Albert Crundall, the brief conversation by the lake would inevitablv be expanded, in memory, during his fairly long life, to fill the entire content of a summer afternoon. What Irma had said, and what he had answered, were relatively unimportant. In actual fact, the very sight of the dazzling creature whose star-black eyes his own had sedulously avoided, had almost deprived him of the power of speech. Now ten minutes later in the damp seclusion of the shrubbery he sank down on to the empty barrow and wiped the sweat from his hands and face. He had plenty of time in which to recover his mental and physical equilibrium, since he knew, with absolute certainty, that he would never speak to Irma Leopold again.

Albert had no sooner disappeared through a gap in the laurel hedge when, with the precise timing of three wooden figures on a Swiss clock, Mike came out of the house and Irma – there is always a little wooden lady – appeared at the boathouse door. She stood there watching him hurry towards her, limping a little, over the dappled grass. 'At last I've met your Albert.' Mike's honest face brightened as it always did at the mention of Albert. 'Well? Wasn't I right?' Dear Michael! Marvelling that the clumsy brick red youth could command such adoration, Irma stepped into the waiting punt.

The weather continued warm and sunny and there were daily outings on the placid lake, soothed by the musical box tinkle of the mountain stream. In expensive green seclusion, the Fitzhuberts lay on long wicker chairs watching the season fade. The air in the Lake View garden was preternaturally still this summer. They could hear the bees murmuring in the wallflower bed under the drawing-room window and now and then Irma's light laughter drifting out over the lake. Beyond the oaks and chestnuts one of Hussey's wagon-ettes went creaking by on the steep chocolate road, scattering the pigeons on the lawn. The white peacock slept, the two spaniels dozed all day in the shade.

Together Michael and Irma had explored every inch of the Colonel's rose garden, the vegetable garden, the sunken croquet lawn, the shrubberies whose winding walks ended in delicious little arbours, ideal for the playing of childish games – Halma and Snakes and Ladders – on straight-backed garden chairs composed entirely of cast-iron ferns. There is no need for anything much in the way of conversation, which suits Mike very well. When Mrs Fitzhubert comes upon them holding hands on the rustic bridge she sighs. 'How happy they look! How young!' And asks her husband, 'Whatever do those two find to talk about all day long?'

Sometimes Irma finds herself chattering as she used to do long ago at school, for the sheer delight of tossing out words into the bright air, as children enjoy sending up a kite. Unnecessary for Mike to answer, or even to listen, so long as he is there beside her, leaning over the rail with a lock of thick hair falling over one eye with every turn of his head, and aiming endless pebbles at the gaping mouth of the stone frog in the pool.

Now in the late afternoon the little lake grew cold under the slanting shadows and a few yellowing leaves floated amongst the reeds. 'Darling Mike – I can't bear to think that summer is almost over and no more rows on the lake.'

'Just as well,' Mike said, expertly nosing the punt through the lily pads. He grinned. 'Actually, the old punt isn't safe to take out again.'

'Oh, Mike! . . . Then it *is* over.'

'Oh, well – it's been good fun while it lasted.'

'Miranda used to say that everything begins and ends at exactly the right time and place . . .'

Mike must have been leaning too heavily on the pole. Irma

could hear the water gurgling under the rotting floor boards as the punt lurched clumsily forward. 'Sorry ... did I splash you? Those confounded lily roots ...'

At the landing stage the lilies were already closed and secret in the half-light. A white swan was rising gracefully out of the reeds ahead. They stood for a moment watching it flapping away over the water until it disappeared amongst the willows on the opposite bank. It was like this that Irma would later remember Michael Fitzhubert most clearly. Quite suddenly he would come to her in the Bois de Boulogne, under the trees in Hyde Park; a lock of fair hair hanging over one eye, his face half turned to follow the flight of a swan.

That night the mountain mist came rolling down from the pine forest and lingered far into the morning. At the Lodge the view of the lake from Irma's window was blotted out and Mr Cutler went off to see to his glasshouses, predicting an early winter. At Manassa's store an occasional customer calling in for the morning paper enquired with flagging interest, 'Anything more about the College Mystery?' There wasn't – at least nothing that could be remotely classed as news on Manassa's verandah. It was generally conceded by the locals that the goings-on at the Rock were over and done with and best forgotten.

A last row on the lake. A last light pressure of a hand ... Unseen, unrecorded, the pattern of the picnic continued to darken and spread.

11

Mrs Fitzhubert at the breakfast table looked out on to the mist-shrouded garden and decided to instruct the maids to begin putting away the chintzes preparatory to the move to velvet and lace in Toorak.

'This ham is distinctly over-cooked,' said the Colonel. 'Where the deuce has Mike got to?'

'He asked for some coffee in his room. You must admit those two are ideally suited.

'Positively ragged at the knuckle! Who?'

'Michael and Irma Leopold, of course.'

'Suited for what? Reproduction of the species?'

'There's no need to be vulgar. I saw them going down to the lake yesterday.... Have you no heart?'

'What the devil's my heart got to do with overdone ham?'

'Oh, bother the ham! Can't you understand, I'm trying to tell you that our little heiress is coming to lunch today!'

For the Fitzhuberts, the punctual appearance of the delicious meals borne on enormous trays to the dining-room was a sacred ritual, serving to define and regulate their idle otherwise formless days. Simultaneously with the striking by the parlourmaid of an Indian gong in the hall, a sort of gastronomical timepiece located in the Fitzhubert stomach would inwardly proclaim the hour. 'I shall take a short nap after lunch my dear. ... We shall be having tea on the verandah at a quarter past four.... Tell Albert to bring round the dog-cart at five.'

Luncheon at Lake View was at one o'clock sharp. Irma, warned by the nephew that unpunctuality was a cardinal sin in a visitor, smoothed out her crimson sash in the porch and glanced at her tiny diamond watch. The mist had cleared at last to a sultry yellow light in which the rambling

123

facade of the villa under its mantle of Virginia creeper seemed strangely unreal. As Mike was nowhere in sight, she made her way to a less forbidding entrance on a side verandah. The bell brought a parlourmaid from a dark tiled passage where a sorrowful moose's head presided above a miscellany of hats, caps, coats, tennis racquets, umbrellas, fly veils, solar topees and walking sticks. In the drawing-room overlooking the lake the very air seemed pink, heavy with the scent of La France roses in silver vases. Flanked by yesterday's pink satin cushions, Mrs Fitzhubert rose to greet her guest from a little pink sofa. 'The men will be here directly. Here comes my husband now, walking straight into the hall with clay from the rose garden all over his boots.'

Irma, who had seen sunset on the Matterhorn and moonlight on the Taj-Mahal, truthfully exclaimed that Colonel Fitzhubert's garden was quite the loveliest she had ever seen. 'Clay is very difficult to remove from a good carpet,' Mrs Fitzhubert said. 'Wait till you have one of your own, my dear.' The girl was certainly a beauty and wore her deceptively simple frock with an air. The Leghorn hat with the crimson ribbons was probably Paris. 'My mama had two – the first was French.'

'Aubusson?' Mrs Fitzhubert enquired.

Oh, Heavens! If only Mike would come! 'I mean husbands – not carpets …' Mrs Fitzhubert was not amused. 'The Colonel used to tell me in India that a really good carpet is the best investment after diamonds.'

'Mama always says you can judge a man's taste pretty well by his choice of jewellery. My papa is quite an expert on emeralds.' The older woman's neat little faded mouth had fallen open. 'Indeed?' There was simply nothing else to be said and both ladies looked hopefully towards the door. It opened to admit the Colonel followed by two ancient slobbering spaniels.

'Down dogs! Down! I forbid you to lick this young lady's lily white hand. Ha! Ha! Fond of dogs, Miss Leopold? My nephew tells me these brutes are too fat – where *is* Michael?' Mrs Fitzhubert's eyes swept the ceiling as if the nephew might conceivably be concealed in the pelmet drapes or hanging head downwards from the chandelier. 'He knows perfectly well we lunch at one.'

'He mentioned something last night about a stroll up to the Pine Forest – but that's no excuse for being late the very first time Miss Leopold comes to luncheon,' said the Colonel turning a glassy blue stare on the visitor and automatically registering the emeralds on the slender wrist. 'You'll just have to put up with us two old fogies. No other guests I'm sorry to say. At the Calcutta Club eight was always considered the perfect number for a small luncheon party.'

'Fortunately we are *not* lunching off those detestable Indian chickens,' said his wife. 'Colonel Sprack kindly sent us over some mountain trout from Government Cottage last night.' The Colonel looked at his watch. 'We won't wait for that young scapegrace or the fish will be ruined. I hope you like grilled trout, Miss Leopold?' Irma obligingly adored grilled trout and even knew about the right sauces. The Colonel thought that damned idiot Mike would be lucky if he landed the little heiress. Why the devil didn't Mike turn up?

A shared appreciation of the trout's delicate flavour could hardly be expected to keep a three-handed conversation going throughout the long leisurely meal. Mike's place was presently removed from the table. An uneasy silence accompanied the mousse of tongue despite the host's monologues on rose growing and the outrageous ingratitude of the Boers towards Our Gracious Queen. The two ladies discussed with desperate animation the Royal Family, the bottling of fruit – to Irma the most boring of mysteries – and as a last resort, music. Mrs Fitzhubert's younger sister played the piano, Irma the guitar, 'with coloured streamers and those divine gypsy songs.' As soon as coffee was served the host lit a cigar and left the ladies marooned on the pink sofa behind the carved Indian table. Beyond the French windows Irma could just see the lake, leaden under a sombre sky. The drawing-room had grown uncomfortably warm, with Mrs Fitzhubert's little puckered face coming and going on the pink air like the face of the Cheshire cat in *Alice in Wonderland*. Why, oh, why had Mike failed to appear at luncheon? Now

Mrs Fitzhubert was enquiring if Mrs Cutler was any sort of a cook? 'Dear Mrs Cutler! She cooks like an angel! I have the recipe for her divine chocolate cake.'

'I remember learning to make mayonnaise at my boarding school – drop by drop with a wooden spoon. ...' Irma descended from the pine forest where Mike wandered incorporeal through the mist. The drawing-room was spinning.

At last the clock on the mantelpiece proclaimed a reasonable hour for departure and Irma rose to go. 'You look a little fatigued,' Mrs Fitzhubert said. 'You must drink plenty of milk.' The girl had pretty manners and quite an air for seventeen. Michael was twenty – exactly right. She accompanied the visitor to the hall door – unfailing sign of social approval – and hoped, for reasons too complicated to be entered upon here, that Irma would visit them in Toorak. 'I don't know if our nephew has told you that we intend giving a ball for him after Easter. He knows so few young people in Australia, poor boy!'

After the suffocating warmth of the drawing-room the damp pine-scented air of the garden was blessedly cool. A sudden flurry of wind sent a long shiver through the Virginia creeper, scattering its crimson leaves on the gravel before the house, bowing the heads of the prim standard roses in the circular flower bed. Then stillness again and the distant striking of the stable clock echoing across the lake. Gone now the misty transparencies of the morning. Opaque saffron clouds piling up on a muddy sky; the pine forest an iron crown encircling the mountain's crest with stiff spikes. On the other side of the forest, far below, the unseen plains forever shimmering in waves of honey-coloured light, and rising out of them the dark reality of the Hanging Rock. Doctor McKenzie was right : 'Don't think about the Rock, dear child. The Rock is a nightmare, and nightmares belong to the Past.' Try to follow the old man's advice and concentrate on the Present, so beautiful here at Lake View with the white peacock spreading its tail on the lawn, fat grey pigeons waddling on little pink feet, the stable clock striking again, bees going home in the fading light. A few drops of rain plopped on the Leghorn hat. Mrs Cutler was coming out of the Lodge with an umbrella. 'Mr Michael reckons there's a storm coming up. My corns are shooting something cruel.'

'Michael? You've seen him?'

'A few minutes ago. He called in with a letter for you, Miss. If ever a young man had lovely manners it's him – oh, my! your pretty hat!' The Leghorn was tossed aside on Mrs Cutler's shining linoleum. 'Don't bother – I shall never wear it again – the letter, please.' The door of her best bedroom closed disappointingly on the cosy chat Mrs Cutler had been looking forward to all day. The hat, however, was presently retrieved, its ribbons tenderly ironed, to appear for many a year at church on Mrs Cutler's devoted head.

In Irma's room the venetian blinds were closed against the heat of the day. She had just thrown up the window and was about to open Mike's letter when a streak of lightning zig-zagged across the pane. In a flash of blue light the weeping elm stood out with not a leaf stirring. Suddenly a mighty wind rose up from nowhere, strangely warm, the elm began to shiver and shake, the curtains billowed out into the room. To drum rolls of thunder, the storm broke, with full bellied clouds exploding in the heaviest rain the Macedon people could remember on the Mount, within minutes washing the gravel from the carriage drives and swelling the mountain streams. In the Lake View pool the muddied water came swirling down over the head of the stone frog. Out on the lake, the punt, torn from its moorings, rocked wildly on the lily pads. Driven by the gale, half-drowned birds fell to the ground from the tossing trees and a dead dove went sailing past the window like a mechanical toy. At last the wind and rain lost their initial fury. A pallid sun came out; the sodden lawns and ravaged flower beds took on a theatrical glow. It was over, and Irma, still at the window, opened the stiff square envelope.

Formally addressed and strictly impersonal, it might have been an invitation card or a bill, except for the oddly childish handwriting with neat copy book loops and a sprinkling of spiky verticals painfully acquired during a brief encounter with the classics at the University of Cambridge. Cambridge or no, for Mike the very act of taking up a pen put his head in a whirl and made him forget what he was trying to say. Whereas Irma, who spelled by the light of nature and confined her punctuation to the impulsive dash or exclamation mark, was entirely herself in the briefest of notes. The letter began with apologies for having stayed too long in the pine forest this morning and for having forgotten to look at his watch until it was too late to be on time for the trout ('all the more for you'). With a mounting sense of irritation she turned the page : *I had a letter from home this morning asking me to call on our banker immediately. A bore, but there it is. I am up to the eyes in packing and will have to be off by the early train tomorrow. Long before you are awake! As Lake View will be closed for the winter in a few days now, I've decided not to come back here, which means I'm afraid that I won't be seeing you to say good-bye. It's rotten luck but I'm sure you'll understand. So if we don't meet again in Australia thank you for having been so nice to me, Irma dear. The last few weeks would have been impossible without you.*

Love from Mike.

P.S. *I forgot to say I intend taking a fairly long look at Australia beginning with Northern Queensland, do you know it at all?*

For a person who found difficulty in expressing himself on paper, the writer had conveyed his meaning remarkably well.

Although we are necessarily concerned, in a chronicle of events, with physical action by the light of day, history suggests that the human spirit wanders farthest in the silent hours between midnight and dawn. Those dark fruitful hours, seldom recorded, whose secret flowerings breed peace and war, loves and hates, the crowning or uncrowning of heads. What, for instance, is the plump little Empress of India planning in bed in a flannel nightgown at Balmoral, on this night in March in the year nineteen hundred, that makes her smile and purse her small obstinate mouth? Who knows?

So, too, in stillness and silence do the obscure individuals who figure in these pages plot, suffer and dream. In Mrs

Appleyard's heavily curtained bedroom the suet-grey mask of the woman on the bed is literally bloated and blotched by evil vapours invisible by the light of day. A few doors away the child Sara's little peaked face is illumined, even in sleep, by a dream of Miranda so filled with love and joy that she carries it about with her all next day, earning countless order marks for inattention in class, and at the instigation of Miss Lumley, half an hour strapped to a backboard in the gymnasium for 'slouching' with drooping, dream-heavy head. At Lake View, the stable clock striking five awakens the cook who rises yawning to set the oatmeal for Mr Michael's early breakfast. Mike is awake after a restless night, productive mainly of dreams of banking and packing and procuring a seat on the Melbourne Express this morning. Once he dreams of Irma hurrying towards him down the corridor of a swaying train. 'Here, Mike, there's a seat here beside me,' and pushes her away with his umbrella.

Down at the Lodge, Irma too has heard the clock strike five; only half awake and staring out at the garden slowly taking on colour and outline for the coming day. At the Hanging Rock the first grey light is carving out the slabs and pinnacles of its Eastern face – or perhaps it is sunset. . . . It is the afternoon of the picnic and the four girls are approaching the pool. Again she sees the flash of the creek, the wagonette under the blackwood trees and a fair-haired young man sitting on the grass reading a newspaper. As soon as she sees him she turns her head away and doesn't look at him again. 'Why? Why? . . .' 'Why?' screeches the peacock on the lawn. Because I knew, even then . . . I have always known, that Mike is my beloved.

12

At two o'clock on the afternoon of Thursday the nineteenth of March, Appleyard College was cold, silent and smelling of roast mutton and cabbage. The boarders' midday dinner was just over, the maids off duty. Afternoon classes had not yet begun. Dora Lumley lay on her bed sucking her eternal peppermints and Mademoiselle, seated at a window overlooking the front drive, was re-reading a letter from Irma received in this morning's mail.

The Lodge. Lake View.

Dearest Dianne,

In haste – Mrs C. and I up to our eyes in tissue paper – can't find a pen. Mrs C. says why isn't the lovely French lady here to show her how to fold the dresses? This is to tell you the WONDERFUL *news – my darling parents arrive from India this week. I am going to Melbourne to wait for them in our suite at the Menzies Hotel!! It all feels like the end of a long long storey and now suddenly it is the* LAST *chapter and nothing more to read. So dearest Dianne I will be calling in at the College on my way to the station probably Thursday afternoon – my last chance to say good-bye to you – and the dear girls – it makes my heart ache to think of them still there at school – and of course Minnie and Tom but I hope* NOT *Mrs A. if it can possibly be* AVOIDED! *Oh, what a hateful thing to say but the thought of having to talk to her is* MISERY! *Dianne I haven't had a chance to buy your wedding present – Manassa's Store has nothing but boots and jam darling and tin billy cans – so please accept my emmerald bracelet with my love – the one my Grandmother in Brazil gave me the one I told you about with the green parrot – remember? anyway now dead so she won't*

*know or mind. Mrs C. wants to know about the blue chiffon
you used to like I must go.*

Love Irma.

P.S. – *I shall come straight up to your room when I arrive –
or to the schoolroom if you are in class whether Mrs A.
approves or not.*

Mademoiselle's was the first of several heads at several
windows to see Hussey's cab coming up the drive. From it
alighted Irma in a scarlet cloak and a little toque of scarlet
feathers blowing this way and that. The Headmistress at her
desk downstairs had seen her too and to Mademoiselle's
amazement – such a lapse of decorum was unknown at the
College – had herself appeared at the hall door before the
governess was half way down the staircase, and was sweeping
the visitor into the study on a chill wave of formal greeting.

On the first floor landing one of the statues was permitted
on dull afternoons to cast a feeble light. Now Dora Lumley
came shuffling out of the shadows. 'Mam'selle! Are you
ready? We shall be late for the gymnasium class.'

'That hateful gymnasium! I am coming down now.'

'The girls are so seldom allowed in the fresh air nowadays
– surely you agree they need exercise?'

'Exercise! You mean those ridiculous tortures with bars
and dumb-bells? At their age young girls should be strolling
under the trees in light summer dresses with a young man's
arm around every waist.'

Dora Lumley was too deeply shocked to reply.

Irma Leopold's visit as far as Mrs Appleyard was concerned could hardly have been worse timed. Only this morning the headmistress had received a highly disturbing letter
from Mr Leopold, written immediately on his arrival in
Sydney, and demanding a new and fuller inquiry on events
leading up to the picnic. 'Not only on behalf of my own
daughter, miraculously spared, but for those unfortunate
parents who have still learned nothing of their children's
fate.' There was mention of a top-rank detective being
brought out from Scotland Yard at Mr Leopold's expense
and other looming horrors impossible to thrust aside.

Somehow, to Irma's surprise, the study was a good deal smaller than she had remembered. Otherwise nothing had changed. There was the same remembered smell of beeswax and fresh ink. The black marble clock on the mantelpiece ticked as loudly as ever. There was an endless moment of silence as Mrs Appleyard seated herself at her desk and the visitor by sheer force of habit dropped a perfunctory curtsey. The cameo brooch on the silk upholstered bosom rose and fell to the old inexorable rhythm.

'Be seated, Irma. I hear you are completely restored to health.'

'Thank you, Mrs Appleyard. I am perfectly well now.'

'And yet you still recollect nothing of your experiences at the Hanging Rock?'

'Nothing. Doctor McKenzie told me again only yesterday that I may never remember anything after we had begun to walk towards the upper slopes.'

'Unfortunate. Very. For everyone concerned.'

'You need hardly tell me that Mrs Appleyard.'

'I understand you are leaving for Europe shortly?'

'In a few days I hope. My parents think it is a good idea to get away from Australia for a time.'

'I see. To be frank with you, Irma, I regret that your parents didn't think fit for you to complete your education at Appleyard College before embarking on a purely social life abroad.'

'I am seventeen Mrs Appleyard. Old enough to learn something of the world.'

'If I may say so, now that you are no longer under my care, your teachers were continually complaining to me of your lack of application. Even a girl with your expectations should be able to spell.' The words were hardly out of her mouth before she realized that she had made a strategic blunder. It was above all things necessary not to further antagonize the wealthy Leopolds. Money is power. Money is strength and safety. Even silence has to be paid for. The girl had gone alarmingly white in the face. 'Spelling? Would spelling have saved me from whatever it was that happened on the day of the Picnic?' The little gloved hand came down hard on the top of the desk. 'Let me tell you this, Mrs Apple-yard : anything of the slightest importance that I learned here at the College I learned from Miranda.'

'It is a pity,' the Headmistress said, 'that you did not acquire something of Miranda's admirable self-control.' With an effort of her own will that contracted every nerve and muscle in her body she managed to rise from her chair and enquire, quite graciously, if Irma would care to spend to-night in her old room, on the way to Melbourne?

'Thank you, no. Mr Hussey is waiting down there in the drive. But I should like to see the girls and Mademoiselle before I go.'

'By all means! Mademoiselle and Miss Lumley will be taking the class in the gymnasium. For once I think discipline may be relaxed. It is irregular but you may go in and say good-bye. Tell Mademoiselle you have my permission.'

A glacial handshake was exchanged as Irma left for the last time the room where she had so often stood – long, long ago, as a schoolgirl – awaiting commands and reprimands at the Headmistress's pleasure. She was no longer afraid of the woman behind the closed door, whose hand, seized with an uncontrollable tremor, reached for the bottle of cognac under the desk.

Minnie ambushed in the shadowy regions behind the green baize door came running towards her with open arms. 'Miss Irma, dear. Tom told me you was in there. Let me look at you. . . . My! a real grown-up young lady !'

Irma bent and kissed the warm soft neck reeking of cheap scent. 'Dear Minnie. It's so good to see you.'

'And you, Miss. Is it true what we hear that you're not coming back to us after Easter?'

'Quite true. I've only called in today to say good-bye to you all.' The housemaid sighed. 'I don't blame you, neither. Sorry as we all are to be losing you. You've no idea what it's like here these days.'

'I believe you,' Irma said, glancing about her at the gloomy hall which Mr Whitehead's late crimson dahlias in brass vases failed to lighten. Minnie had lowered her voice to a whisper. 'Talk about rules and regulations ! The boarders aren't hardly let open their mouths out of school hours! Well, thank Heaven me and Tom are out of it in a few days' time.'

'Oh, Minnie, I *am* so glad – you're going to be married?'

'Easter Monday. Same day as Mam'selle. I told her I reckoned Saint Valentine had pulled it off for both of us and she says, quite serious : "Minnie, you may be right." Saint Valentine is the patron saint of lovers.'

The gymnasium, commonly known to the boarders as the Chamber of Horrors, was a long narrow room in the West wing, lit only by a row of barred skylights, and designed by the original owner for Heaven knows what domestic purposes : possibly the storage of extra foodstuffs, or unwanted furniture. Now on its bare limewashed walls various instruments for the promotion of female health and beauty had been set out, as well as a rope ladder suspended from the ceiling, a pair of metal rings and parallel bars. In one corner stood a padded horizontal board fitted with leather straps, on which the child Sara, continually in trouble for stooping, was to pass the gymnasium hour this afternoon. A pair of iron dumb-bells which only Tom had enough muscle to lift, weights for balancing on tender female skulls and piles of heavy Indian clubs, proclaimed Authority's high-handed disregard of Nature's basic laws.

At one end of the room, on a platform raised a few feet above floor level, Miss Lumley and Mademoiselle were already on duty; the former engaged on looking out for minor misdemeanours below, the latter seated at the upright piano hammering out the 'March of the Men of Harlech'. *One two, one two, one two.* Three rows of girls in black serge bloomers, black cotton stockings and white rubber-soled canvas shoes listlessly dipped and rose in time to the martial strains. For Mademoiselle, the Gymnasium class was a recurring penance. Presently, when it was time for a five-minute break, she would give herself the pleasure of announcing that Irma Leopold was actually here in the building, and would shortly be coming to the gymnasium to say good-bye. *One two, one two, one two* . . . it was possible, she thought, dreaming and hammering, that they already knew on the College grapevine. *One two, one two* ... 'Fanny,' she said, taking her hands off the keys for a moment, 'you are badly out of step. Pay attention to the music, please!' 'Take an order mark, Fanny,' Miss Lumley muttered, scribbling in her little book. The languid physical movements of arms and legs belied the expression of the fourteen pairs of eyes, sliding from side to side. *One – two, one – two*, alert and sly as the eyes of Normandy hares in their barred wooden cages. *One two, one two, one two, one two* ... the monotonous thumping was inhuman, almost unendurable.

The door of the gymnasium was opening, very slowly, as if the person outside were reluctant to enter. Every head in the room turned as the 'Men of Harlech' halted in the middle of a bar. Mademoiselle rose smiling beside the piano and Irma Leopold, a radiant little figure in a scarlet cloak, stood on the threshold. 'Come in Irma! Comme c'est une bonne surprise! Mes enfants, for ten minutes you may talk as you please. Voilà, the class is dismissed!' Irma, who had taken a few steps towards the centre of the room, now paused uncertainly and smiled back.

There were no answering smiles, no hum of excited greeting. In silence the ranks broke to the shuffling of rubber-soled feet on the sawdust floor. Sick at heart, the governess looked down at the upturned faces below. Not one was looking at the girl in the scarlet cloak. Fourteen pairs of eyes fixed on something behind her, through and beyond the whitewashed walls. It is the glazed inward stare of people who walk in their sleep. Oh, dear Heaven, what do these unhappy children see that I do not? So the communal vision unfolds before them and Mademoiselle dare not pierce the taut gossamer veil by a spoken word.

They see the walls of the gymnasium fading into an exquisite transparency, the ceiling opening up like a flower into the brilliant sky above the Hanging Rock. The shadow of the Rock is flowing, luminous as water, across the shimmering plain and they are at the picnic, sitting on the warm dry grass under the gum trees. Lunch is set out by the creek. They see the picnic basket and another Mademoiselle – gay in a shady hat – is handing Miranda a knife to cut the heart-shaped cake. They see Marion Quade, with a sandwich in one hand and a pencil in the other, and Miss McCraw, forgetting to eat, propped against a tree in her puce pelisse. They hear Miranda proposing the health of Saint Valentine; magpies and the tinkle of falling water. Another Irma in white muslin, shaking out her curls and laughing at Miranda washing out cups at the creek. ... Miranda, hatless with shining yellow hair. A picnic was no fun without Miranda. ... Always Miranda, coming and going in the dazzling light. Like a rainbow. ... Oh, Miranda, Marion, where have you gone ...? The shadow of the Rock has grown darker and longer. They sit rooted to the ground and cannot move. The dreadful shape is a living monster lumbering towards them across the plain, scattering rocks and boulders. So near now, they can see the cracks and hollows where the lost girls lie rotting in a filthy cave. A junior, remembering how the Bible says the bodies of dead people are filled with crawling worms, is violently sick on the sawdust floor. Someone knocks over a wooden stool and Edith screams out loud. Mademoiselle, recognizing the hyena call of hysteria, walks calmly to the edge of the dais with madly thumping heart. 'Edith! Stop that horrible noise! Blanche! Juliana! Be silent! All of you be silent!' Too late; the light voice of authority goes unheard as the smouldering passion long banked down under the weight of grey disciplines and secret fears bursts into flames.

On the lid of the piano stood a small brass gong, normally struck for silence and order. Mademoiselle struck at it now, with all the force of her slender arm. The junior governess had retreated behind the music stool. 'It's no use, Mam'selle. They won't take any notice of the gong or anything else. The class is quite out of hand.'

'Try to get out of the room by the side door without them seeing you and bring the Head. This is serious.'

The junior governess sneered : 'You're afraid, aren't you?'

'Yes, Miss Lumley. I am very much afraid.'

Above a sea of thrusting heads and shoulders where Irma stood hemmed in by the laughing sobbing girls, a tuft of scarlet feathers trembled, rising and falling like a wounded bird. The voice of evil cackled as the tumult grew. Years later, when Madame Montpelier was telling her grandchildren the strange tale of panic in an Australian schoolroom – fifty years ago, mes enfants, but I dream of it still – the scene had taken on the dimensions of a nightmare. Grandmère was no doubt confusing it with one of those villainous old prints of the French Revolution that had so terrified her as a little girl. She recalled for them the mad black bloomers, the instruments of torture in the gymnasium, the hysterical schoolgirls with faces distorted by passion, the streaming locks and clawlike hands. 'Every moment I thought : they will lose control and tear her to pieces. Revenge, senseless, cruel revenge. That is what they wanted ... I can see it all now. Revenge on that beautiful little creature who was the innocent cause of so much suffering ...' Now on a pleasant March afternoon in the year nineteen hundred, it was a hideous reality to be faced and somehow dealt with single-handed by the young French governess Dianne de Poitiers. Gathering up her wide silk skirts she took a flying leap from the dais and was hurrying towards the milling group when something warned her to walk sedately with head held high.

Meanwhile, Irma, limp and utterly bewildered, was near suffocation. Fastidious Irma, who deplored all female odours and protested that she could smell Miss Lumley's peppermint-laden presence in the classroom six feet away, was inexplicably hemmed in by angry faces enlarged in hateful proximity to her own. Fanny's little snub nose hugely out of focus and sniffing like a terrier with an exposure of bristling hairs. A cavernous mouth agape on a gold-stopped tooth – that must be Juliana – the moist tip of a drooling tongue. Their warm sour breath came and went on her cheeks. Heated bodies pressed on her sensitive breasts. She cried out in fear and tried in vain to push them away. A disembodied moonface rose up somewhere in the background. 'Edith. You !'

'Yes, ducky. It's me.' In the novel role of ringleader Edith was beside herself, smugly wagging a stumpy forefinger. 'Come on, Irma – tell us. We've waited long enough.' There was a nudging and muttering. 'Edith's right. Tell us, Irma. ... Tell us.'

'What *can* I tell you? Have you all gone crazy?'

'The Hanging Rock,' Edith said, pushing to the front. 'We want you to tell us what happened up there to Miranda and Marion Quade.' The more silent of the New Zealand sisters, rarely articulate, added loudly, 'Nobody in this rat-hole ever tells us anything!' Other voices joined in: 'Miranda! Marion Quade! Where are they?'

'I *can't* tell you. I don't know.'

Suddenly possessed of a power that drove her slim body between the closed ranks like a wedge, Mademoiselle was standing beside her, holding Irma's arm. She cried in her light little French voice, 'Imbeciles! Have you no brains? No hearts? How can la pauvre Irma tell us something she does not know?' 'She knows all right only she won't tell.' Blanche's doll's face was an angry red under the tousled curls. 'Irma likes to have grown-up secrets. She always *did*.'

Edith's great head was nodding like a Mandarin's. 'Then *I'll* tell you if *she* won't. Listen all of you! They're *dead* ... *dead*. Miranda and Marion and Miss McCraw. All dead as doornails in a nasty old cave full of bats on the Hanging Rock.'

'Edith Horton! You are a liar and a fool.' Mademoiselle's hand had come down smartly on Edith's cheek. 'Holy Mother of God.' The Frenchwoman was praying out loud. Rosamund, who had taken no part in all this, was praying too. To Saint Valentine. He was the only Saint she was acquainted with, and so quite rightly she prayed to him. Miranda had loved Saint Valentine. Miranda believed in the power of love over everything. 'Saint Valentine. I don't know how to pray to you properly ... dear Saint Valentine make them leave Irma alone and love one another for Miranda's sake.'

Not often, surely, is the good Saint Valentine – traditionally concerned with the lesser frivolities of romantic love – offered a prayer of such innocent urgency. It seems only fair that he should be credited with its speedy and practical answer: a smiling messenger from Heaven in the guise of Irish Tom, open mouthed and gloriously solid and masculine at the gymnasium door. Dear kindly toothless Tom fresh from a visit to the dentist at Woodend and overjoyed, despite his aching jaws, to see the poor young creatures having a bit of a lark for once in a way. Tom, grinning respectfully at Mademoiselle and waiting for a suitable interlude in the larks (whatever they can be) to ease off, so that he can deliver Ben Hussey's message to Miss Irma.

The arrival of Tom caused a moment of distraction and turning of heads, in which Irma shook herself free; Rosamund rose from her knees, Edith pressed a hand to her burning cheek. The messenger presented Mr Hussey's compliments, and if Miss Leopold was set on catching the Melbourne express she had best come this minute; adding as a personal postscript, 'And good luck to you Miss from meself and all in the kitchen.' It was all over, as simply and quickly as that, with the girls falling back in the old orderly manner to let Irma pass between them and Mademoiselle kissing her lightly on the cheek. 'You will find your parasol hanging up in the hall, ma chérie – au revoir, we shall meet again.' (Ah, but never . . . never again, my little dove.)

There was a perfunctory murmuring of farewell as they watched her walking with the old remembered grace towards the gymnasium door. Here, filled with an infinite compassion for sorrows unguessed at and forever unexplained, she turned, waved a little gloved hand and wanly smiled. So Irma Leopold passed from Appleyard College and out of their lives.

Mademoiselle was consulting her watch. 'We are late this afternoon, girls.' The gymnasium, always poorly lit, was rapidly darkening. 'Go at once to your rooms and change those ugly bloomers to something pretty for supper tonight.'

'Can I wear my pink?' Edith wanted to know. The governess looked up sharply. 'You may wear what you like.' Only Rosamund lingered. 'Shall I help you tidy the room Mam' selle?' 'No, thank you, Rosamund, I have a migraine and would like to be alone for a little while.' The door closed on the empty room. It was only now that she remembered that Dora Lumley had never come back with the Head.

It is no easy matter to emerge with dignity from a crouching position in a narrow cupboard with one eye glued to the keyhole. Something pretty indeed! Dora Lumley, who now thought it prudent to step out from safe asylum, could hardly believe her ears.

'So! The brave little toad has come out of its hole!' A trickle of saliva moistened Dora Lumley's dry lips. 'You are insolent, Mam'selle!' Dianne, meticulously putting away her music, tossed the junior governess a contemptuous glance. 'I might have guessed! You made no attempt to give my message to the Head?'

'It was too late! Somebody would have seen me. ... It seemed better to stay here until it was over.'

'In the cupboard? Oh, the wise little toad!'

'Well, why not? The girls were making a disgraceful exhibition of themselves. There was nothing I could do.'

'You had better do something now and help me put some order into this horrible room. I don't wish that the servants notice anything unusual tomorrow morning.'

'The point is, Mam'selle, what are we going to tell Mrs Appleyard?'

'Nothing.'

'Nothing?'

'You heard me! Exactly nothing.'

'You astound me! If I had my way they should be whipped.'

'There is a word in the French language that fits you à merveille, Dora Lumley. Malheureusement, decent people do not use it.' The sallow cheeks flushed. 'How dare you speak to me like that! How dare you! I shall inform Mrs Appleyard myself of these disgraceful goings on. This very night.'

Dianne de Poitiers had picked up an Indian club from the floor. 'You see this? I have the wrists exceptionally strong, Miss Lumley. Unless you give me a promise, before you leave this room, that you will not tell one little word of what happened here this afternoon ... I will hit you with it very hard indeed. And nobody would suspect the French governess. You understand what I say?'

'You are not fit to be in authority over innocent young girls.'

'I agree. I was brought up expecting something much more entertaining. Alors! C'est la vie. You promise?'

Dora Lumley, looking desperately towards the closed door, decided the necessary dash was too much for her fallen arches and heaving chest.

The Frenchwoman was idly twirling the Indian club. 'I am perfectly serious Miss Lumley. Though I don't intend to give you my reasons.'

'I promise,' gasped the other, now trembling and marble white as Mademoiselle calmly replaced the club on top of the pile. 'Mercy on us! What's that strange sound?'

From the far corner of the room now almost in darkness came a single rasping cry. Miss Lumley, under the stress of a most unpleasant afternoon, had forgotten to unfasten the leather straps that held the child Sara rigid on the horizontal board.

13

Whether the events just related were eventually made known to Mrs Appleyard can only be surmised. It is unlikely under the circumstances that Dora Lumley broke her promise of silence to Mademoiselle. At supper that evening, over which the Headmistress presided as she occasionally liked to do, the boarders were quiet and orderly, if not particularly hungry. A little desultory conversation was indulged in, and to all appearances as far as Dianne de Poitiers could judge nothing special was amiss apart from Sara Waybourne's absence with a migraine and Edith Horton complaining to Miss Lumley of a touch of neuralgia in the right cheek. Edith supposed she must have been sitting in a draught in the gymnasium. 'The gymnasium can be a very draughty room,' put in Mademoiselle from her end of the table.

The Headmistress, gloomily attacking a lamb cutlet at the opposite end, might have been engaged in expertly dismembering a man-eating shark. Actually she had far more important fish to fry, the cutlet being no more than an outward symbol of inner conflict concerning the two letters, one from Mr Leopold and one from Miranda's father, still unanswered on her desk. However, she felt it was necessary for purposes of morale to keep the conversational ball rolling and forced herself to enquire of Rosamund, on her right hand, whether Irma Leopold was travelling to England by the Orient or P. & O. Line?

'I don't know, Mrs Appleyard. Irma stayed such a very short while this afternoon we hardly spoke to her.'

'My sister and I thought she looked rather pale and tired,' piped up the more articulate of the New Zealand pair.

'Indeed? Irma assured me herself she is in perfect health.' The gold padlock on the Head's heavy chain bracelet rattled against her plate, She felt herself start and fancied that the French governess at the other end of the table was looking at her in rather a peculiar way; noted the emeralds sparkling on her wrist and wondered if they were too large to be real. The sight of the jewels brought her thoughts back to the Leopolds, said to own a diamond mine in Brazil. She made a vicious stab at the cutlet and decided to sit up all night if necessary and get Tom to post both letters by the early mail on Friday morning.

Directly the meal was over and the Lord duly thanked for rice pudding and stewed plums, the Headmistress rose from the table, retired to the study, locked the door, and sat down, pen in hand, to her odious task. Most women faced with a situation so dangerous, so entangled by a thousand side issues, would long ago have taken the simplest way out. It would still have been possible, for instance, to plead urgent business in England and regrettably close down the College for good. Even to sell it for what it would bring while it remained a going concern. What was it called in business? 'Goodwill.' She ground her teeth. Precious little of *that* ! The College was already being talked about as haunted and God knows what other mischievous nonsense. She might sit in her study behind closed doors for the better part of the day but she had eyes in her head, and ears. Only yesterday Cook had mentioned quite casually to Minnie, that 'they' were saying in the village that strange lights had been seen moving about the College grounds after dark.

In the past Mrs Appleyard and her Arthur had skated hand in hand over some remarkably thin ice. But never before had they been confronted by a situation impregnated with such personal and public disaster. To take a sword and plunge it through your enemy's vitals in broad daylight is a matter of physical courage, whereas the strangling of an invisible foe in the dark calls for quite other qualities. Tonight her whole being cried out for decisive action. Yes, but what kind of action? Not even Arthur could have worked out a plan of campaign while the damnable mystery at the Hanging Rock remained unsolved.

Before settling down to either of the letters, for the second time that day she took the Ledger from the bottom drawer and studied it closely. On present calculations it seemed probable that only about nine of the former twenty pupils could be expected to return when the new term began after Easter. Once again she ran down the list of names. The last to be crossed off was Horton, Edith, whose insufferably stupid mother had written only today announcing 'other plans' for her only daughter. A few months ago the news would have been only too welcome, and the school dunce easily replaced. Without Edith only nine other names were left, including Sara Waybourne. There was a bottle of cognac in the cupboard behind the desk. She unlocked it and half filled a glass. The thread of fiery spirit touched off a train of clear factual thinking. She sat down at the desk again and made a few notes in the impersonal copperplate hand that gave away nothing of the background character and iron will of the woman who held the pen. It was nearly three o'clock when at last the letters were stamped and sealed and the Headmistress dragged her weary body upstairs.

The following day passed without incident. There was a note in the post from Constable Bumpher saying that he had nothing fresh to report, but one of the Russell Street men would like to see Mrs Appleyard some time next week when convenient. There were one or two points concerning matters of school discipline prior to the day of the Picnic which some of the parents had suggested should be elucidated. ... The weather was mild and fine and Mr Whitehead had requested a long-deferred day off, which he passed in reading the *Horticultural News* with his boots off. Tom went about his duties with his raging jaws tied up in a strip of Minnie's flannel petticoat, and Sara Waybourne, on special instructions from Mademoiselle, spent most of the day in bed. Otherwise, all was as usual.

Saturday was usually a day taken up with small domesticities and household tasks. The boarders did their mending, wrote their letters home – their correspondence rigorously censored at Headquarters with the aid of a spirit lamp on the desk – played croquet or lawn tennis in fine weather or wandered aimlessly about the grounds. Tom was making heavy weather of a chat with Miss Buck beside the dahlia bed when the arrival of Hussey's cab at the front door set him free. There was no luggage to be taken off, however – only a seedy-looking young man of about his own age carrying a small seedy-looking bag who asked the driver to wait out of sight of the front windows until further instructions. Insignificant as he was in appearance, Tom at once recognized Miss Lumley's cocky little squirt of a brother. It was the first time for several months that Reg Lumley had paid his sister a visit at the College. Why in the name of Heaven had he chosen today? thought the Headmistress, watching him pulling on a pair of gloves and smoothing down a shabby overcoat preparatory to ringing the doorbell. Mrs Appleyard, who secretly prided herself on being able to get rid of an unwelcome visitor within three minutes – if necessary with all graciousness – had recognized Reg at the very first handshake as a sticker and stayer. In short, like his sister Dora, a fool and a bore. However, here he was, or rather his not very clean card with his business address in the township of Warragul. 'You may show Mr Lumley in, Alice, and tell him I am very much occupied.'

Reg Lumley, dank, pompous and half-baked, was a clerk in a Gippsland store, holding Views and Opinions on every subject under the sun from Female Education to the incompetence of the local Fire Brigade. Which of them, thought the headmistress, drumming impatient fingers on the desk, was he going to bring out today? And what could have brought him all the way from Warragul without warning? 'Good morning, Mr Lumley. I wish you had thought to write and tell us you intended calling today. I happen to be extremely busy this afternoon and so is your sister. Put your hat down on that chair if it's worrying you – and your umbrella.'

Reg, who had lain awake half the preceding night picturing himself delivering his ultimatum from a vertical position of authority, reluctantly seated himself on a chair with his umbrella between his knees. 'I may say I had no intention of calling today, Ma'am, until I received a telegram from my sister Dora late yesterday afternoon. It upset me considerably.'

'Indeed? May I ask why?'

'Because it confirmed my own opinion that Appleyard College is no longer a suitable place for my sister to be employed.'

'I am not concerned with matters of purely personal *opinion*. Have you any *reason* for this extraordinary statement?'

'Yes, I have. A number of reasons. In fact –' he was fumbling in his shiny pockets, 'I have a letter here – in case you were not in, you know. Shall I read it to you?'

'Thank you, no.' She looked up at the clock over her shoulder. 'If you can tell me what you have to say as briefly as possible.'

'Well, to begin with, it's all this publicity concerning the College. In my opinion, there has been far too much publicity ever since this – er these – er unfortunate occurrences at the Hanging Rock.'

The Headmistress said acidly: 'I don't recall your sister being mentioned at any time in the Press ...?'

'Well, perhaps not my sister ... but you know how people talk. You can't open a paper nowadays without reading something about all this business. It's not right, in my view, that a respectable young woman like Dora should be connected in any way whatsoever with crime and all that sort of thing.' (If young Lumley's heart could have been exposed to view like the poet's it would have had graven upon it RESPECTABILITY. Publicity was hardly ever respectable in Reg's opinion, unless you were somebody frightfully important like Lord Kitchener.)

'Be careful how you express yourself, Mr Lumley. Not crime. Mystery if you like. A very different matter.'

'All right then – Mystery. And I don't like it, Mrs Appleyard. And nor does my sister.'

'My solicitors are confident there will be a solution shortly, whatever you and your friends in Warragul may choose to think. Is that all you have to say?'

'Only that Dora has told me she wishes to terminate her employment with you, as from today, Saturday, March the twenty-first. In point of fact I have a cab outside waiting to take her away; and if you will kindly tell her her brother is here, and have her pack her bags, the heavy luggage can be sent on later.'

At this juncture, as he later remarked to his sister in the train, the young man had noticed a strange mottled colour creeping up Mrs Appleyard's neck under the net collar. Her eyes, which he had never looked at before one way or the other, had gone round like a couple of marbles and appeared to be jumping out of her head. The next minute the old girl had let fly. 'Phew, Dora, I wish you'd heard her! Luckily I had complete control of the situation and didn't attempt to answer back.'

An impartial witness might have observed that the visitor himself had gone a curious shade of waxen green, and was visibly trembling.

'Your sister is a pink-eyed imbecile, Mr Lumley. I should have given her notice before Easter, even without your interference. Fortunately, you have saved me the trouble. You understand, of course, that by her extraordinary behaviour she forfeits her salary for such a breach of contract?'

'I'm not so sure about that. However, that can be adjusted later. And by the way, I understand she would like a written reference.'

'I daresay she would! Although any reference from myself, with a grain of truth in it, would be unlikely to gain her a position!' Her hand struck the blotting pad with such force that it nearly jumped off the desk, at which Mr Lumley jumped, too. 'I am a truthful woman, Mr Lumley, and if you don't know it already allow me to tell you that your sister is a bad-tempered, ignorant dunce and the sooner she gets out of this house the better.' She pulled the bell rope at her elbow, rose from the desk. 'If you will kindly wait in the hall, one of the maids will bring your sister and you may tell her to start packing her bag at once. If she hurries, you can catch the Melbourne express.'

'But Mrs Appleyard! I insist on you hearing me out!

Surely you want to know my point of view about all this? I mean there are quite a number of people who −' The door of the study was somehow behind him. Hatless and trembling with suppressed fury Reg stood alone in the hall. Here, in an agony of frustrated oratory and punctured self-esteem, he was obliged to pass the time as best he could, on a high-backed mahogany chair, devising ways and means of retrieving his hat from the study without loss of face.

Within an hour Dora Lumley had succeeded in compressing her meagre stock of clothing and few personal possessions − a Japanese fan, a birthday book, her mother's garnet ring − into a wicker dress basket, several bags and brown paper parcels, and was seated beside her brother in Hussey's cab. It is hardly necessary to add that the cab bowled down the drive under the scrutiny of numerous pairs of unseen eyes. Curiosity has its own peculiar means of expression; the spoken word assisted by raised eyebrows, nods, headshakings and the shrugging of shoulders. On the evening of Saturday, the twenty-first, curiosity at Appleyard College was at fever heat. Despite the restrictive rules of silence, a highly sensitized ear would have been aware of a ceaseless gnat-like buzzing on stairs and landings; the wordless hum of female curiosity aroused but as yet unsatisfied. Ever since Miss Lumley and her brother had been seen driving away together late in the afternoon the weird assortment of hastily packed belongings on the box seat had given rise to the wildest speculation. Was the junior governess actually leaving the College for good? And if so, why such haste? It was generally agreed that it was unlike Miss Lumley to miss a chance of a spectacular farewell. The housemaid was implored to repeat what the brother had said on arrival and how long he was left stranded in the hall. And what Miss Lumley had said when informed by Alice that her brother was waiting below with a cab. All very mysterious and in its way serving as comic relief in an otherwise colourless day: Dora Lumley and her impossible brother having been long ago pigeonholed as figures of fun.

The only member of the household to show no interest in Miss Lumley's departure was Sara Waybourne, who had passed the afternoon in wandering about the grounds with a book. Struck by the child's increasing pallor, Mademoiselle made up her mind to 'take the bull by the tail' and ask Mrs Appleyard to send for Doctor McKenzie. Ever since the scene in the gymnasium Dianne had been conscious of a strange new strength. She was no longer afraid of Mrs Appleyard's individual wrath, now rendered impotent by the impersonal wrath of Heaven.

There were only five more days left until Wednesday, when the College broke up for the Easter Vacation. After that, Appleyard College would be little more than a bad dream as she lay in her Louis' arms. Rosamund, glancing across the supper table, saw her sudden smile above a plate of Irish stew and rightly guessed her thoughts. Life at the College without Mam'selle's endearing presence would be unsupportable. She thought, 'Why am I here, with all these stupid children?' and decided to ask her parents to let her go home for good at Easter.

Not only Sara Waybourne, but Mrs Appleyard was in need of Doctor McKenzie's attention. She had lost a great deal of weight in the past few weeks and the full silk skirts hung loosely about her massive hips. The flaccid cheeks were sometimes pale and sunken, sometimes mottled a dull red and 'blown up' as Blanche whispered to Edith, 'Like a fish left too long in the sun.' The two girls giggled in the shadow of Aphrodite, watching their Headmistress slowly mounting the staircase from the hall. Halfway towards the first landing the Headmistress caught sight of Minnie coming up from the back stairs with a tray, nicely set out with a lace trimmed cloth and Japanese china. She enquired acidly, 'Have we an invalid in the house?'

Minnie, unlike Cook and Alice, was never intimidated by Mrs Appleyard. 'It's Miss Sara's supper, Ma'am – Mam'selle asked me to slip up with something, seeing there's no homework for the young ladies of a Saturday night and the child's feeling poorly.'

The girl had just reached the door of Sara's room when Mrs Appleyard, retiring early to her vast bedroom directly above the study, called her back. 'Kindly tell Miss Sara not to put out her light until she has had a word with me.'

Sara was sitting up in bed with the gas turned very low, her heavy hair unbraided and falling about her narrow shoulders; and looking, Minnie thought, almost pretty, thanks to a fevered flush and dark glittering eyes. 'See, Miss, I've brought you a nice boiled egg on Mam'selle's special orders. The jelly and cream is something I pinched for you myself off Madam's dinner tray.' A thin arm shot out from under the coverlet. 'Take it away. I won't touch it.'

'Now, then, Miss Sara, that's real baby talk! A great girl of thirteen – isn't that right?'

'I don't know. Even my guardian doesn't know for certain. Sometimes I feel as if I was hundreds of years old.'

'You won't feel that way when you leave school and all the boys are after you – Miss – all you need is a bit of fun.'

'Fun!' repeated the child. 'Fun! Come over here. Close to the bed and I'll tell you something nobody at the college knows except Miranda, and she promised never never to tell. Minnie! I was brought up in an orphanage. Fun! Sometimes I dream about it even now, when I can't go to sleep. One day I told them I thought it would be fun to be a lady circus rider on a lovely white horse in a spangled dress. The matron was afraid I was going to run away and shaved my head. I bit her in the arm.'

'There, Miss. Don't cry.' The kind-hearted Minnie was horribly embarrassed. 'Look, lovey, I'll leave the tray here on the washstand in case you change your mind. Lor', that reminds me! Madam said to tell you not to turn out your light till she comes in to see you. Sure you won't try a bit of the jelly?'

'Never! Not if I was starving!' She turned her face to the wall.

In a second-class compartment of the Melbourne train Reg and Dora Lumley had talked without ceasing; the sister now and then dabbing at angry tears with interjections of 'Monstrous! Oh surely not! You don't say! How dare she!' as the wayside stations flew past in the gathering dusk. Already the brother was planning ways and means of extracting the full term's salary, in Reg's opinion a matter of extreme urgency. 'Why, Dora, for all we know the old girl may be bankrupt any day – or getting that way.'

When the train drew in at Spencer Street Station it had been decided that Dora would accompany her brother back to Warragul, there to housekeep for three in the dilapidated cottage of an ageing aunt. 'In my opinion, Dora, you might do a great deal worse. After all, Aunt Lydia cannot live for ever.' On which inspiring note they stepped out of the train and boarded a tram to a respectable small hotel in a respectable city street. Dora was filled with admiration for her strongminded capable brother who had even engaged beforehand two cheap single rooms for the night, in the back wing. They were just in time for a late evening meal and after swallowing some cold mutton and strong tea the brother and sister retired exhausted to bed. About three o'clock in the morning an oil lamp, left alight too close to a blowing curtain on the wooden stairs, fell to the floor. The flames began licking up the shabby wallpaper and blistered paintwork. Curls of smoke poured unseen into the street from the staircase window. Within minutes the whole of the back wing was a roaring vault of fire.

14

Reg Lumley's final exit, although perfectly respectable, was accompanied by such lurid flames of publicity that in death the young man took on an almost phoenix-like quality of colourful resurrection from the burning hotel. The Warragul Store where for fifteen insignificant years he had worked and argued and held forth, was closed for half a day on the occasion of the Lumleys' funeral, a public tribute that might or might not have been appreciated by the deceased, at last unable to voice his opinions.

In the previous chapter we witnessed a segment of the pattern begun at Hanging Rock literally burning itself out, five weeks later, in a city hotel. During the week-end of the fire, yet another was gradually coming to a freezing standstill amongst the mountain mists at Lake View. Mike had been nearly a week in town and the Fitzhuberts had returned to Toorak for the winter when a solicitor's letter, mislaid, had obliged him to spend a couple of nights at Mount Macedon. Albert had met him at the Macedon station with the cob on the evening of Saturday the twenty-first – actually his train passed within inches of the Lumleys, en route for Melbourne. As the dog-cart passed under the now leafless avenue of chestnuts it had begun, almost imperceptibly to sleet. 'Winter coming early this year all right,' Albert said, turning up his collar. 'Don't wonder all the nobs that can afford to clears out for the winter.' There were only a few lights burning in the usually brilliantly lit facade of the house. 'Cook hasn't left for her holiday yet but the Biddies have gone with the family to Toorak. Your old room's ready and a fire laid.' He grinned. 'You know how to light a wood fire?' A single light burned dimly in the hall and through the open door of the drawing-room they glimpsed the shrouded sofas and chairs.

'Not too lively up here, is it? Better eat your dinner and come on down to me at the stables. I've got a bottle of grog the Colonel give me the day he left.' Mike however was tired and dispirited and promised to come tomorrow.

The Lake View house emptied of the day-to-day presence of its owners was dull and lifeless. It existed only as a comfortable holiday background for his Aunt and Uncle and had no personality of its own. Michael, eating his chop on a tray by the fire, was dimly conscious of the difference between Lake View and Haddingham Hall, whose ivied walls had existed and would go on existing for hundreds of years, dominating the lives of succeeding generations of Fitzhuberts who had at times gone as far as to fight and die for the survival of its Norman tower.

Next morning the solicitor's letter turned up exactly where Mike had expected – stuffed into the back of the little drawer in the spare room writing table. It was Sunday, and as Albert had a mysterious appointment concerning a horse on an outlying farm, he passed the greater part of the day in wandering aimlessly about the grounds. About midday the wreathing mists lifted to show a clear view of the pine forest against a pale blue sky. After lunch when the sun came out in fitful primrose gleams, he strolled down to the Lodge and was met with open arms by the Cutlers and regaled with hot scones and tea in the cosy kitchen. 'And how's Miss Irma? My, you wouldn't guess how we miss her about the place.' Mike confessed that he hadn't seen her while he was in town, but understood she was sailing for England on Tuesday, at which Mrs Cutler's face fell in genuine consternation. As soon as the visitor left, Mr Cutler, who like most people who live in close daily contact with nature was aware of elemental rhythms, said mildly, 'I always reckoned there was something between them two. Pity!'

His wife sighed, 'I couldn't believe my ears when he spoke so casual-like about my poor dear lamb.'

At twilight Mike had gone down to the lake where the dry rattle of the reeds and bare willow streamers dipping in and out of the little cove (in summer a shaded anchorage for the punt) filled him with a restless melancholy. The swans had disappeared, and the water lilies, whose dark green pads dotted the black sunless surface. The oak where he had seen the swan drinking at the clam shell on a summer afternoon was naked to the sky. In the distance he could hear the little stream tumbling down from the forest under the rustic bridge. The tinkling music seemed to accentuate the stillness and silence of the interminable day.

As soon as he had finished his evening meal, he took the hurricane lamp that always hung in the side passage and made his way, in drizzling sleet, to the stable. There was a light in the window of Albert's room and the trapdoor propped open with a boot for the reception of the visitor. On the table a bottle of whisky and two glasses were set out. 'Sorry I can't make a fire up here – no chimney – but the grog keeps the cold out and Cook knocked us up a sandwich. Help yourself.' Mike thought there was an air of welcome, even of comfort, unknown in his Aunt's drawing-room. 'If you were a married man,' he said, settling down into the broken rocking chair, 'you would be what the women's magazines call a Home Maker.'

'I like a bit of comfort when I can get it – if that's what you mean.'

'Not only that ...' Like so many things one would have liked to say, it was too complicated to embark on. 'I'd like to see you in a place of your own some day.'

'Oh, you would, would you? I'd soon be getting itchy feet, Mike, even if I had the dough to settle down and raise a pack of kids. How are you liking city life with the nobs?'

'Not at all. My Aunt can think of nothing but giving one of her ghastly parties – for *me*. I haven't told them yet I'm going up North in a week or two – probably Queensland.'

'Now there's a place I never really seen – except the Brisbane waterfront and the lock-up at Toowoomba – oh, only for one night. I told you before, I was with a pretty tough mob in them days.'

Mike glanced affectionately at the brick red features, more honest in the flickering candlelight than the faces of many of his Cambridge friends who let their tailors' bills run on for years and had never passed a night behind bars. 'Why not take a holiday and come up North with me?'

'Jeez. You mean that?'

'Of course I mean it.'

'Where would you be stopping?'

'There's a big cattle station I want to see – away up near the border. It's called Goonawingi.'

Albert said thoughtfully, 'I reckon I could easy get a job on one of them big runs. All the same, Mike, I can't walk out on your Uncle and the horses unless I got someone to suit him at Lake View. The old bastard's treated me pretty good, taking it all round.'

'I understand that,' Mike said. 'Anyway, start keeping your eyes skinned for the right bloke to take over and I'll write to you as soon as I know my plans.' Money was noticeably not mentioned. At this stage the offer of a train fare to Queensland would have been out of keeping with the dignity of a perfect understanding. The stuffy little room was almost cosy what with the whisky and the light of the two candles. Mike helped himself to another drink and felt the gentle glow running through his veins. 'When I was a child I always thought whisky was some kind of remedy for toothache. My Nannie used to dip cotton wool into the bottle. Lately I find a stiff whisky's quite a help when I can't sleep.'

'Still thinking about that bloody Rock?'

'I can't help it. It comes back at night. Dreams.'

'Talk about dreams!' Albert said. 'I had a bobbydazzler last night. Talk about real.'

'Tell me. I'm an expert on nightmares since I came to Australia.'

'Not exactly a nightmare this wasn't. . . . Oh, Hell! I can't explain.'

'Go on. Try! Mine are so real sometimes I can't even be sure they *are* dreams.'

'I was bloody well dead asleep. Had a big Saturday. Must have been round midnight when I got to bed. Well, all of a sudden I'm as wide awake as I am this minute and there's such a stink of pansies in the room I opens my eyes to see where it's coming from. I never knew pansies has that much perfume. Sort of dainty but no mistaking it. Sounds bloody silly, don't it?'

'Not to me,' Mike said, his eyes fixed on his friend's face. 'Go on.'

'Well, I opens my eyes and the joint's as bright as day although it's as dark as hell outside. Never struck me as funny until I'm telling you now.' He paused and lit a Capstan cigarette. 'That's right. Like the gas was full on. And there she is standing at the end of the bed – exactly where you're sitting now.'

'Who was? Who was it?'

'Jeez, Mike! There's no call to get worked up over a bloody dream . . .' He pushed the bottle across the table. 'My kid sister. You remember – the one I told you about that was nuts on pansies? She seemed to be wearing some kind of nightgown. And that didn't strike me as funny either – not until now. Otherwise she looked about the same as when I seen her last . . . oh about six or seven years ago, I suppose. I forget now.'

'Did she say anything – or just stand there?'

'Mostly just stand there looking down at me and smiling. "Don't you know me, Bertie?" she says. And I says, "Of course I know you." "Oh, Bertie!" she says, "your poor arms with the mermaids and the way you was laying there with your mouth wide open and that broken tooth I would've known you anywhere!" I'm just sitting up to get a better look at her when she starts to sort of . . . what the Hell do you call it when a person starts to go all misty-like?'

'Transparent,' Mike said.

'That's right. How did you know? I calls out, "Hi! Sis! Don't go yet." But she's almost gone, all but her voice. I could hear it as plain as what I'm hearing you now. She says, "Good-bye, Bertie. I've come a long way to see you and now I must go." I sung out good-bye but she'd gone. Clean through that wall over there . . . you reckon I'm batty?'

Batty! If Albert's bullet-head so firmly screwed on to the squared shoulders wasn't to be relied on for glorious commonsense sanity, what was? If Albert was batty there was no sense in believing in anything. In hoping for anything. Or praying. No more sense in praying to the God Mike had been told to believe in ever since Nannie had dragged him to Sunday school in the village church. And there was God Himself in a red and blue glass window – a terrifying old man rather like his grandfather, the Earl of Haddingham, sitting on a cloud and interfering with everyone down below. Punishing the wicked, caring for the sparrows fallen from their nests in the park, keeping an eye on the Royal Family in their various palaces, saving – or allowing to be shipwrecked according to whim – 'Those In Peril On The Sea' … Finding and Saving, or allowing to perish, the lost schoolgirls on the Hanging Rock. All of which and a good deal more flashed through poor Mike's brain in a jumble of imagery impossible to digest – let alone communicate – as he sat staring at his friend, now grinning and repeating, 'Batty! Just you wait till *you* have a dream like that!' Mike rose, yawning, 'Batty or not, you'll do me, Albert. Think I'll have another drink and turn in. Good night.'

Although the mist had cleared and the sun been up for some time when Mike was at breakfast next morning, daylight had not yet reached the gardens on the shady side of the Mount. From the dining-room window he looked out for the last time at the little lake, still in deep shadow, like a slab of cold grey stone. Mount Macedon robbed of its summer beauty might well be as bleak as the sodden Cambridge fields. He shivered as he picked up his valise, put on his overcoat and walked down to the stables. Albert, who was driving him down to the Melbourne train, was whistling through his teeth as he hosed down the bricks, with Toby standing ready in the dog-cart.

The cob was eager to be off, tossing its smartly hogged little head and jingling its shining bit. 'Take your time, Mike. Little brute's got a mouth like iron but I can hold him while you get in.'

They had just turned out of the avenue into the road when Albert jerked the lively cob to a standstill at sight of Manassa's boy, wobbling along on his sister's bicycle and bearing the morning's mail in a hand mottled with cold. 'This is

Cook's cough drops, Mr Crundall, will you take 'em? Half a mo – there's a letter here for you.'

'What's the joke? Nobody writes *me* no letters.'

'I can read, can't I? Your name's Mr A. Crundall, ain't it?'

'Here then, hand it up and none of your cheek. Well I'll be buggered. Who the hell can it be from?' As no answer was expected or given the boy went wobbling off down a side lane in a huff and the drive proceeded in silence until they pulled up outside the Macedon station. There was a good ten minutes to spare before the arrival of the train, and Albert being on friendly terms with the stationmaster, they were invited to come in out of the cold and warm themselves at the fire in his office.

'Aren't you going to open your letter?' Mike enquired. 'Don't mind me.'

'Tell you the truth, I'm not too clever at making out this kind of fancy writing. Better on the print. How about you reading it out to me?'

'Good Heavens, there might be something private.' Albert grinned. 'Not unless the cops are after me. Fire away.' The Albert who had no inhibitions about the Toowoomba Lock-up or having his private correspondence opened and read aloud continued to surprise and stimulate. At home the family letters laid out in orderly rows by the butler on a Boule table had an almost divine right of privacy. Feeling as if he were about to rob a bank, Michael took the letter, opened it and began to read. 'It's written from the Galleface Hotel ...'

'Don't know the joint. Where is it?' 'At least it seems to have been written there and posted later, from Fremantle.' 'Cut the frills – just tell me what it's about and I'll nut it out again when I get home.'

It was a letter from Irma Leopold's father, thanking Mr Albert Crundall for his part in the finding and rescue of his daughter on the Hanging Rock. *I understand you are only a young fellow, and unmarried. My wife and I will be most happy if you will accept the enclosed cheque as a token of our everlasting gratitude. I understand from my solicitor that you are at present employed privately as a coachman ... if*

*you have any wish to change your present employment at
some future date, please do not hesitate to communicate with
me at my Banker's address, below* . . . 'Jeez!' Further comment, if any, was cut off by the roar of the Express coming
into the station as Mike pushed the letter into Albert's seemingly frozen hand, picked up his valise and jumped into
the nearest compartment just as the train pulled out of the
platform. Five minutes later, Albert was still standing in
front of the stationmaster's fire gazing at a cheque for one
thousand pounds.

The hotels were not yet open in the township, but Mr
Donovan of Donovan's Railway Hotel was presently awaken-
ed by insistent knocking that brought him, still in his
pyjamas, to the side entrance of the closed and shuttered
Bar. 'What the blazes . . . oh, it's you Albert! Hell, we're not
open for another hour.'

'I don't care if you're open or shut. A double brandy, as
quick as you can get it. This bloody cob won't stand —' Mr
Donovan, a good-natured soul accustomed to the demands
of persons in desperate need of strong liquor before breakfast,
opened up the bar, produced a bottle and glass and asked no
questions.

Albert by this time was reduced to much the same state of
mind and body as on the memorable occasion when he had
been knocked out in the tenth round by the Castlemaine
Wonder. He was heading for home and half way down
Main Street when he caught sight of Irish Tom from the
College, driving a hooded buggy on the opposite side of the
road. Albert was in no mood to talk to Tom or anyone else
and merely raised his whip in greeting. Tom, however, was
pulling up at the kerb with such urgent nods and grimacings
that he reluctantly reined in the cob. Whereupon Tom
sprang from the buggy, threw the reins over the neck of the
patient brown mare, and crossed the road to the dog-cart.
'Albert Crundall! I haven't clapped eyes on you since that
Sunday on the Rock with the Johns. Seen this morning's
paper?'

'Not yet. I don't go much on the papers — only for the
racing.'

'Then you haven't heard the news?'

'Stone the crows! Don't tell me they've found the other two sheilas?'

'Oh, no, nothing like that, poor young creatures! See here – on the front page – FIRE IN CITY HOTEL. BROTHER AND SISTER BURNED TO DEATH. Glory be! What an end. As I said to Minnie if it's not one thing it's another nowadays.' Albert glanced hurriedly at the paragraph which revealed that the couple were on their way to Warragul and that Miss Dora Lumley's previous address was entered on the hotel register as 'Care of Appleyard College, Bendigo Road, Woodend'. Albert was sorry enough for anyone unlucky enough to be burned alive in their beds but at the moment he had other and more important matters on his mind. 'Well, I'll be off now. Toby don't like standing for long.' Tom, however, was disposed to linger by the wheel of the dog-cart for further conversation. 'That's a nice wee cut of a cob you got there, Albert.'

'Lively,' said the other. 'Mind your hand – he don't like his tail touched when he's in the dog-cart.'

'I don't blame him. There's one like that down at the College. By the way, you wouldn't be knowing anyone on the Mount would be wanting a married couple? Me and Minnie's getting married on Easter Monday. After that we'll be looking for a job.'

Still more or less stunned by the impact of Mr Leopold's letter, the coachman could hardly wait to get back to the privacy of his attic room to read it again, and was gathering up the reins when something about the word job rang a bell. Tom was rambling on: 'Minnie's Auntie wants us to give her a hand with a bit of a pub she owns at Point Lonsdale – did I tell you that's where we're going for our honeymoon? But I fancy something with horses meself, and Minnie – you don't know my Minnie – dainty as a fairy about a house though I say it – never seen the likes of her with the silver!'

'I'll keep my eyes skinned for you, Tom. It's on the cards I might know of something after Easter, but you never know. Ta-ta.' And off he clattered round the turn into the Upper Macedon Road.

Thus was decided within less time than it took Tom to cross the road to the buggy, a future of blissful domesticity for himself and Minnie beyond their wildest dreams. Another segment of the Hanging Rock pattern was nearing completion, in this instance with a spectacular flourish embellished with unguessed-at future joys, including a comfortable cottage to be erected behind the stables at Lake View and later to be filled with merry-eyed infants the spit and image of Irish Tom. One of them subsequently became a strapper in a racing stables at Caulfield and achieved undying fame for himself and parents by coming in second in a field of twenty-seven in the Caulfield Cup. At which point we can no longer concern ourselves with the fortunes of Tom and his Minnie who, after all, are only minor threads in the pattern of the College Mystery, soon to take on a new and unpredictable turn in which they were fortunately not involved.

As soon as Albert had unharnessed Toby he sat down in the rocking chair and took out Mr Leopold's envelope which had been burning into his right hip the whole way home from the railway station. After laboriously deciphering the contents several times, he knew it by heart, address and all – a boon granted to the non-reading fraternity that accounts for their safe storage of any necessary factual information. The unlettered farmer who sows and reaps according to the seasons has no need of writing down the dates in a notebook. Thus Albert, who always knew to the day precisely when Toby's mane was last hogged and when the mare was shod in Woodend, carefully placing the Leopold cheque in a jam tin under his bed, had no further need to refer to the letter, and after burning it over a stump of candle sat down to think things over. Just as he himself by a few casual words this morning had effectively shaped the destinies of Tom and Minnie, so had Irma's father, in a moment of generous impulse, altered the entire course of Albert's life. It is probably just as well for our nervous equilibrium that such cataclysms of personal fortune are usually disguised as ordinary everyday occurrences, like the choice of boiled or poached eggs for breakfast. The young coachman settling down in the rocking chair after tea that Monday evening had no sense of having already embarked on a long and fateful journey of no return.

Albert felt he could do with a short holiday. He had always wanted to have a look at Queensland and now, surely, was his chance? It was a decision easily made and far less onerous than the necessity of writing at least three letters this very night, that involved the borrowing of Cook's writing pad and three envelopes, and unearthing a pen, thickly encrusted with stale purple ink. In spite of these minor drawbacks, he knew what he wanted to say to each of his three correspondents, which is not always the case with people who can spell a good deal better and write more legibly than Albert Crundall. Even so, the nib was licked clean before he had actually got going on letter number one which began smoothly enough with *Dear Mr Leopold Sir – You could of nocked me down with a fether when your letter and enclosed cheque receeved this morning (March 23)*. After which it struck the writer that apart from an occasional tip and the Colonel's sovereign at Christmas, he had never within his memory been given a present until today's magnificent gift. Except once, at the orphanage, when some well-meaning old hen had handed him a Bible. As it seemed necessary to say something more than a bare Thank You for a cheque of £1000 (Yes, there it was large as life in the jam tin) he decided on telling Mr Leopold how he had traded the Bible for five bob, in the hope of someday buying himself a pony. *Well, sir, I was only a nipper and of course I never got same having to ern my living when I turned twelve so will start now looking round for somethink with a bit of blood – about fourteen hands. There is some reel good horses about if you have say thirty pound cash which I now have sir thanks to your jennerosity. The rest of the money can sit tite in the Bank till I have had a good think wot to do with it for the best. Well Mr Leopold sir I am still nocked sideways at your jennerous gift so will now close being near midnight. Again with grateful thanks and wishing yourself and family long and prosperus life.*

> *Yours gratefully,*
> *Albert Crundall.*

There was still something to be added in a postscript that took nearly as long to compose and get written down as all the rest of the letter. *It was reely nothink wot I done for your dauter on the Rock. Anyone round here will tell you the same. It was my mate. A young chap by the name of Hon. Fitzhubert saved her life. Not me. Albert Crundall.*

Letter number two, to Colonel Fitzhubert, was much easier, giving the coachman's notice on a date suitable to both parties and recommending Tom from the College as a reel good man with the horses and ending up, *You was always a good boss to me. I appreciate same and if you want lancer's new saddle before the Spring is hanging on a nail in my room better kep dry this damp wether your faithfully Albert Crundall.*

The last letter, to Mike, was dashed off at breakneck speed with spelling thrown to the winds. Good old Mike knew he was no hand with a bloody pen. *Dear Mike. By Jeez that check is a bobbydazzler all rite.* The rest is of no special interest except perhaps the last sentence : *Well Mike meet me any day you say in the City do you know the Post Office Hotel in Burke Street? We could have a beer and fix a date for Q'land? I have wrote to your Unkle re turning in the job at Lake V. and all in order there so you name the day. Albert.*

15

In the morning of Sunday the twenty-second of March, Appleyard College presented the usual scene of bustling preparation as the boarders arrayed themselves for church-going in Woodend. Deliberately cut off nowadays from unnecessary contacts with the outside world, the household had remained ignorant throughout the long boring Sunday of the shocking news that would have set every tongue in the place wagging, rules or no rules. There were no Sunday newspapers and dinner was consumed while the charred timbers of the Lumleys' hotel lay smouldering in pale autumn sunshine. Constable Bumpher had actually taken Sunday off for a day's fishing at Kyneton, gleefully returning at midnight with a solitary blackfish to be grilled for Monday morning's breakfast : a meal cruelly interrupted by the arrival of young Jim with requests for information from the Melbourne papers, the dramatic death of the obscure little governess immediately linked up with the almost defunct College Mystery in the journalist mind.

The staff at the College was shorthanded that Sunday and Mademoiselle and Miss Buck had both been called into action. Although it was Minnie's day off, the place was all anyhow with Miss Lumley clearing out like that yesterday afternoon and the good-natured housemaid had remained on duty. Rubbing up the table silver in the pantry she saw, through the narrow window, the two governesses marshalling the gloved and hatted girls into the waiting wagonettes, and presently Tom with Alice and Cook in the buggy. Minnie had just come through the baize door leading into the hall when to her surprise she saw the Headmistress almost running downstairs carrying what looked like a small basket in one hand. At sight of the housemaid she stopped, hanging on to the stair rail, Minnie thought, as if she were feeling giddy, and beckoned her over. 'Minnie! Surely this is your Sunday off?'

'It don't matter, Ma'am,' Minnie said. 'We're all behind this morning – after yesterday.'

'Come into the study for a moment. Is Alice on duty?'

'No Ma'am, Tom took her and Cook into church in the buggy. Did you want her for anything?'

'On the contrary. You look tired, Minnie. Why don't you go and lie down?' (And there was poor Tom with not a tooth in his head since Thursday and never a word of sympathy.) 'I'll lay my tables first. Besides, somebody might call.'

'Exactly. I was about to tell you that I am expecting Mr Cosgrove some time this morning. Miss Sara's guardian. I can see him through the window when he arrives and can easily answer the door myself.'

'Well, Ma'am, it don't seem right,' Minnie said wavering, as a delicious little shoot of pain ran through her stomach.

'You're a good reliable girl, Minnie. You shall have five pounds on your wedding day. Now do as I say and leave me. I have some business letters to attend to before Mr Cosgrove comes.'

'And Laws, Tom,' said Minnie that night, 'the old girl looked something awful – white as chalk and breathing like a steam engine. Five pound? You could have knocked me down with a feather.'

'Glory be – wonders will never cease,' Tom said, putting his arm round her waist with a smacking kiss. He was right. They never will.

As soon as Mademoiselle had returned from church and removed her hat and veil she applied a soupçon of colourless face powder and lipsalve and presented herself at the study door. It was then nearly one o'clock. As usual nowadays it was locked. 'Come in, Mam'selle. What is it?'

'Might I have a few words with you, Madame, before déjeuner? A propos de Sara Waybourne?' Although the governess was aware that Sara was anything but a favourite with the Head, she was unprepared for the expression that creased the older woman's face like an evil wind. 'What

165

about Sara Waybourne?' The pebble eyes were alert, watchful – almost, Dianne decided afterwards, as if she were afraid of what I was going to say. 'I had better tell you, Mam'selle. You are wasting my time and your own. Sara Waybourne left here this morning with her guardian.'

The governess let fly an irrepressible, 'Oh, no! No! When I saw her yesterday the poor child was not fit to take a journey. Actually, Madame, it is of Sara's health that I wished to speak.'

'She appeared well enough this morning.'

'Ah, the pauvre enfant . . .'

The Head eyed her sharply. 'A trouble maker. From the very first.' 'An orphan,' Mademoiselle said boldly. 'One must for those lonely ones make the excuses.'

'In fact, I doubt whether I shall accept her here for another term. However, that can be dealt with later. Mr Cosgrove was insistent on taking the child with him there and then. It was most inconvenient but I had no choice in the matter.'

'You surprise me,' Mademoiselle said. 'Mr Cosgrove is a charming man with the perfect manners.'

'Men, Mam'selle, are often inconsiderate in such things. As you will shortly be finding out for yourself.' The thin humourless laugh belied the unchanging watchful eyes.

'Sara's things,' Dianne said, rising. 'I regret that I was not here to help her pack.'

'I myself helped Sara to put a few things she specially wanted in her little covered basket. Mr Cosgrove was waiting downstairs in a hurry to get away – he had a cab or a carriage ordered.'

'We may have passed them on the way home from church. I wish very much that I had seen them and waved goodbye.'

'You are sentimental, Mam'selle – unlike most of your race. However, there it is – the child has gone.' Still the governess lingered at the door. She was no longer afraid of the woman whose crackling Sunday taffeta disguised an ageing body in aching need of rest, hot water bottles, the small feminine humanities.

'Is there anything else you wish to say, Mam'selle?' Recalling an elegant little grandmother reclining for two hours every afternoon on a chaise longue, Dianne, greatly daring, enquired if Madame would perhaps consider asking the good Doctor McKenzie for a little something for herself? There had been much fatigue ... the early autumn ...

'Thank you. ... No. I have always been an indifferent sleeper. What time is it? I forgot to wind my clock last night.'

'Ten minutes to one, Madame.'

'I shall not be coming in to luncheon. Kindly tell them not to lay a place for me.'

'Nor for Sara,' Mademoiselle unaccountably said.

'Nor for Sara. Is that rouge I see on your cheek, Mam'-selle?'

'Powder, Mrs Appleyard. I find it becoming.'

As soon as the impertinent hussy had left the room the Headmistress rose and bent over the cupboard behind the desk. Her hand was trembling so badly she could hardly open the little door. She kicked at it savagely with the rounded toe of her black kid slipper. It flew open and a small covered basket fell out on to the floor.

The Headmistress remained in her private rooms for the rest of the day and retired early to bed. On the following morning it was Irish Tom's melancholy pleasure – there being certain warmhearted persons who find some consolation in being first with the worst – to deliver to Mrs Appleyard in person the newspapers filled with lurid accounts of the Lumley tragedy. Somewhat to Tom's disappointment the news had been received at Headquarters in stony silence with a peremptory 'Hand it to me!' Whereas in the kitchen regions there had been a dramatic throwing of aprons over horrified heads and shrill incredulous cries that such a thing could happen only two days after Miss Lumley and her brother had been actually here in this very house : which somehow underlined and intensified the dreadful thing and made the flames nearer and more real.

Tuesday passed without incident. Rosamund had arranged for a joint telegram of farewell to be sent to Irma during the afternoon, when the Leopolds sailed for London accompanied by a ladies' maid, secretary, groom and half a dozen polo ponies. With the relaxing of Dora Lumley's petty disciplines there was a welcome sense of freedom, the ghostly presence of the little figure in brown serge obliterated, at least for the boarders, by excited preparations for Wednesday's wholesale exodus for the Easter holidays. It was a long time since so much whispering and comparing of notes and even occasional laughter had been heard at Appleyard College. To add to an atmosphere of wellbeing a few days of Indian summer were brightening the garden and Mr Whitehead was obliged to turn the sprinklers on to the hydrangea bed where the heavy blue and purple heads were still blooming under the windows in the west wing. The newspaper forecasts predicted a fine mild Easter gradually working up to a change on Easter Monday.

The two brides-to-be compared notes on their respective trousseaux and Dianne, joyously indiscreet, confided to the goggle-eyed housemaid the story of the emerald bracelet. 'I have no other jewels,' the governess told her. 'Ours will be a very simple wedding. We have very little money and no relations except those in France.' Minnie giggled. 'My Auntie's giving us our wedding reception and Tom reckons she's asked that many relations on both sides there won't be room for the bride and bridegroom to get into the church.'

Miss Buck having proved herself during her brief term of office useless for anything but the imparting of rudimentary Euclid and arithmetic, Mademoiselle found herself occupied most of the day in all manner of small domesticities. Everyone – even Cook and Mr Whitehead – turned to the French governess for orders.

During the morning she had run upstairs for a packet of pins when Alice the under-housemaid appeared on the landing armed with a bucket and brooms. 'Minnie says for me to do out the big double room but there's that many clothes and things lying about I don't know where to begin.' 'I'll help you,' Mademoiselle said. 'Australian schoolgirls are very untidy I find – I have had much practice of late in packing and folding their dresses.'

'Miss Irma was the one!' Alice said admiringly. 'Gee! Gold-backed brushes all amongst her shoes, and brooches pinned in her petticoats. If it had been Miss Sara, the Madam would have been on to her like a ton of bricks! That's what it is to be an heiress.' Miranda's old room that used to be filled with light and air from the garden outside the two tall windows, was almost in darkness when they opened the door, with the venetian blinds all drawn except on the narrow window above Sara's bed, still unmade and rumpled as she had slept in it last. 'A bit spooky in here, isn't it?' said the big blowsy girl, throwing down her brooms and getting to work. The blinds rattled up on a scene of depressing disorder. Sara's dressing-gown over the back of a chair, a pair of bedroom slippers on the washstand. 'Well, I never! She don't seem to have taken much with her,' she said, dragging at the bed covers. 'Here's a nightdress case and a sponge bag,' Mademoiselle said, 'with the sponge still in it. Madam told me she only packed a few necessary articles in a small basket, for the journey. It is best we put everything away in the wardrobe until Miss Sara returns after the holidays.' 'They say the guardian's got plenty of cash,' Alice said cheekily. 'Won't do him any harm to buy the kid a new dressing-gown – shall I put fresh sheets on the bed over there? That was Miss Miranda's, wasn't it? Now *there* was a lovely girl for you! A real toff and never too high and mighty to have a bit of a laugh with Minnie and me.'

The blundering creature was insupportable. 'No. Take all the bed linen away and make the coverlets neat. Comme ca.' Miranda would never again sleep in this house ...

'Beats me why young Sara didn't go off on Sunday morning in this nice blue coat with the fur collar. I'll say a kid of thirteen don't have much sense when it comes to clothes.'

'Miss Sara left in a hurry and what she chose to wear for the journey has nothing to do with you, Alice. If you would please attend to the dusting – it must be nearly lunchtime.' She glanced up at the stopped clock on the marble mantelpiece, where a photograph of Miranda smiled calmly down from a small silver frame. Unlike the majority of photographs this one had an extraordinary feeling of life and reality. Alice went on dusting in offended silence and Mademoiselle stood looking up thoughtfully at the portrait of Miranda. 'Alice,' she said suddenly, 'was it you who brought Miss Sara her breakfast on Sunday morning?'

'Yes, Miss. Minnie was having a sleep in.'

'I hope she had an egg – and some fruit? She had a migraine all day Saturday and had eaten nothing.' Alice, who had completely forgotten Minnie's instructions about the sick child's breakfast and had in fact brought her nothing on Sunday morning, merely nodded, which somehow seemed less of a mortal sin than a barefaced lie. Anyway she was sick and tired of the boarders and their nonsense. And made up her mind, even as she finished dusting behind the two beds, to get herself a job as a waitress after Easter.

Dianne de Poitiers was especially wakeful on Tuesday night. The Easter moon, already large and brilliant, threw a silver shaft between the partly drawn curtains at her open window which overlooked a part of the west wing. There was a light burning in Minnie's room, otherwise the whole building – or as much as she could see of it – was in darkness. When she leaned out over the sill she could see the steeply pitched slate roof shining under the moon and beyond it the squat little tower, black against the sky. Could it be true that the moon actually had something to do with the thoughts and even the actions of human beings millions of miles below on the earth? She could feel the tide of silver light flowing over her sensitive skin. Not only her mind but her whole being was preternaturally awake and aware. She lay down again on the bed but the faint zing-zing of a mosquito hovering close to the pillow twanged on the silence like a harp. Sleep on such a night was impossible. The moment she closed her eyes she began thinking about the child Sara. Was she too wide awake under the moon? What sort of man was the guardian behind his charming façade of good manners? Where had he taken her for the holidays? What did the future hold for the lonely unloved child? Miranda was the only one at the College who had ever made Sara smile and now Miranda was gone ... Miranda ... Miranda smiling down from the mantelpiece in the oval frame was Sara's most treasured possession. 'Imagine, Mam'selle! Miranda gave it to *me* for my birthday!'

'You should colour it, Sara – vou are clever with your paint brush,' Mademoiselle had suggested. 'Miranda's hair is such a lovely colour – like ripe yellow corn.'

'I don't think Miranda would like that, Mam'selle. Irma Leopold was crazy to curl it up for her – for the photograph – but Miranda said "straight hair or nothing. Like it always is at home. Baby Jonnie wouldn't recognize his sister with curly hair".' And that other day, in the Ballarat Gardens. How clearly it all came back to her now. 'Sara – your pocket. It bulges like the toad!' 'Oh, no, Mam'selle! It isn't a toad.'

'Then what is it? It looks very ugly.'

'It's Miranda, Mam'selle. No, don't laugh. Please! If Blanche and Edith found out they would never stop teasing. You see I take it everywhere – even to church – it just fits, in that little oval frame. But promise me never to tell Miranda.' That small pointed face was flushed and solemn. 'Why not?' Dianne said, laughing. 'It is amusante, ça – nobody has ever taken *me* to church in their pocket.'

'Because,' said the child earnestly, 'Miranda wouldn't approve. She says she won't be here much longer and I must learn to love a whole lot of other people besides her.'

What could have occurred on Sunday morning to make her forget to take the portrait off the mantelpiece as usual? Such a little thing. So easily carried. ... In a hurry, Alice. I have just told you ... Miss Sara was in a hurry and forgot her dressing-gown. A dressing-gown. A sponge bag. Easily forgotten by the excited child and grimly undomesticated adult who had helped to pack a few things in the little covered basket. But not the portrait. Never, never the portrait forgotten and left behind. Was she perhaps seriously ill? So ill that Madame had refused to admit it? Had the guardian, sworn to secrecy, driven the child away to a hospital? A puff of night air blew the lace curtains into the room ... she was cold, dreadfully cold. And afraid. Throwing a wrapper over her shoulders, she lit a candle and sat down at her dressing-table to write to Constable Bumpher.

By the afternoon of Wednesday the twenty-fifth, the last of Hussey's cabs had carried the last of the boarders down the drive. The silent rooms overflowed with drifts of paper, dropped pins, scraps of ribbon and string. In the dining-room the fire was out, the carnations in tall glass vases on their last legs. From the staircase the grandfather clock had become so loud that Mrs Appleyard fancied she could hear its everlasting tick-tock through the study wall. Minute by minute, hour by hour : like a heart beating in a body already dead. Minnie had come in at dusk with the mail on a silver salver. 'It's late today, Ma'am. Tom says it's because of the Easter trains. Shall I draw your curtains now?'

'As you like.'

'There's one here for Miss Lumley – will you take it?'

The Headmistress held out a hand. 'I shall have to find out the brother's address in Warragul.' Who but the Lumleys would have died without leaving an address? Dora Lumley had always been a muddler with her letters. Even now. She sat staring at the heavy curtains that shut out the gentle twilit garden, thinking how few things in life were un-muddled, firmly outlined as they were surely intended to be? One could organize, direct, plan each hour in advance and still the muddle persisted. Nothing in life was really water-tight, nothing secret, nothing secure. Take people like Dora Lumley and the child Sara. Weaklings ... you had them firmly under control and the moment you turned your head they wriggled through your fingers. ... Mechanically she picked up the pile of letters and began sorting them out as she always insisted on doing with her own hand. Two or three for the staff – one in Louis Montpelier's thin purple ink for Mademoiselle, a coloured postcard for Minnie from Queenscliff. The baker's preposterous account left by hand in a dirty envelope. No cheques. Directly after Easter she would have to go to Melbourne and sell some shares, and she could go to Russell Street at the same time. If ever construc-tive action was called for it was now. Much as she would have preferred the privacy and solitude of dinner alone this evening she pulled the bell by the fireplace. 'Alice, I shall be dining downstairs with Mademoiselle and Miss Buck. Kindly tell Cook and ask her to send in a tray after dessert with black coffee, sugar and cream for three.' No detail at this juncture was unimportant – a specially careful toilet with a velvet bow at her throat and an extra brooch. Mademoiselle would notice such trifles and find them reassuring. Miss Buck of the blank toothfilled grin and thick spectacles might well be a suspicious type. One never knew with young women supposed to be brainy. There were dolts and dullards who saw too much, others who saw nothing. Oh, for the guiding hand of Arthur! Even the cool appraisement of Greta McCraw. For the first time in many weeks she thought of the mathematics mistress and brought her fist down on the dressing-table with such force that the combs and brushes and curling pins danced on its polished surface. It was inconceivable that this woman of masculine intellect on whom she had come to rely in the last years should have allowed herself to be spirited away, lost, raped, murdered in cold blood like an innocent schoolgirl, on the Hanging Rock. She had never seen the Rock but its presence was often with her of late – a brooding blackness solid as a wall.

At dinner that evening the two young women had never seen the Head so gracious. Positively loquacious. The governesses were already stifling their yawns after the hectic activities of the day when Miss Buck was requested to ring for Minnie. 'There is a little brandy, I think, in the decanter in the pantry? You remember, Minnie – the day the Bishop of Bendigo came to lunch?' The decanter and three glasses were brought. They sipped at it delicately and even drank to the health and good fortune of Mademoiselle and M. Montpelier. Dianne wearily taking up her candle at eleven o'clock thought it was the longest evening she had ever spent.

The clock on the stairs had just struck for half past twelve when the door of Mrs Appleyard's room opened noiselessly, inch by inch, and an old woman carrying a nightlight came out on to the landing. An old woman with head bowed under a forest of curling pins, with pendulous breasts and sagging stomach beneath a flannel dressing-gown. No human being – not even Arthur – had ever seen her thus, without the battledress of steel and whalebone in which for eighteen hours a day the Headmistress was accustomed to face the world.

From the window at the top of the staircase moonlight

fell upon the row of closed cedar doors. Mademoiselle slept at the far end of the corridor, Miss Buck in a small room at the rear of the tower. The woman with the nightlight stood listening to the tick-tock, tick-tock, coming up out of the shadows below. A possum scudding across the leads overhead made her start so violently that the little lamp almost fell from her hand. By its feeble light the big double bedroom appeared in perfect order; fresh, chintzy and smelling faintly of lavender. The blinds were all drawn to the same level, disclosing identical rectangles of moonlit sky and the dark tops of trees. The two beds, each with a pink silk eiderdown quilt neatly folded, were immaculate. On the dressing-table, flanked by two tall pink and gold vases, the heart-shaped pincushion where she had found and instantly destroyed the note. Again she saw herself bending over the child in the smaller of the two beds. Eyes, hardly a face now – only those enormous black eyes, burning into her own. Again she heard her cry out, 'No, no! Not that! Not the orphanage!' The Headmistress shivered, wishing she had put on a woollen spencer under her nightdress. She put the nightlight down on the bedside table, opened the cupboard where Miranda's dresses were still hanging on the left hand side and began methodically to go through the shelves. On the right, Sara's blue coat with the fur collar, a little beaver hat. Shoes. Tennis racquets. Now the bureau. Stockings. Handkerchiefs. Those ridiculous cards ... dozens of them. Valentines. Directly after the holidays she would have Miranda's things removed. Now the dressing-table. The washstand. The little walnut work table where Miranda kept her coloured wools. Lastly the mantelpiece. Nothing of any significance there – only a photograph of Miranda in a silver frame. The first grey light was showing under the blinds as she closed the door, put out the nightlight and threw herself on to the great fourposter bed. She had found nothing, deducted nothing, decided nothing. Another dreadful day of enforced inaction lay ahead. The clock was striking five. Sleep was out of the question. She rose and began taking the curlers out of her hair.

Thursday was unseasonably warm and Mr Whitehead,

who was taking Good Friday off, decided to do as much as he could in the garden today. No more rain yet by the looks of it although the top of the Mount was shrouded as usual in fluffy white mists. He thought the hydrangea bed at the back of the house could do with a watering. The place without the young ladies was strangely quiet but for the peaceful clucking of fowls and distant grunting of pigs, and now and then the rumble of wheels going past on the highroad. Tom had gone into Woodend in the buggy for the mail. Cook, with only a handful of adults to cater for instead of the usual complement of hungry schoolgirls, was having a grand clean up in the vast flagged kitchen. Alice was scrubbing the back stairs, she hoped for the last time. Miss Buck had gone off in a cab for an early train. Minnie was snatching ten minutes in her bedroom, greedily devouring a bunch of ripe bananas for which she had developed a passion during the last month, and joyfully letting out the waistband of her print frock, already too tight for comfort.

Dianne de Poitiers in a flurry of tissue paper was packing her small but elegant wardrobe. The very sight of the simple white satin wedding gown made her heart turn over. In a few hours' time Louis would be escorting her to the modest Bendigo lodging house where he had engaged a room for his fiancée until Easter Monday. She felt like a bird about to be set free after years of captivity in the cheerless room where she had so often cried herself to sleep, and began, very softly, to sing 'Au clair de la lune, mon ami pierrot'. From the open window the bittersweet little tune floated out over the lawn where Mrs Appleyard was discussing with Mr Whitehead the planting of a new border for the drive. 'Have to be getting on to it after Easter, Ma'am, if you want a nice show for the Spring.' Salvias? They were a useful sort of flower, Madam suggested. The gardener half-heartedly agreed. 'A lot of young ladies have their favourites. Funny thing I can never see a Christmas lily without thinking of Miss Miranda. "Mr Whitehead," she used to say, "lilies always make me think of angels." Well, she's probably one herself now, poor young creature.' He sighed. 'How about pansies?' The Headmistress forced her thoughts to pansies

175

and observed that they made a good show from the front gate. 'Now little Miss Sara – she's the one for pansies. Often begs a few off me for her room. You feeling cold, Ma'am? Could I fetch you a shawl?'

'One expects to feel chilly in March, Whitehead. Is there anything else you want to discuss before I go indoors?'

'Only about the flag, Ma'am.'

'Good gracious, what flag? Is it important?' Her foot tapped impatiently on the gravel. 'I have a good deal to attend to today.'

'Well,' said the gardener, an avid reader of the local papers, 'it's like this. The *Macedon Standard* is asking anyone in the district who has a flag to fly it on Easter Monday. It seems the Lord Mayor is coming from Melbourne for lunch at the Shire Hall.'

A double brandy after breakfast had made her head as clear as a bell. In a flash she saw the Union Jack floating out from the tower, a signal to the prying gossiping world that all at Appleyard College was well. She said graciously : 'By all means run up the flag. You will find it under the stairs – you remember we put it there after the Queen's birthday last year.'

'That's right. I folded it up and put it away myself.' Tom was beside them with the mail bag. 'Only one letter for you, Ma'am. Will you take it here or shall I bring it inside?' 'Give it to me.' She turned and left them without another word. 'She's a funny one, that,' the gardener said. 'I wouldn't mind betting she don't know a pansy from a chrysanthemum unless I tell her which is which.' And he made up his mind to put in begonias all down the drive.

The letter was addressed to Mrs Appleyard in a distinguished hand, precise and unfamiliar. Dated two days ago from an expensive Melbourne hotel, it read :

Dear Mrs Appleyard,

I regret that as I have been looking into my mining interests in North Western Australia, with no possible means of communication, I have been unable to forward the enclosed quarterly cheque for Sara Waybourne's fees until today. The purpose of this letter is to let you know that I intend calling at the College for Sara on the morning of Easter Saturday (28th). I trust this arrangement will be convenient to you as I am occupied all day on Good Friday and don't care for her to be here alone at the hotel, excellent though it is. If Sara is in need of any new clothes, books, drawing materials, etc., could you kindly have a list made out so that we can do some shopping together in Sydney where I shall be taking my ward for a few days holiday. As Sara must now be nearly fourteen, which I find hard to realize, I imagine something more sophisticated in the way of a party dress would be appreciated? Anyway, you can give me your views when we meet.

With kindest regards and hoping once again that you will not be inconvenienced by looking after Sara (of course, at my expense) until Saturday.

I remain,
Yours sincerely,
Jasper B. Cosgrove.

16

Constable Bumpher was inured to varying degrees of shock and surprise. Nevertheless the letter marked CONFIDENTIAL that had just been handed to him at his desk had left him, to use his own words, 'with a nasty taste in the mouth'.

Appleyard College,
Tuesday, March 24th.

Dear Monsieur Bumpher,

Forgive me if I address you incorrectly, as I have never before written to a gentleman of the Australian Police. I find much difficulty, in English, to explain just why I write to you at this moment—nearly midnight—except that I am a woman. A man would perhaps have waited for more definite proof. However, I feel that I must act, from my heart, without delay, and you may think, without sufficient reason.

Last Sunday morning (March 22nd) when I returned to the College from Mass, about midday, Madame Appleyard informed me that Sara Waybourne, a girl of age about thirteen years and our youngest pupil here, had been taken away by her guardian shortly after most of the household had left for church. I was very surprised, as Monsieur Cosgrove (the child's guardian) has excellent manners and had given Madame no warning. He has never to my knowledge acted in this impolite way before. As I write this I know you will see little reason for my uneasiness. The truth is Monsieur, that I fear this unhappy child has mysteriously disappeared. I have asked a few questions – very discreet – of the only two persons at home during the time of Monsieur Cosgrove's visit, besides Madame herself – both women honest and good. Neither of these women, Minnie the femme de chambre and the cook, saw Monsieur Cosgrove arrive at the house, nor

did they see him leave, with or without the child Sara. I
understand, however, that there may be an explanation for
this. Other reasons for my fears seem to be much more im-
portant, and much more difficult to make clear to you in
English. It is late, and the house is in darkness. This morning
I have passed an hour in the bedroom usually occupied by
Sara, and in the beginning, by Miranda. Here I observed
very carefully while helping a servant to tidy the room, cer-
tain things which I shall explain to you later. I have neither
the Time, nor the good English without my dictionary, to
write down here the shocking thoughts which have gradually
come to me, with a clearness quite horrible, after leaving that
empty room this morning. As I shall be leaving the College
on the day after tomorrow (Thursday) and will be married
on Easter Monday in Bendigo I enclose my new name and
address if you should wish to write to me on this matter.
Meanwhile M. Bumpher I am gravely troubled and shall be
most grateful if you can visit the College as soon as possible
and make some enquiries. You will not of course disclose to
Madame or any other person that I have written this letter.
You will I hope receive it on Thursday morning. Unfortu-
nately I have no way to post it earlier as Madame herself sees
everything that is put into the mail bag and so I must wait
to give this to someone whom I can trust to post. I am ex-
hausted, and shall try to sleep a little before dawn. I can do
nothing more without your help. Forgive me for troubling
you.

    Goodnight Monsieur . . . Dianne de Poitiers.
    Minnie the femme de chambre tells me today that
Madame A. had insisted on opening the front door herself,
on Sunday morning. Because of my terrible suspicions I find
this disturbing.

                                  D. de P.

Bumpher had formed an excellent opinion of the French
governess ever since the day when they had driven to the
Picnic Grounds with Edith Horton Not the type of young
woman to lose her head without any reason. He read the letter again with growing uneasiness. The Bumphers' neat

weatherboard villa was close to the Police Station in a neigh-
bouring back street, and here he presently surprised his wife
by appearing on the verandah with a request for a cup of
morning tea. 'Right here in the kitchen – I happened to be
passing our gate with a few minutes to spare.' While the
kettle was boiling he asked casually, 'You off to one of your
bun fights this afternoon?' Mrs Bumpher sniffed. 'Since
when have I been out to tea? If you'd like to know, I'm
going to clean right through the house for Easter.'

'I was only asking,' said her husband mildly. 'Because last
time you went to a social you brought home those cream
puffs I like – from the Vicarage – *and* a lot of gossip.'

'You know very well I'm not one for gossip. What is it
you want to find out?'

He grinned. 'Shrewd little woman, aren't you? I've been
wondering if you ever heard any of your lady friends mention
Mrs Appleyard at the College?' In Bumpher's experience it
was amazing how an ordinary housewife seemed to know by
instinct things that might take a policeman weeks to find out.
'Let me see. Well, I have heard it said the old girl's a bit of
a Tartar when she flies into one of her rages.'

'Flies into rages, does she?'

'I'm only telling you what I hear. Smooth as silk to me,
if I happen to run into her in the village.'

'You know anyone who's actually seen her in a rage?'

'Drink up your tea while I think ... you know the Comptons down at the cottage with the quince trees where the
College gets their jams? Anyway, the wife told me she was
terrified of making a mistake in the account because once
when her hubby was away she had to take it over by hand
and it was a pound out and Mrs Appleyard sent for her and
gave her hell. Mrs Compton thought the old girl was going
to have a stroke.'

'Anything else?'

'Only that a girl by the name of Alice who works at the
College told that woman in the fruit shop that she drinks a
bit. This Alice hadn't ever seen her tiddly or anything but
you know how people talk in this town! Especially since the
College Mystery.'

'Don't I just!' Over a second cup of tea he tried to extract a few crumbs of information about the French governess by announcing she was to be married next week. 'Go on! I'm not much of a one for the Frogs, as you know (remember that fellow who played the flute?), but I must say I thought this one was a real pretty girl the only time I was close enough to see her face.'

'Where was that?'

'At the Bank. This Mademoiselle was cashing a cheque and Ted – that's the teller with the ginger hair – gave her too much change. She'd gone half way down the street before she noticed it and brought it back. I remember because Ted remarked to me at the time: "My word Mrs Bumpher, there's honesty for you! I would've had to pay back that money out of my own pocket."'

'Well, thanks for the tea – I'll be off now,' said Bumpher, pushing back his chair. 'Expect me when you see me this evening. I may be very late home.' There was a lovely piece of rump steak for tea but Mrs Bumpher had been married for fifteen years and knew better than to ask why.

The promise of fine weather for Easter continued all through Thursday. By twelve o'clock it was almost hot, and Bumpher taking notes in the stuffy privacy of his office took off his jacket. Mr Whitehead too had taken off his coat to fork over the dahlias. As soon as he had finished his early dinner the gardener went into the tool shed and dragged out the hose, already rolled up for the coming winter, with the intention of watering the hydrangeas before the bed got too dry. Tom asked if he could lend a hand, otherwise he was going to take Minnie for a stroll down the road. The gardener said no, he had the place in pretty good shape to leave for a day tomorrow, but would Tom give the hydrangeas a bit of a sprinkle if the sun came out again strong, like today, on Good Friday? Tom promised, and taking Minnie by the arm was mercifully spared from participation in subsequent happenings during the next few hours.

The hydrangea bed, eight feet wide and running along the back of the house for most of its length, was the apple of Mr Whitehead's eye. This summer some of the flower heads were at least six feet above the ground. He had just fixed his hose on to the nearest garden tap when he noticed an offensive smell which seemed to be coming from the direction of the hydrangeas. Before turning on the tap he thought he had better investigate or Cook would be kicking up a shine with a stink so close to the kitchen door. He had been too busy with the autumn pruning the last few days to stop as he often did to admire the close growing hydrangea bushes, their dark glossy leaves crowned with clusters of deep blue flowers. Now to his annoyance he saw that one of the tallest and most handsome plants, in the back row, a few feet out from the wall directly below the tower, had been badly crushed and broken, the beautiful blue heads limp on their stalks. Possums! The darned things were always gallivanting about on the leads. Tom had even found a possum nest in the tower last year. Tom would have gone crashing into the bushes there and then in his heavy boots in search of a dead possum. The gardener, however, removed his waistcoat, took a pair of secateurs from his trouser pocket in order to make a clean snip at the broken flower stalks, and began crawling carefully between the bushes on his hands and knees so as not to disturb the young growth at the base of the roots. He was within a few feet of the damaged bush when he saw something white beside it on the ground. Something that had once been a girl in a nightdress, soaked with dried blood. One leg was bent under the tangled body, the other wedged in the lower fork of the hydrangea. The feet were bare. The head was crushed beyond recognition, even if he could have forced himself to look at it more closely. Even so he knew that it was Sara Waybourne. No other girl at the College was so small, with such thin arms and legs.

He managed to crawl out on to the path that ran beside the bed and was violently sick. The body from here was entirely hidden by the dense screen of foliage. He and Tom and the maids must have passed it dozens of times during the last few days. He went into the wash-house and splashed his hands and face. There was a bottle of whisky in his room. He sat down on the edge of the bed and poured himself a small drink to settle his wildly leaping stomach and went straight round the house to the side door and across the hall to Mrs Appleyard's study.

Extract from a Statement by Edward Whitehead, gardener at Appleyard College, as given to Constable Bumpher on the morning of Good Friday, April the twenty-seventh.

All this was a terrible shock to me and a terrible thing to have to tell Madam after what she'd had to go through lately. I think she must have been walking up and down the room when I knocked. Anyway she didn't answer so I went in. She nearly jumped out of her skin when she saw me. She was looking something awful – even for her. I mean to say, we all said in the kitchen she had been looking ill. She didn't ask me to sit down but my legs were shaking that badly I could hardly stand up and I took a chair. I can't remember exactly what I said about finding the body. At first she just stood there staring as if she hadn't heard a word I'd been saying. Then she told me to say it all again, very slowly, which I did. When I'd finished she asked, 'Who was it?' I said, 'Sara Waybourne.' She asked if I was quite sure the girl was dead? I said, 'Yes, quite sure.' I didn't tell her why. She let out a sort of smothered scream, more like a wild animal than a human being. I won't forget the sound of that scream if I live to be a hundred.*

She got out a bottle and poured out a stiff brandy for herself and one for me which I refused. I asked if I would fetch the cook who was the only other person in the house at the time. She said, 'No, you fool. Can you drive a horse?' I told her I wasn't much of a hand at it but I could put the pony in the trap. She said, 'Then you can take me into the police station. For God's sake hurry and if you see anyone don't open your mouth.' About ten minutes later she was out in the drive waiting for the trap at the front door. She was wearing a long navy blue coat and a brown hat with a feather sticking up that I've seen her wearing when she goes to Melbourne. She was carrying a black leather handbag and black gloves because I wondered why a person would think of gloves at

* Author's Note: Edward Whitehead actually lived to the age of ninety-five years.

such a time. We drove to Woodend as fast as the pony would go and neither of us said a word the whole way. When we were within a hundred yards of the Police Station, opposite Hussey's Livery Stables, she told me to pull up. She got out and went over to the seat where Hussey's passengers wait for the cabs. I thought she was going to fall over. I asked if she wanted me to go with her to the Station or wait outside. She said she would sit there for a few minutes and then go to the Station alone. She said there would be plenty of questions for me to answer later and I was to drive straight home. I didn't like leaving her there in the street looking so ill and all. However, she seemed to know exactly what she wanted, like she always does, and I thought it best to obey orders. Especially as I was feeling terribly sick in the stomach after what I had seen that afternoon. Before I left her Mrs Appleyard said she would get a cab back to the College from Hussey's after she had seen the police. She was still sitting on the seat straight as a poker when I turned the pony round to go home. And that was the last time I saw her.

> Signed . . . Edward Whitehead,
> Woodend, Friday, March 27th, 1900.

Statement by Ben Hussey of Hussey's Livery Stables as given to Constable Bumpher on the same date as above.

We were very busy on the Thursday before Good Friday because of the Easter holidays. I was sitting in my office at the Stables checking on the orders for cabs when Mrs Appleyard came in and said she wanted one straight away. I had hardly set eyes on her since the day of the picnic to Hanging Rock and was shocked at the change in her appearance. I asked how far she wanted to go — she said she thought about ten miles; she had just had bad news from friends out on the Hanging Rock Road, she would know the house when she saw it. As all my drivers were out on jobs meeting trains and so on I told her I'd take her myself if she didn't mind waiting while I harnessed up a pretty lively mare I've just broken in, and won't let anyone handle but me. I could see Mrs Appleyard was very upset, especially for somebody like her who don't show her feelings. I asked her if she'd like to sit down and have a cup of tea at my place while she was waiting but she came and stood beside me all the time I was putting the mare in the buggy and we got away at ten minutes to three. I know the time as I had to write it down for my drivers on the office pad. After we had gone a couple of miles in silence I remarked it was a nice sunny day. She said she hadn't noticed. Nothing else was said until we came to the bend in the road where you can first see the Hanging Rock coming up out of the trees in the distance. I pointed it out to her and said something about the Rock having made a lot of trouble for a lot of people since the day of the Picnic. She leaned right across me and shook her fist at it and I hope I never have to see an expression like that on another face. It gave me quite a turn and I wasn't sorry when we came in sight of a small farm with a gate on to the road but no track and she told me to stop. I said are you quite sure this is the place? 'Yes,' she says, 'this is it and you don't need to wait. My friends will bring me back later.' There was a tumble-down sort of a cottage across the paddocks and a man and a woman holding a baby were standing outside. 'All right,' I said, 'the mare's not used to standing yet and if you're sure you can manage I'll be off and I hope things won't be as bad as you think.' We got off to a flying start and I didn't look back.

Signed... Ben Hussey,
Livery Stables, Woodend, March 27th, 1900.

The shepherd and his wife who later testified in Court that they had seen a woman in a long coat getting out of a one-horse buggy at their gate, stood watching her walking off along the road in the direction of the Picnic Grounds. Very few strangers passed that way on foot. The woman appeared to be walking fast and was soon out of sight.

Although she had seen the Hanging Rock for the first time this afternoon, when Ben Hussey had pointed it out from the buggy, Mrs Appleyard was only too familiar with its general aspect and the various key points of the Picnic Grounds, as depicted in the plans, drawings and photographs in the Melbourne press. Here, after a more or less level stretch on the seemingly endless road, was the sagging wooden gate through which Ben Hussey had driven his five-horse drag. There was the creek, holding the last of the afternoon light in its placid pools. To the left, a little way ahead, the much photographed spot where the picnic party from Lake View had camped beside their wagonette. To the right, the vertical walls of the Rock were already in deep shade, the undergrowth at the base exuding the dank forest breath of decay. Her gloved hands fumbled with the catch of the gate. Arthur used to say : 'My dear, you have an excellent head but you are no good with your hands.' She left the gate open and started to walk along the track towards the creek.

And now, at last, after a lifetime of linoleum and asphalt and Axminster carpets, the heavy flat-footed woman trod the springing earth. Born fifty-seven years ago in a suburban wilderness of smoke-grimed bricks, she knew no more of Nature than a scarecrow rigid on a broomstick above a field of waving corn. She who had lived so close to the little forest on the Bendigo Road had never felt the short wiry grass underfoot. Never walked between the straight shaggy stems of the stringy-bark trees. Never paused to savour the jubilant gusts of Spring that carried the scent of wattle and eucalypt right into the front hall of the College. Nor sniffed with foreboding the blast of the North wind, laden in summer with the fine ash of mountain fires. When the ground started to rise towards the Rock, she knew that she must turn to the right into the waist-high bracken and begin to climb. The ground was rough under the large soft feet in kid button-up boots. She sat down for a few minutes on a fallen log and took off her gloves. She could feel the perspiration trickling down her neck under the stiff lace at her throat. Now she was on her feet again looking up at the sky faintly streaked with pink behind a row of jagged peaks. For the first time it dawned on her what it meant to climb the Rock on a hot afternoon, as the lost girls had climbed it, long, long ago, in full-skirted summer frocks and thin shoes. Stumbling and sweating upwards through the bracken and dogwood, she thought of them now, without compassion. Dead. Both dead. And now Sara lying under the tower. When presently the monolith came into view she recognized it at once from the photographs. With her heart pounding under the heavy coat it was as much as she could do to clamber towards it over the last few yards of stones that slid from under her feet with every step. To the right a narrow ledge overhung a precipice at which she dared not look. To the left, on higher ground, a pile of stones ... on one of them a large black spider, spread-eagled, asleep in the sun. She had always been afraid of spiders, looked round for something with which to strike it down and saw Sara Waybourne, in a nightdress, with one eye fixed and staring from a mask of rotting flesh.

An eagle hovering high above the golden peaks heard her scream as she ran towards the precipice and jumped. The spider scuttled to safety as the clumsy body went bouncing and rolling from rock to rock towards the valley below. Until at last the head in the brown hat was impaled upon a jutting crag.

17

Extract from a Melbourne newspaper, dated February 14th, 1913.

Although Saint Valentine's Day is usually associated with the giving and taking of presents, and affairs of the heart, it is exactly thirteen years since the fatal Saturday when a party of some twenty schoolgirls and two governesses set out from Appleyard College on the Bendigo Road for a picnic to Hanging Rock. One of the governesses and three of the girls disappeared during the afternoon. Only one of them was ever seen again. The Hanging Rock is a spectacular volcanic uprising on the plains below Mount Macedon, of special interest to geologists on account of its unique rock formations, including monoliths and reputedly bottomless holes and caves, until recently uncharted (1912). It was thought at the time that the missing persons had attempted to climb the dangerous rock escarpments near the summit, where they presumably met their deaths; but whether by accident, suicide or straight out murder has never been established, since the bodies were never recovered.

Intensive search by police and public of the relatively small area provided no clue to the mystery until on the morning of Saturday, February 21st, the Hon. Michael Fitzhubert, a young Englishman holidaying at Mount Macedon (now domiciled on a station property in Northern Queensland), discovered one of the three missing girls, Irma Leopold, lying unconscious at the foot of two enormous boulders. The unfortunate girl subsequently recovered, except for a head injury which left her without memory of anything that had occurred after she and her companions had begun the ascent of the upper levels. The search was continued for several years under great difficulties, owing to the mysterious death of the Headmistress of Appleyard College within a few months of the tragedy. The College itself was totally destroyed by a bushfire during the following summer. In 1903, two rabbiters camped at the Hanging Rock found a small piece of frilled calico, thought by the police to be part of a petticoat worn on the day of the picnic by the missing governess.

A somewhat shadowy figure appears briefly in this extraordinary story; a girl called Edith Horton, a fourteen-year-old boarder at Appleyard College, who had accompanied the three other girls for a short distance up the Rock. This girl returned at dusk to the other picnickers by the creek below in a state of hysteria, and was unable then, or ever after, to recall anything whatever that had occurred during the interval. In spite of repeated enquiries over the years, Miss Horton recently died in Melbourne without having provided any additional information.

Countess de Latte-Marguery (the former Irma Leopold) is at present residing in Europe. From time to time the Countess has granted interviews to various interested bodies, including the Society for Psychical Research, but has never recalled anything beyond what she was able to remember after first regaining consciousness. Thus the College Mystery, like that of the celebrated case of the Marie Celeste, seems likely to remain forever unsolved.

penguinclassics.com.au

View an old friend in a different light.

Access the complete range of Penguin Classics:
read and listen to extracts; download reading group
notes; view themed reading lists and much more.